Tickety Tock

Manda Mellett

Wicked Warriors MC - Arizona Chapter

Manda Mellett

Copyright

Production Acknowledgments

Cover Design by Wicked Smart Designs

Edited and formatted by Maggie Kern @ Ms.K Edits

Proof reading by Darlene Tallman

Cast List Wicked Warriors Arizona Chapter

Officers:
Prez: Toad – Curtis Mckenzie
VP: Raider
Sergeant-at-arms: Metalhead
Enforcer: Stumpy
Treasurer: Cash
Medic: Scalpel
Tech Expert: Cloud

Members:
Bonkers
Midnight
Crumb

Prospect:
Punchbag

Club girls:
Easy
Cilla

Old Lady:
Ruby (Princess) – Toad's old lady

Prologue

DWARF

A s I stand at the top of the ramp leading into the single-storey house, I gaze at the sight of the sun setting, just visible over the roofs of the houses opposite. I don't much care for the location. Personally, I'd hate being hemmed in by other buildings, but apart from that, my old Marine buddy, Miles, seems to have it all. The house, the family, and the girl. Of course, what he hasn't got probably balances it out in my favour. Despite that, some effort is needed on my part to make the visits to keep in touch. It still hurts to see what I missed out on.

Turning at the whishing sound behind me, I see Miles rolling his wheelchair out of the widened front door. When his wistful gaze lands on my bike, it's not hard to see him longing for the freedom it represents.

"You sure you don't want to stay the night? Won't take but a moment for Jolene to make up a bed."

Suppressing my shudder, I shake my head. In a few moments, I'll be throwing my leg over the seat of my bike. Shortly after, I'll be feeling the wind in my hair and seeing the pavement go by beneath my wheels. Guilt has me mumbling something about having to get back to the club, and not mentioning that I need to escape the atmosphere around here. A few hours, and already it's stifling.

Miles and I had served together, him signing up for one tour more than I. Though it was done without an ounce of premonition, the fact is, had I put my name on that dotted line just like he had done, I might not be alive. Miles was the only survivor of the IED that took his transport out, and sometimes I believe he'd prefer to have died. As well as his physical injuries, he wrongly blames himself that the rest of his team didn't survive. It's one of the reasons I make this annual visit to see him. Maybe I come because I share that survivor's guilt. I'd gotten out in time.

"She'd have been better off with you." His voice catches as he expresses the thought on the topic I'd hoped we'd continue to avoid until I'd ridden out of sight.

She's the reason I have to prepare before I come to see him, gritting my teeth and swallowing my anger before I come darkening his door. Now he's brought it up, I can only hope I find the right words to reply.

I wave my hand dismissively, wishing to shut this discussion down. "Long time ago, man." In the early days, it had been hard to continue a friendship with him, but like many things, time had deadened the hurt and gradually it mostly got swept under the rug. No blame could ever have been attached to him, but seeing him with her was always difficult.

Miles, though, isn't going to let the matter drop. "She's going to leave me."

Having picked up that impression, I don't respond. I'd stayed with them for a day and any fool could see it wasn't marital bliss. To be honest, it had been obvious for a while. I give her credit, though, for not immediately walking away. Jolene had at least stayed with the broken man out of a sense of duty, proving she had some loyalty, after all.

Miles gives me a moment, then says, "She made a mistake, and she knows it. Look, Liam. If you want to rekindle—"

I cut him off. A relationship with the woman who'd dropped

me like a hot cake, impossible to consider. "It's too late now. That ship has passed." And that's if it ever left port in the first place. Or if it had, it had only been my feet on the gangway. She had stayed with hers on solid ground. Turning to face him, I give him more. "If what we'd had had been worth anything, she wouldn't have left my side."

Again, I find the slowly disappearing sun a more interesting direction in which to focus my eyes, unwilling to load Miles with any more burdens. Although I might not be giving voice to it, it doesn't stop the memories going through my mind.

I should have been used to it. I was a Marine. Girls were drawn to me like a moth to a flame, attracted by my uniform and the danger of my job. But it wasn't the man under the clothes that they wanted. I knew exactly what I was, a poor substitute for the type of man they were really after. Miles wasn't the first man the girl I'd thought could have been mine had gravitated to. They'd used me to get an introduction to the man they really wanted. At best, they'd let me into their pussy before moving on, at worst, I'd be short the dollars for the drinks that I'd bought.

They'd wanted a man like Miles. Miles, when he had both his legs, had stood six foot three, handsome in ways even a cisgender male like me could admire. He'd been fit and well proportioned. In contrast, I was short and rotund, and my face could in no way be described as pretty.

Jolene? Well, I'd thought she was different, and it certainly went more than a few drinks. I'd gotten lucky. After a couple of weeks of dating, I thought I'd found one who would stick. I'd even started to believe this attractive, intelligent, fun girl could really be mine. Although it was still early, I was already considering a ring.

Up until the night we'd ended up at a bar frequented by my fellow Marines, that was. One look at Miles and, without apology, she'd left my side and glued herself to his.

Of course, I hadn't told him I'd considered her mine. Once I saw the way the wind was blowing, I accepted what happened all the time. All he knew was that an available female had plastered herself to him, dismissing me without even a glance. When he'd glimpsed down, he'd smiled like he'd won the jackpot when he saw how fucking gorgeous she was. As he'd put his arm around her, I watched as she'd leaned in close, my fists clenching, but knowing there was fuck all I could do about it.

Her choice. I couldn't force the woman, *any* woman, to stay by my side.

I'd have kept quiet. He wasn't responsible for Jolene's actions. He was a good friend, a man who'd had my back time after time. If it was up to me, he'd never have known. If I'd had to bite my tongue and find excuses for not attending their wedding, well, so be it. But on their first night of marital bliss, Jolene had come clean, had chosen to joke about the short ass of a man who'd tried to get her attention.

Miles wasn't stupid. He'd read between the lines. Something he refers to now, even though I'd rather he kept quiet. "I never would have fuckin' gone there had I known."

I shrug. "No worries, man." He wouldn't have, unlike some others. But why would I want to hold on to a woman who felt the grass was greener on the taller side? It had only revealed her true nature.

The sun's almost disappeared now. It's time for me to ride. Already it will be late when I get back to the clubhouse, even if I leave now, but there's no way I'm taking up his offer of hospitality. It was bad enough before.

Sure, I've read the signs. I know Jolene's now looking for a way out, and even if it might be with Miles's blessing, I'm never going to settle for being second best, a consolation prize. I'd rather never have an old lady, not if she wasn't going to choose me first.

As I reach down to pick up my saddlebags, he again glances toward my bike with a look of envy. "It was good to see you, Liam. You'll be back this way soon?"

"Hopefully in a few months." I jerk my head back to the

4

house behind me. "Let me know..." How can I ask him to let me know when the inevitable happens and his wife leaves him all alone? I start again, "Keep in touch, man."

My heart breaks for him, though this has been coming for some time. Jolene, having enough of looking after a disabled man, will leave him, taking the kids with her. To be honest, I'm surprised she stayed with him as long as she has. It's been six years since that explosion.

Bending, and slightly awkwardly, I give Miles a man hug, telling him to take care and to look after himself—all the platitudes you normally say upon leaving someone.

"Take care of yourself, Liam."

With a mock salute, I go to my bike, settle my saddlebags in their rightful places, then ride off into the night.

Chapter One

DWARF

Knocking down a gear, I carefully take the next bend in the road, then speed up once I've rounded the curve. Trees, lit by the light of the full moon, flash past in a blur as I twist the throttle hard. I'm riding on my own, and it feels like I'm in the middle of nowhere. In daylight, it would be exhilarating, but in the dark, for some reason, I'm feeling unnerved.

Give me the desert every day where I can see what's coming for miles. Here in the midst of a forest, I'm out of my element.

Frustrated by the stationary traffic on the highway, I hadn't thought twice about using this road as a shortcut when I'd turned on to it. Sure, it was dark, but hell, all I need is the beam of my headlight. But an hour or so later, noting there's no other traffic about, I have pricking at the back of my neck and a sense I can't shake that something's not right.

PTSD, I tell myself. *I don't like being hemmed in, that's all.* It's just my imagination that the road seems to be narrowing, as if the conifers are joining forces and corralling me. But fuck, I'm sure the road was wider than it now is. *Could I have taken a wrong turn?*

Nah. That's fucking stupid. While it might be a long detour, my glance at the map on my phone has showed me it was just one road that more or less takes me in the direction I want to go. The way that will eventually get me back on the highway that will take me back to my home, to the compound of the Wicked Warriors MC Arizona chapter.

Should have waited until morning to make the trek back.

Yeah, should have done. But a night spent under the same roof as Jolene and Miles hadn't held much joy. Their marital issues and our past history seemed to suck most of the oxygen out of the room, and I'd been pleased to get gone. Weighing it up, driving through the night to return to my own bed, which I could probably persuade a sweet butt to warm for me, was a far better option. But who could have guessed a fucking eighteen-wheeler would have jack-knifed, lost its load and blocked the whole damn freeway?

Should have been an easy ride.

The idea that keeping moving was better than sitting on my bike twiddling my thumbs drove me to choose this route. Longer by far, but at least I'll get back tonight. *Or so I'd thought.* Is it just in my head that this route's turning out to be several miles further than I estimated it would be?

Am I riding in circles?

Another bend coming up, I shift down, feeling my engine growl as it ascends the slight incline, then, taking the middle line, lean into the curve. I've started straightening my bike when the blur of a dark shape runs out in front of me.

What the fuck?

Deer?

Christ! I'm going to hit it.

As I'm still at an angle, I fight my bike, trying to swerve to avoid whatever the fuck it is, knowing a motorcycle hitting something that size at the speed I'm going is certain to cause some damage both to it and me. My brain's working at the speed of light, issuing instructions to my muscles.

Front brake, rear brake, get that fucking speed down. Don't lock the wheels.

Despite my efforts, I'm heading straight for it. I try to take evasive action, but off-balanced, being still on a lean, I'm quickly losing my fight with gravity.

I feel a thud and wrench the handlebars. That action has me almost horizontal, skidding toward a tree. Knowing there's no saving the bike now, I make the decision to part company with it. Though I've slowed sufficiently and I'm not going too fast, my dismount is ungainly, and I land awkwardly on my ankle and twist it.

Fuck. Fuck. Fuck! Gritting my teeth, I use the trunk of a tree to help me stand. Putting as little weight as possible on my injured foot, I manage to hop over to my bike to turn the engine off. Taking out my phone to use the flashlight, I see it's clipped the tree hard and fallen on its side in a ditch. As I inspect it, I find the front wheel bent out of shape.

Just my fucking luck. I'm in the middle of nowhere. The shortcut I'd taken was not much more than an old logging trail. As the main roads provided a far quicker solution to get from A to B, I hadn't come across any other idiot using it but me.

For a moment I stand cursing, listening to the ticking of the cooling engine, rubbing my leg, while coming to terms with the fact that neither my bike nor I are going to make it out of here without help tonight.

As my bike grows silent, other sounds invade my psyche, including the loud rustling in the bushes behind me. *What the fuck's that?* Spinning fast, I try to make out a shape.

There's nothing there. Or nothing that the light of my phone allows me to see.

My heart rate's still high, adrenaline still coursing through me from the accident. I'm so on edge, a hoot of an owl from close by actually makes me jump. I'm not kidding. I have two feet in the air. Then something brushes into me. Putting up my hand to fight it off, I find I'm battling with a leaf falling off a tree.

Christ, I'm spooked tonight.

Taking several deep breaths, I bend over, deliberately trying to slow my fast-beating heart. That fucking owl hoots again and another answers, destroying all my efforts to calm myself down.

Give me engine noise over nature any day.

I may be a fucking biker, a Marine who'd served too many terms, but this deserted forest at midnight is really fucking with me.

A growl rises in my throat as I remember the reason for my current predicament. *Fucking deer.* Turning so the beam from my light falls on the offending animal, I hope to see it dead, so I might at least end up with a haunch of venison to share with my brothers when they show up to save me. One thing's for certain, with that fucked wheel on my bike, I won't be riding out of here by myself. But there could be a plus side to this. I've already got several recipes running through my head.

Concentrating on those thoughts rather than my unease of the situation I find myself in, I begin to limp over toward the carcass, when *goddamnit.* I slide my gun out of my holster when I see movement from the shape on the road, showing I hadn't made the kill cleanly. Now I'm going to have to help what's going to be on the menu on its way.

I've killed before, of course I have, but I'm not looking forward to doing what I have to. Disposing of a man equally as intent on taking my life is one thing. An innocent animal is something else. Contenting myself that putting it out of its misery is a service and not a crime, I approach. I also find consolation in that the offer of a few venison steaks and other concoctions I can come up with, is sure to take the sting out of my brothers having to come to the Bumfuck of nowhere to rescue me in the middle of the night.

I cook 'em, but I don't like killing them, so sue me. It's just the way that I am.

Justifying most of the damage has probably been done

already, I start to cover the remainder of the distance between the downed animal and my bike.

Oh fuck. My steps falter, and my brain freezes as I approach. I'd hit something. That was what the thud had been, but it was no four-legged creature.

Is that a fucking ghost? Goosebumps go up my spine.

Giving myself a mental slap, I remind myself that I'd definitely hit a corporal body and try to get my mind to accept that the robed figure just pulling themselves up from the road can't be a spectre. It's flesh and fucking blood, I'm sure of it.

Worse than a spirit, I'd hit a fucking human being.

"What the hell do you think you were doing?" I roar as I near it. I'm hurt, and my bike's unrideable. I think I deserve the anger that's welled up so fast. Whoever it is, is lucky I'm lame, otherwise I'd be stomping my way to them and shaking some sense into them. "You must have fuckin' heard me coming." A Harley's not quiet, yet this fucking idiot ran right out in front of me.

"Well?" When I get no response, I forget and put weight on my twisted ankle as I try to get closer. It hurts like hell but holds. Gingerly, I use a sort of hop/tiptoe action and start to make my way faster over to them.

My anger must be palpable as they reel back when I approach. Their head shakes and their hands come up to ward me off.

"I... I'm sorry."

It's the soft female voice that makes me come to an abrupt halt. *A fucking girl?* Drawing closer, I shine my light on her. *What the hell?* Yeah. It's a woman, quite young, from what I can tell. She's dressed in a black satin robe and what I'd thought was a hood is her own long dark hair, cascading over her shoulders, the moon shining down, making it glisten like a thousand stars. Apart from the robe and whatever she's got on underneath it, she's wearing nothing else. Her bare feet gleam in the beam of the flashlight like beacons.

11

When she sees I'm not going to draw closer, she brushes herself off. Assessing her quickly, I gather she can't be badly injured, though she is rubbing her elbow.

"What on earth were you doing?" As I repeat my question, the incongruousness of her clothing and the speed she'd been running hits me at last. My brain kicks into gear as I put the pieces together. *Girl, running, barefooted at night.* Immediately, my protective instincts slam into me as I remember the rustling and look around cautiously, my weapon, which I hadn't yet holstered, grasped firmly.

"Someone after you?" I bark.

Her eyes go in the direction of the woods from which she'd appeared. When she shivers, I, too, stare back into the trees as if to spot whoever it is who she so obviously fears.

"Husband? Boyfriend?" I snap. *What the fuck am I dealing with?*

"What? Oh. Uh…" Her stammering gets me looking at her again. "No one's after me. I, I was just spooked."

Just fucking spooked? I eye the wreck of my bike a few yards up the road, ire once again rising inside me. "Where the fuck did you come from?"

"Up there." She jerks her head toward the dark interior of the woods.

Well, she's not dressed for hiking, and I doubt that kind of robe would be carried as camping gear. I presume she's come from a cabin or something.

She looks scared out of her wits, but if it wasn't a man, what got her out of her bed? "What spooked you?" I snap. "A bear?"

"Bear?"

I roll my eyes. "You know, furry creature, four-legged, big claws. You leave food out or something?"

My light's still on her, and I can't see any comprehension on her face. Is she stupid, or did she take a blow to her head?

"You hurt?" Belatedly, I realise that while my first thought had been the damage she'd done to my ride, I had knocked into her. I nod to the way she's cradling her arm.

That she seems to understand. Experimentally, she stretches out her limb. "I think it's just bruised." She rubs her temple, and adds ruefully, "I banged my head when I fell."

Is that blood? Anger gives way to concern. It's my bike that hit her. Do I bear some responsibility? Fuck knows. But I can't walk off and leave her. Not that I've any means of getting out of here anyway. Well, not until I summon my brothers.

She's also still half lying in the middle of the road. "Think you ought to move out of the way." While no other traffic has passed, I don't want any other fucker coming round that bend and running into her. Though the thought of my twisted front wheel makes me want to pick her up and shake her, in all honesty, I don't want more harm to befall her. "Do you need help?"

"Oh." She glances around as if realising she's still there. Pressing her uninjured palm to the asphalt, she pushes herself up, then staggers slightly as if the fall she'd taken had stunned her. She takes the couple of steps that bring her to my side of the road, the same side she exited from. I don't miss the way she glances back into the woods warily.

She's upright and moving under her own steam. She can't be hurt that badly.

Feeling for a fleeting moment that it's a shame I'm having to say goodbye to my visions of free venison, I turn back to my main concern. My bike. After staring at it for a moment, seeing the second glance hasn't changed a darn thing, and that wheel will need to be straightened before I can ride it again, I decide to summon help.

Taking out my phone, I click on the prospect's number, unwilling to wake up anyone else at this ungodly hour. But the call won't connect.

There's no fucking signal.

Just my luck. I eye the woman again. "You got a phone?"

Instead of answering, she indicates her robe. I presume whatever the fuck scared her, she'd just run without stopping to put on shoes or to collect her phone.

That pricking at the back of my neck starts again.

I'm a man who can look after himself. I might not be tall, but my width is muscle, not fat. I don't turn away from any man, but something about this situation doesn't feel right.

There's been no car passing since I came off the road, and the last sight of civilisation I'd seen had been several miles back. Too far to walk with one ankle out of action. *I'm fucking stranded.* My only companion may or may not be in possession of all her senses.

She ran because she was spooked.

Shit. Actually, as the breeze picks up, I have some sympathy for her. The trees are swaying and rustling as though having some private conversation between themselves, and the darkness seems eerie. And those damn fuckin' owls keep screeching, as if arranging some kind of ambush on us.

"What the fuck?" I step back and throw up my hands as a shape flies over me.

"It's just a bat." She'd ducked herself but had regained her senses more quickly.

Automatically, I rub my hand over my hair, even though logically I know it would mean no harm to me. But my nerves are stretched taut right now, and my sixth sense warns me it could be Dracula himself.

I don't like it here.

I go through my options. Wait here by my bike until someone does pass, and hope they stop with good intentions, or go to wherever she's come from, get her phone and see if she's got a signal? There's no competition.

I approach her again. "You come from a cabin or something?"

"Yes." Her voice is cracked, and she tries it again. This time it comes out a little stronger. "Yes."

Glancing again at my bike, satisfying myself from its position

14

in the ditch, a passing driver probably wouldn't be able to spot it —not that anyone could ride it off—I determine the only course of action. "Take me to your cabin. I need your phone to call for assistance."

It's the least she owes me. It was her fucking fault I came off my bike.

"G-g-go back?"

Again, I question her level of intelligence. "You must have come from fuckin' somewhere, sweetheart. Take me there."

Fuck, but I'm tired. Driving half the night will do that to you. I've got shooting pains coming up from my ankle, and my heart hurts at the damage done to my Harley. I had little patience with her from the start.

"Let me make this clear to you. You ran out in front of me. You caused the fuckin' crash. Least you can do, *sweetheart*, is whatever you can to help me."

Chapter Two

RAVEN

I s it stupid that I'm glad I'm no longer alone, even though my only company is this rightfully angry man?

My head hurts, my arm throbs, and my feet feel numb, but all in all, I think I probably got off lightly. I'd run from the cabin like the demons of hell were after me, which I'd felt like they were. While I wouldn't deliberately have chosen to crash into any vehicle, it had proved an effective way of getting someone to stop.

There's no way I can admit to him what did actually put the fear of God into me. I'm sure he's already questioning my sanity. If I told him the truth, he'd summon the men in white coats to come for me for sure.

I don't want to return to that cabin again.

I pull my robe more tightly around me, knowing I'm naked and vulnerable underneath. He's actually lucky I'd reached out my hand to grab something that would cover me. I'd been so scared, if it hadn't been close, I'd have been running in my birthday suit through the trees.

I eye the man who'd knocked me off my feet. He's quite short, maybe just an inch or so taller than me, but he's broad. He's waving that beam from his phone around, almost at times blinding me. The moon's shining down, and I can see his muscular torso, and I don't miss the weapon he still holds in his hand.

At any other time, he might have scared me. But now? Well, I'm less wary of him than the thing that's after me.

Ignoring his request for me to take him to the cabin, I eye his bike optimistically. "Can you give me a ride?"

"Christ, you *are* fuckin' stupid." I suspect from his tone, he's rolling his eyes. "My bike's fucked, *sweetheart.*" Again, he sneers the endearment.

My heart drops. "You can't ride it?"

"You think I'd still be standing here if I fuckin' could?"

Wrapping my arms around me, I shiver slightly. The autumn night's got a chill, but that's not the most of my worries. It's fear that's got hold of me.

I try to come up with options. "We could stay here. When someone comes, we could wave them down."

"And how the fuck long will that be?" His growl goes right through me. "I don't know about you, woman, but I want my fuckin' bed."

That's exactly where I want to be. Safely tucked up between the sheets, knowing nothing can hurt me. But back in my apartment and not here, where I'd been woken by a nightmare all too real.

"Where's this fuckin' cabin?" He turns to head into the woods from the direction I exited from.

He's leaving me? No, I can't allow that. If I'm alone, I don't know what will happen to me. I've run, but I can't be sure I'm safe. *It, he, could still be following me.*

"Please don't go," I cry out. "Don't leave me."

He sighs, the sound loud in the night air. "I don't want to fuckin' leave you. I'm hurt. You're hurt. My bike ain't going nowhere. We need help."

Rubbing at my injured arm, I close my eyes, straining to hear the sound of an engine approaching. But this road isn't normally used as a through road—only foresters or people who stay in the odd few cabins would be likely to come along.

The isolation and lack of neighbours was the exact reason my family settled here.

He's making what to him seems to be a very reasonable request, and I can't voice my objections without him thinking I'm crazy. A man like him would never believe it was real. But my rational side disappears as the words echo in my head.

Tickety tock.

"I can't go back," I suddenly scream. "He's waiting for me." Again, I raise my hands as if to ward something off, but it's not the flesh-and-blood man standing in front of me.

While he's favouring one leg, he's at my side in a flash. "Who, woman? Who the fuck is up there?"

My lips tremble, and my voice shakes. "M-m-my f-f-father."

He takes in a sudden sharp breath and does a quick shake of his head, as though wondering why I hadn't told him earlier. His hand snakes out, tangles in my hair, and he turns my face up so he can examine it. I blink as the moon's light hits me.

"Why the fuck didn't you say that? He going to hurt you?"

With my movement restricted, I raise my head and dip it slightly.

"You said no one was after you," he reminds me. Then, as if what he thinks is a lie of no consequence, he moves his gun into my line of sight. "I've had about all I can take tonight. I'll come with you to your cabin. Your pa goes to touch you? Well, he'll be eating a bullet."

"Bullets can't hurt him," I rasp out.

"Oh, sweetheart." He scoffs. "Never yet seen a man who doesn't change his mind when he's staring at the wrong end of a barrel."

Still trapped in his hold, which for some reason is reassuring rather than threatening, I'm bold enough to spit out to him, "Maybe that would work if he was still alive. He was buried fifteen years ago."

He releases me and steps back. His body straightens, and the moon glints off his widened eyes. For a moment, his mouth gapes like a grounded fish.

"You're running from a fuckin' *ghost*?"

Oh, he has every right to sound incredulous. I wouldn't have believed it myself. Would have resigned that rasping voice to the nightmare I thought I'd been having until I'd woken. Once fully awake, I believed I'd shaken it off. Until I heard it again.

Tickety tock.

"Hey." His hands reach out to steady me before I realise I'm falling. "You hit your head, sweetheart. Reckon you're not thinking straight. Let's get you back home and take a look at it." For a moment, I swear he caresses my hair, his touch so light, I might have imagined it. "Yeah, probably hit your head a bit too hard." His voice hardens. "Need a phone, and that's the end of it. We're going back to your cabin. Trust me, babe. Whatever's scaring you, I'll fuckin' deal with it."

Oh, to be able to trust someone, to put my problems in their lap and have them deal with them. I'm tired of fighting on my own. The thought is so tempting. This man is clearly so strong and so capable. But would he be able to deal with my father?

He actually reminds me of another man who could, the man who's the reason my father's no longer breathing. My grandaddy.

I strain my ears once again, hoping to pick up the distant roar of an engine, but it's clear no help's coming our way. The chill's starting to eat into my bones, and while I've no desire to return, I also can't spend the night out in the forest. Taking a deep breath, I make the decision I'd never intended.

"It's this way." I indicate the gap in the trees I'd, a lifetime ago it seems, exited from.

"Through the woods?" He eyes my bare feet dubiously.

"There's a paved track, but it's about a mile that way." I wave my hand down the road. When I'd run, I'd taken the direct route. Not that I'd stopped to calculate anything, I'd just bolted.

He glances down at his own feet. Well, the one he's standing on. Experimentally, he puts weight on the other, and swears loudly.

"Fuck it." He stares back into the woods. "Won't be able to get far on this."

"I'll help you." I hold out my hand.

He chuckles, but there's no mirth in it. "Might have to take you up on that, sweetheart." Instead of taking my hand, he places his on my shoulder, using me as a crutch. "Lead the way."

Fleeing in terror is different from walking purposefully back to my doom. Before, I hadn't noticed the brambles and stones under my feet, but I sure do now. Every step is painful, and it's hard to suppress exclamations of protest coming out of my mouth.

"Wish I could fuckin' carry you," he murmurs, his fingers squeezing into my shoulder. He removes his weight once he understands my predicament. "Hell, you wait here. Give me directions—"

"Don't leave me." Determinedly, I stride forward again, trying to hide that I'm hurting. I can't lose his company.

He shines his phone light downward. "Hunters work these woods? There likely to be traps or anything?"

My eyes widen. In my panic, that's something I hadn't considered. "Er, maybe?"

"Fuck it," he swears again.

Our progress is slow. He manages to find a stick and leans heavily on it. I try to pick my steps carefully. I tread on a particularly sharp stone and wince loudly, just as a purr of an engine sounds behind us.

I swing around, but he grabs hold of me.

"You won't make it to the road in fuckin' time."

"We should have waited," I cry out.

He snorts. "Should have, would have, could have. Gotta deal with the hand we're dealt, sweetheart. Need to keep moving forward. Never go back."

Oh, how I've tried. That should be the mantra for my life, but somehow the past has gotten hold of me. I came back. That was my mistake.

We start moving again, but after only a few more steps, his battery runs out, and the light that had been guiding us dies.

The trees are thick, the moonlight barely penetrates. We're moving blind, and now I'm wary of the traps he'd suggested could be about. Each step I take, I think of metal teeth closing around my ankle.

But it's not just a hunter's traps that worries me. Each step closer to the cabin, I become more and more terrified of the one I'm heading into.

Tickety tock.

It had only taken me minutes to make my panicked exit from the cabin and down through the woods, but the way back is torturously slow, due to my sore feet, and my companion's limp. But all too soon, I see the familiar clearing appear.

He holds me back. "That it?"

"Yes," I whisper, keeping my voice low.

His weapon, which he had holstered for our hike, now reappears in his hand. "Stay here," he says harshly.

I'm torn. I have no desire to set foot in the place ever again, but on the other hand, I'm in too close a proximity to the place that holds such terrors for me to wait here alone. "We need to get the generator running." Lights are a necessity. "I'll show you where it is."

"Just tell me."

"It's temperamental—"

"I can get a fuckin' generator running, woman."

"Not mine." Taking the decision out of his hands, I use his instability to push past him. With a growl, he's hot on my heels as I lead the way toward the outbuildings. I pause at the entrance, my heart threatening to beat out of my chest, listening carefully.

It's dark inside, and I'm grateful that his hand is again

clutching at me. Though I know it's not to offer comfort but to keep his balance, it does help steady me. *I'm not alone.*

Fumbling, I head for the generator, perform my magic and get it working. The shed fills with the satisfying rhythmic beat of the ancient engine thumping away.

Behind me, he stiffens and shakes his shoulders as if preparing for a fight. As he pulls away from me and faces the doorway, that gun is held out in front of him.

"Keep behind me," he warns, as he starts to cover the short distance to the door to the cabin.

I grab on to the garment he's wearing which happens to be a leather vest. He tenses as I touch it, but I'm not letting him loose. If something's coming for me, I want to be close to him.

I'd left the door open. He pushes it easily, his fingers feeling for the light switch on the wall which he finds in the expected place.

Lighting floods the interior of the main room.

"Christ, it's bigger than I expected," he observes, his eyes going right and finding the hallway. Then his face rises, and he notes the stairs. "How many fuckin' bedrooms has this place got?"

"Six," I tell him. "Four upstairs, two down."

Instead of entering, he looks around for a moment, probably noting the old-fashioned furniture which has definitely seen better days. That hole in the couch I'm pretty sure has been a home for mice.

There's still a glow of embers in the fireplace from the fire I'd lit earlier to cheer and warm up the place.

Now he moves forward. "I'll check everything out."

I could tell him there's nothing here, or nothing human at least, but he doesn't seem like he'll settle until he's seen that for himself. As he moves forward in the direction of the hallway, the light falls on the back of his vest.

It reads *Wicked Warriors MC* at the top. The middle is a patch of a skull and crossbones surrounded by wings. At the bottom it reads *Arizona Chapter*.

Oh my God. I've not just been knocked off my feet by a biker, but a real one at that. A member of a motorcycle club. I recall reading about them, and that they're into some shady stuff.

And I invited him into the cabin. Or, more accurately, he invited himself.

Is he going to rape me or kill me? What's more of a threat? The disembodied voice that continued long after my nightmare, or this man who's now searching my childhood home?

Chapter Three

DWARF

I s this night ever going to stop with its surprises?

First the closure of the freeway, then me taking that lonesome road, then crashing into a deer only to find it was nothing of the sort. Then she brings me to this cabin, and I was expecting just one or two rooms. Instead, it's a fucking mansion.

Okay, that's a bit of an exaggeration, but I hadn't expected something of this size. Granted the two first-floor bedrooms I've explored aren't large, but functional enough, with room for a bed but little else. There are still even bedframes in them, but the bare mattresses haven't stood up to the ravages of time. Mildew has discoloured them, and I'm certain several creatures have made them their home.

What is this place and why's she here? It doesn't look particularly habitable. The main room was warm and dry enough, thanks to the fire she'd had burning.

Still, it's none of my business. I won't be here long. I just need a moment to use her phone and then only as long as it takes for help to arrive. But first, given the terror that had led to her running into my path, I need to satisfy myself, if not her, that there's no threat here. Well, flesh-and-blood ones I can deal with.

As I don't believe in ghosts, if I find no one breathing, I'll leave it at that.

She probably had a fucking nightmare. Yeah, that was what must have driven her into the night.

She's still hanging onto my cut as I turn around and retrace my steps, now wanting to check out the rest of the cabin and go upstairs. It's only because I can feel her trembling that I don't snarl out for her to take her fucking hand off. My cut is sacred, and no one touches it.

But I bite back my comment, glad that I have when I glance down at the floor to see bloody footsteps on the boards. Looking at her feet, I inwardly curse when I see how cut up they are. *She must be in agony.* Yet she's not said a word. My eyes go to her face, examining her properly for the first time in good light.

Her eyes are wide, her pupils dilated, her lips slightly parted to let in and out her shallow breaths. Her chest is heaving. She's showing all the symptoms of being scared out of her wits. That she's not mentioned the pain she's in, shows me either she's so crazy she's immune to the pain, or that she's brave.

It makes me wonder again about her mental state. Is she completely out of her head or is her terror greater than physical discomfort? Real or imagined, something has put her in a state.

She doesn't look mad, though, of course, I'm not quite sure I'd recognise if anyone was certifiably insane. They don't exactly go around with it tattooed on their foreheads. Except perhaps for Bonkers, my brother, it's easy to tell he's completely mad. Just a moment's conversation will do it.

With the jury still out on whether she's firing on all cylinders, I check out the rest of the first floor. There's a rudimentary kitchen with a wood-burning stove, and a hand pump for water.

It's like the blind leading the blind, or some kind of three-legged race, I muse as I limp my way across to the stairs, and she tiptoes, trying to keep her weight off her feet.

To ease her discomfort, I suggest, "Wait for me down here."

"I'm coming with you," she stubbornly replies.

Not bothering to argue, I just proceed up the stairs, taking them carefully one at a time, with her hanging on.

The first bedroom we come to is where she must have slept. The bed has a sleeping bag on it, though open and thrown back as though she left it in a rush. Although I can't see the mattress underneath, I'm hoping it's cleaner than the others I've seen. A small suitcase is lying open in the corner.

Her eyes must land on it at the same time as mine. "Do you mind if I get dressed?"

Her robe is insubstantial, and I've a suspicion she's wearing nothing underneath, so her request is quite reasonable. No one likes being caught undressed, and however unprotective it is, there's a comfort being clothed as though it's armour.

"I'll check out the—"

"No, stay here." Her voice is high, and she anchors herself to my back.

As I turn, reflecting getting her to loosen her grip is like trying to remove a limpet from a ship's hull, I try to persuade her. "I'll just be out there."

"Please, don't go." Her shrill plea, the way the skin around her eyes tightens, and the sheer look of horror on her face, has me taking the easiest route and complying.

Like a gentleman, I turn my back, fold my arms, and impatiently wait, balanced on one leg as I hear rustling behind me. To give her her due, she doesn't take long. In moments, I find a woman dressed in jeans and a form-fitting t-shirt in front of me.

She's got a great figure. Nice tits, and her jeans show off a shapely ass.

Hey, I'm a man, don't judge me.

"Ready?" My tone is irritable. I just want to make sure I can relax my guard and there aren't any threats. Then I'll make that call and as soon as I can, I'll be out of here.

She gives a little nod. Instead of letting her grab my leather again, I take hold of her hand with my left—the one not holding my gun.

The next bedroom is unused, not even an old bed in sight. The next door reveals a room used for junk, nothing to write home about. I notice she hangs back and doesn't seem to want to look into the door at the end of the corridor, but I take a glance in and see it's also unoccupied with nothing to interest me.

"There a bathroom?" I could do with a piss.

"There's an outhouse." She snorts. "And a stream. And further up in the woods a pond if you want a better wash."

Hmm. Like a dog, I'll be watering the trees. The lack of facilities confirms the conclusion I'd reached seeing the state of the place. "I take it you don't live here?"

"No." I think her confirmation is all she's going to say, but then she adds, "But once I did. When I was a kid."

As a kid, she probably didn't notice the lack of amenities. It's hard to miss something you've never had.

But I'll be damned if I'm interested. Why she's here now, and why she left, it's of no consequence. "It all checks out." There's nothing and no one that could harm her here. My conscience is salved. When my brothers come, I can safely leave her. "Now where's your phone?"

"In the bedroom I'm using." A little braver as we've discovered nothing amiss in the house, she leads the way into the room where she's been staying.

I'm close on her heels as she marches in and crouches by the side of the bed. "Here." As she stands, she taps in a code, then puts a satellite phone into my hands.

Thank fuck she was prepared.

It takes me only a moment to input the prospect's number, having taken a minute longer to remember it since my phone has died. While I wait for the ring tone to start, with a slight grin, I resurrect my thoughts of getting to my own bed in time to convince a sweet butt to join me. Shifting more weight to my good ankle, it's only then I note silence is the only sound coming from the device I'm holding to my ear.

I pull the phone away, glare at it, but it still doesn't work. I stare at it more closely.

"You've got no fuckin' signal. Who's your carrier?"

"It should work." She scowls at me as if I'm doing it wrong and takes it away from me.

I watch her face. Her cheeks slowly pale. Her teeth bite her lip. Her jaw clenches. Then she looks up, her eyes dark and troubled. "I don't understand. I got it only last week, set it up myself. But now there's no plan for me to connect to."

"You forget to pay your fuckin' bill?" I thunder.

The first sign of spirit I get from her is now as she places her hands on her hips. "No, I did not. I paid up front when I got the phone. I knew I was coming here and knew I had to have some way of contacting the outside world. I am not stupid."

No. Just scared of ghosts. Wanting to keep my balls attached to my body, I keep that to myself.

Jeez… What do I do now? Car. She must have one.

"Where are your car keys?"

Her head tilts to the side as she narrows her eyes. "Car keys?"

I stare at the beamed ceiling for a moment, then back down. *Give me strength.* "Yeah, the things you stick into the ignition, and boom, start the engine."

"My car keys are in my purse…" I start looking around for it and find it on the floor next to her suitcase. As I take a step forward, she continues, "But they won't be much good to you."

I spin around, grimacing as I'd wrenched my ankle again. "What? That doesn't work? You forgot to put gas in it?"

"No, Mister…" She approaches, her finger stabbing at my chest. "Because it's in an airport parking lot in San Francisco. I got a taxi to bring me here and drop me off. I was only going to stay a few days."

She's here, all alone? No means of escape?

"So how the fuck were you going to get out of here?"

She gestures toward the useless phone. "I was going to use that to summon a cab."

I stare at her. She stares at me. Both of us realising we're fucked. *Damnation.* I sink onto her bed and drop my head into my hands.

She drops down beside me. "I can call 911 without a plan, can't I?"

The pigs are the last people I'd approach, even in an emergency. "What the fuck for? You being murdered or robbed?"

"I don't know. Am I?" She gives a calculating look toward me. "I mean, I don't know you, except that you're a biker."

Yeah. She'd had an upfront and personal look at my cut for the past half hour. I tap at my name badge. "I'm Dwarf."

"Dwarf?" Her eyes open wide, but she doesn't ask me to explain.

Instead, she responds in kind. "Raven." And fuck me if she doesn't hold out her hand.

Not wanting to appear an oaf, I take it and shake it. I hold my palm against hers for a second longer than necessary, marvelling how small it seems. It's dwarfed in my large paw. I grin at my own comparison.

Then I sigh heavily. "So, Raven. Seems like we're stuck here. At least for the night."

She looks around uneasily. "I don't want to stay."

I drop her hand. "You think I fuckin' want to? I had plans for tonight, woman."

"You know my name. Use it," she snaps.

Oh yes. I quite like her spirited rather than scared, but I can't help but retaliate. "I can call you whatever the fuck I want. Bike wrecker comes to mind."

She winces and turns her head away.

I glance at the useless phone by my side. The time's still displayed. It's two in the morning. Maybe we should both get some rest, then in the daylight, get back to the road again. There might be more chance there will be traffic passing. Or maybe if I climb higher up, I'll be able to get a signal on my cell, if she's got a charger but I'm starting to doubt that.

But I won't be going anywhere if my ankle seizes up overnight.

"You got a first aid kit, babe?"

She turns wide eyes on me and snorts. "Yeah, sure." She waves her hand around. "This place comes with all the amenities."

It's no Airbnb, that's for certain. I start to wonder what the fuck she's doing here. I grit my teeth. "I need to find something to strap up my ankle, and you need to wash and clean your feet before you get an infection."

Wincing, she rises from the bed and goes to her suitcase. She extracts a pair of trainers and is just about to slip her feet into them, when I remind her, "Your feet are bloody. Better clean them first."

She huffs and swaps them for a pair of socks. Then she starts toward the door, stops, turns, and waves at me. "Come on then, what are you waiting for?"

For you to tell me what the fuck we're doing.

But I keep that thought to myself as I get to my uninjured foot. Even a couple of moments of sitting makes it more painful to put my weight on the other one. But I wave off her offer of help, and doing that tiptoe step shuffle again, follow her back into the hall and down the stairway.

Chapter Four

RAVEN

There wasn't much gas here at the cabin when I arrived, and I should have thought to bring more. So while I should be worried about the amount of fuel we're wasting, I prefer to keep the lights on all over the cabin, the brightness helping to push the night's horrors to the back of my mind.

Maybe I wouldn't have panicked if I'd been able to vanquish my demons by switching on the lights earlier, but I'd turned off the generator before settling to sleep, wary of the low fuel level.

I suppose it would be hard to maintain the level of terror I've experienced tonight, but whether it's the lights, Dwarf's presence, or that we've searched and there's nothing to be seen, and no noises heard, my heart rate has decreased to an almost acceptable level. As my panic fades, other feelings take precedence.

My feet hurt. They're cut, bruised and sore. Dwarf—and what kind of name is that anyway? He's short, yeah, but still taller than me, and I'm no midget—was right to remind me, they need cleaning. God only knows what I might have stepped on.

There's nothing in the cabin itself, but... as I lead Dwarf back down the stairway, I have a half-grin on my face.

"Got any plans as to what we can use?" he asks me, looking around disdainfully. "Sheets I can tear up, something like that?"

I just might have a plan. "I've got some ideas where we might find something."

His mouth turns down, dubiously. "Hope you're fuckin' right. You've come up with nothing so far."

That's just wrong. I grit my teeth. Whatever he thinks of me, I purchased a good enough plan when I bought that satellite phone. I know only too well how out of the way this place is and didn't want to be isolated here for a week, with no way of calling for help if I needed any.

Help that it turns out I need.

I pause, causing him to bump into me. I hadn't questioned why the phone hadn't worked up to now, just accepted it as one more thing going wrong. Now I start wondering, can ghosts affect phones? Cause them not to work?

I don't ask the question out loud. I've already guessed Dwarf doesn't think much of me. *Well, I did cause him to crash his bike.* He has no reason to look kindly on me.

"Why you stopped?" he grunts.

To cover my unanswerable queries about the powers of the supernatural, I ask my own question. "You ever met a prepper?"

Taken by surprise, his brow scrunches. "Prepper? Know of them. Seen some of them. But met one of them? Nah, not as I remember."

"Well, I lived with one. When I was young." I move into the kitchen, kick the rug to one side, and grab the handle of the trap door.

His gun once again appears in his hand like a magician's trick. "What the fuck's down there?"

"Down there," I tell him, with a quirk of my lips, "is my grandaddy's lair." I grimace slightly, remembering it doesn't belong to Grandaddy anymore. "Well, it was."

Pushing me aside, he demonstrates his manly muscles by

pulling up the hatch, then eyes the stairs going downward. "Got a flashlight, doll?"

Doll? That's a new one. Maybe it goes along with the spark of interest in his eyes. What is it about men that something secret intrigues them? Instead of answering, I go to a drawer and get out the requested item. Astonishingly, given the time since it was last used, it still works.

Flashlight held in his teeth, one hand on the wall to balance him on his wrecked ankle, Dwarf slowly descends the stairs. I don't have long to wait before I hear the shouted question.

"What's the combination?"

Rolling my eyes, me holding that information was the reason I intended to go down first, but I have no hesitation letting him know. It was my grandmother's birthdate. "One-zero-one-one-four-one," I shout back to him, and add helpfully, "There's a light switch to your right as you enter."

A gust of wind blows up, knocking a branch against the kitchen window. Logically, I understand the sound, but that's enough to again stretch my nerves to the breaking point. I shiver and run down the stairs after him.

"What the fuck you doing? I was going to check it out."

"Here's the safest place in the cabin," I explain, shooting a cautious look behind me. "No one can get in unless they know the code."

"Which you've just given me." He snorts.

I don't bother explaining, as I don't intend to hold on to this cabin for long, security doesn't matter to me. Pushing past him, I flick on lights as I descend the sloping path into the depths of the extended cellar, heading for the room that I want.

Dwarf follows behind me, soft exclamations letting me know his surprise at what my grandfather constructed. He pulls off into a kitchen and opens the cupboards.

"Haven't seen this many MREs since I was serving." He takes one out and looks at it.

I grimace. "They're probably well out of date, but there might be something in the tins which are still edible."

"As these weren't particularly edible when they were fresh, I doubt time will make much of a difference." He chuckles, and glances around. "How long has it been since your grandaddy was here?"

"He moved to a residential home five years ago," I tell him, a wave of sadness washing over me as I remember the old man who'd been more of a father than grandfather. When I'd found out and had gone to see him, he was only a shadow of the man he'd once been. It wasn't only his body but his mind that had given up on him. He hadn't recognised me, and I barely recognised him.

Dwarf's eyeing the microwave. "Power come from the generator?"

"No. From solar panels. Grandaddy updated his refuge. Didn't much care about modernising the cabin above though."

"To hide this was under here?"

I shrug. "He spent more time down here than in the cabin. Anyway, come." I lead him along the corridor and into the room at the end.

His eyes widen seeing the chemical toilet and rudimentary shower. "I can see why. It's got better facilities." When I open a cupboard, he exclaims, "Well fuck me."

Again, I raise and lower my shoulders. "He was prepared for any eventuality." I delve into the medical cupboard and take out a box of painkillers. "How long past their use by date do you think these are good for?" I eye them dubiously.

"Don't fuckin' know, babe." He reaches past me, grabbing a roll of crepe bandage. "But this is what interests me." Immediately, he sits himself on the commode and starts to wrap his ankle tightly. Once he's finished, he gingerly tries to stand on both feet, and gives a grin. "That's better." He sighs with relief. "Some support was all I needed." His eyes sharpen. "Got disinfectant in there?"

When I bring it out, he motions me to take his makeshift seat, and grabs some cotton balls as well. Then he sinks to his knees, places one of my feet in his lap, and proceeds to clean my injuries.

I hiss as it stings and try my hardest not to pull away. He holds onto one foot firmly, doing what he needs to. Then he moves onto the next.

Frowning, he informs me, "You're going to be sore for a while."

Tell me something I don't know, why don't you?

After he searches for and finds an antiseptic cream and has applied it gently, he looks up into my eyes. "Fuck, Raven. I don't know how you kept moving when your feet were cut up so badly."

Terror, I reply, but only in my head.

But just my expression is all he needs. "Something really scared you, huh?"

Yes. Something had really scared me. Had made me run for my life which I almost ended up losing as I ran into his bike.

As if he can read my mind, his jaw clenches. He shakes his head. "You're lucky I didn't fuckin' kill you."

I know I could have just as easily have killed him. If he'd been going faster, if he hadn't seen me, if...

I close my eyes and force myself to breathe. There's no point considering what could have happened. All I've got is a bruised elbow and sore feet, and his ankle is sprained, not broken. That's something to be thankful for at least.

Suddenly, he yawns widely. It's infectious, and soon I'm trying to stifle one of my own. He regards me carefully. "Not much we can do until daylight, babe. Why don't we try and get some sleep?" He glances toward the corridor. "Grandaddy got a bedroom down here?"

I shudder. "Yes, but it's not where I can stay." At his cocked eyebrow, I explain, "Claustrophobia. Grandaddy always tried to get me to stay with him, but I couldn't... it's okay for a short time, but if I try to relax, all I can think of are the walls closing in, and how we could be trapped down here for days."

One side of his mouth turns up. "Isn't that the point, babe? That you could live here for days, weeks, months?"

The thought doesn't fill me with any pleasure. "I don't think I'd be able to survive that long without going out of my mind."

He considers my words, then raises his chin. "Let me use the facilities, have a quick look around to satisfy my curiosity, then we'll go upstairs and get our heads down."

As he shoos me out then closes the door to the bathroom to give himself privacy, I glance around, considering my options. Here seems to be an oasis, unlike the building above ground. Would I be able to overcome my nerves and stay down here to sleep? But though going back to the bed I was so rudely awoken from holds little desire, I can already feel my palms beginning to sweat, and know my breathing is getting shallow. If I don't get out of here soon, I know the signs. I'll have a panic attack.

Dwarf said he'd come with me. Maybe a man like him will keep even the ghosts away. In life, he'd have been enough to scare my daddy.

Propping myself against the wall, I rest my head into my hands. I've been running on adrenaline since I jerked awake from sleep. My feet throb, my eyes feel sore, and I know I'm just running on fumes. He's right, there's nothing we can do until morning, and the cabin's the only place we can use unless I want to brave a night under the trees.

Dwarf will keep me safe.

I don't know why, but I'm sure of it. I may have only just met him, but he's got that air about him. I sense he's a dangerous man, but none of that's been directed at me, even though I caused him to crash his bike. Sure, he was angry when it had first happened, but he seems to have moved on. I sense he's a good man to have on my side, and while I'm uncertain the effect bullets would have on someone who's already crossed over to the other side, I believe he'd do his best to protect me.

Once he reappears shaking water off his hands, I indulge his curiosity. I let him explore, taking a moment to explain the water filtration and ventilation systems, or at least as much as I remembered being told as a young girl. When he opens the door to the final room, I crash into his back as he stops quickly.

"It's a fuckin' shortwave radio." He claps his hand to his forehead. "Should have fuckin' thought about that in the first place. Of course, Grandaddy would have had a way to communicate."

I hadn't remembered it myself. My heart leaps. We can summon help for him and a taxi for me and get out of this place.

As he eagerly steps forward, flicking switches, I watch in anticipation. But to his obvious disgust, and my disappointment, the radio stays dead.

"Fuck it!" He slams his hand down on the desk and starts checking the power leads. He opens the cupboard underneath and then swears again.

"Fuckin' rodents have made a nest." He shines the flashlight so that I can look. "Chewed right through the wires, see?"

I do. There's a big battery underneath the old-fashioned radio, and even to me, it's clear the terminals are corroded. Slumping against the wall, I feel my burst of optimism leave.

He stares in, picking up one wire then the next. He rubs at his eyes and shakes his head. "Fuck, I'm too tired to focus tonight, but maybe I can fix this in the morning."

"You can fix it?"

He gives me a cocky grin. "Baby, I'm a Marine. I can fix anything."

A useful man to have around indeed, I think to myself. But I'm impatient. "You can't do anything now?"

Easing himself out and to his feet, he shakes his head. "I've been riding for hours. I'm beat." He waves his hands around. "I'm sure your grandaddy's got tools somewhere, but we're going to have to search them out. I'm gonna need to concentrate if I'm to get this thing working and not fuck it up. I'll be better after a couple of hours of downtime." He looks at the devastation on my face. "Raven, I'm not going to leave you alone. There's nothing in the cabin, I've already checked, and in any event, I'll keep my gun close to me. The only things here are the ghosts that haunted your sleep."

Only, he hasn't a clue. "It wasn't a nightmare," I say through gritted teeth.

He doesn't believe me. Physically, he turns me around and pushes me into the corridor. "Let me recharge my batteries then we'll get out of here. Okay?"

Chapter Five

DWARF

Whatever scared her out of the cabin tonight is still lurking in her head. Actually, I'm certain it's always been in her mind.

I'm sure the cabin will be safe enough. There was no sign of a physical intruder when I checked it out—no noticeable footsteps other than hers, and nothing looking out of place or disturbed. Though she's clearly loathe to go back to bed, I'm convinced that with me with her, both of us will get some rest.

I do get she doesn't want to sleep in this dugout. While being under the earth wouldn't bother me, I have a similar dislike for submarines. I can swim like a fish, but none of that's any good at the depths they go under the sea. I'd only had to experience it once but being under the water severely fucked with my head. So, yeah, I can understand how she feels. Claustrophobia's a bugger when it hits.

My ankle, while better now with the support on it, still throbs to the extent I optimistically take a couple of the out-of-date painkillers, knowing they won't kill me, just might not do anything to counteract the ache. Then I lead the way up out of the bunker that I'm fucking impressed Raven's grandfather had built. It was a serious endeavour, and I suspect his life's work.

From what I'd seen, I'd like to have met him. He probably was an interesting, if obsessed, dude.

Raven might not have liked being underground, but her tension seems to grow worse when we emerge into the cabin again. With my hand to the small of her back, I encourage her forward, snagging a second flashlight from the drawer as we pass. She'd already explained it would be prudent to turn off the generator, else there was a danger we'd run out of gas.

Not for the first time, I wonder what had brought her to this cabin. If I wasn't dead on my feet, maybe I'd have asked her, but it seems irrelevant at this point. We're both trapped here. Plenty of time to salve my curiosity when we get out.

Although strapping my ankle had made me able to walk a little easier, the rest of my body needs sleep. The early start this morning, the draining time spent with Miles, and then that nightmare journey, I've nothing in reserve to give.

That radio is going to be a bugger to fix, and I'll need all my wits about me. But after silence descends as we turn off the thump and grind of the generator, I feel happier than I had earlier. I won't let that radio defeat me, and once it's working, then help will soon be on its way. Right now, I'd even kiss Bonk if he appeared in front of me.

My fears of being trapped in this isolated spot, unable even to walk out due to my injury, somewhat appeased as I walk up the stairs beside Raven, I allow myself to analyse the rest of my pains. Fighting to keep the bike upright had pulled at a range of muscles that weren't used to being used for that reason. My back, shoulders and chest all ache.

A good sleep, and then awakening refreshed for the new day is just what the doctor ordered. I'm looking forward to getting my head down.

Raven's steps start to drag as we approach the room where her sleeping bag is. Her need for more rest is obvious, but her reluctance to close her eyes is palpable.

As we enter the doorway, I pull her into my arms, unable not to notice how well she fits there. She's a couple of inches shorter than myself. In heels, she'd possibly be taller. But being a short shit myself, I'm used to girls towering over me. She's slight, but soft with curves in proportion to her figure.

My cock twitches and I tell him to back down. It's only that I was so focused on using a sweet butt when I'd returned to the club that it now senses a target. Raven might be female, but I doubt she'd be willing. I know my drawbacks and that I'm not the most desirable man on the planet. For some reason, most women like someone they can look up to. A protector in their eyes is someone they can shelter under. Time after time, I've been passed over in favour of my brothers who stand over six feet tall.

They overlook that I might have other things to offer. I may not have the height, but I've big feet and hands, and a cock which doesn't fail to deliver.

Not that Raven will see that tonight. Though mores the pity. If I overlook that I'm not sure whether all's right in her head, she's really quite attractive.

Maybe I can persuade her sex is a good stress reliever? Nah, citizen women want more than a casual fuck. She'd probably be looking for a happy ever after, and there's no way I could even consider giving this unbalanced woman that.

She wrecked my bike for starters.

I slide out of my cut, glance around, and finding nothing better on offer, drape it carefully on top of her open suitcase.

Raven's standing, unsure what to do with herself.

I decide she could do with direction. "Get into your sleeping bag."

"You staying here?" Her voice seems to wobble.

I search her face, but the worry seems more that I'd leave her, not that a strange man would be sleeping in the same bed.

"I'll be here. Along with my gun." And knife, but of that I don't enlighten her. Looking down at the useless phone that's still by the bed, I notice it's four a.m. The late hour seems to make me feel even more tired, and I want nothing more than to get some shut-eye.

She glances to the bed, then back at me. By the flashlight, her face looks haunted. "Will you... will you hold me?"

As long as she doesn't mind my dick poking into her. "I can do that, sweetheart."

My assurance seems to get her moving at last. Without undressing, and who can blame her, she slides into the sleeping bag. Without further ado and only removing my boots, I slide on the mattress behind her. It's not the best place I've ever prepared to sleep, but certainly not the worst either.

I fidget as I find the best place to evade the lumps and broken springs. Then I put my arm over her, pulling her to me. A quite unpleasant, musty smell fills my nostrils, so I try to concentrate on the womanly smells coming from her. Those, in contrast, are more than palatable.

"Relax, I'm here. I'm not leaving you." She's still too tense. I slow my breathing, hoping she'll pick up my cue and follow. It takes more than a moment, but slowly it starts to work. Gradually, she synchronises the movement of her lungs to my own. I wait until she goes lax in my arms and only then allow my body to fall limp. I have a few minutes where my brain can't keep hold of any thought, then know no more as I fall fast asleep.

"Tickety tock. Tickety, tickety tock. Come to Daddy."

What the fuck? I come awake like a shot, my hand reaching out for my gun. I blink my eyes in the darkness.

I've had a dream. Inwardly, I snort. Raven's fear must be catching. I close my eyes and force my body to relax once again.

Until I hear a whisper, *"Tickety tock. Time's running out. Don't make Daddy come to find you."*

I inhale sharply. I'm wide awake. I hadn't dropped back to sleep. Had I? I pinch myself to make sure.

"Tickety tock!"

The loud shout makes me sit up fast, while Raven gasps and goes rigid by my side.

"*Tickety tock. Tickety, tickety tock.*" The distinctive sound of footsteps distantly clomping on wood come to my ears.

"Stay here," I rasp at her.

"Don't leave me." Her voice is shrill, dripping with fear.

"*Tickety, tickety tock. Where's my little mouse? Clock's ticking.*" The footsteps sound closer and louder, like they're on the stairs.

As Raven whimpers, I grab the flashlight and ease off the bed, but keep the beam switched off for now. My eyes have become accustomed to the darkness, and I don't want to lose that. Ignoring the protest of my ankle, I move quietly in my stockinged feet toward the door and ease my head around the doorway.

As quietly as I'd moved myself, Raven's beside me. She's got enough sense not to grab my arms, but her hands are flat on my back, as if reassuring herself that I'm there.

Clomp, clomp, clomp.

The footsteps are getting nearer.

"*Tickety, tickety. My little mouse, are you ready for me?*"

It sounds like someone's reached the top step, but there's fuck all that I can see. As the next footfall sounds, I throw caution to the wind and press the button on the flashlight. My eyes blink, but nothing is revealed.

Clomp, clomp, clomp. The footsteps are in the hall and coming toward us.

But there's no one fucking there.

Raven's whimpering sounds in my ears like an animal fatally injured. My heart's beating loudly in my chest.

"*Tickety, tickety tock. Tickety, tickety, tickety, tock, tock, tock!*"

Although I can see nothing, I push back against the doorway as the footsteps seem to come level with me. I hold my breath as they falter, then pass on, each footfall sounding like it's being placed deliberately.

"*Tickety tock. Come to Daddy.*"

"*Tickety tock. Tickety tock. The mouse can't win against the clock. Daddy's here.*"

My eyes open and in the glare of the light, I see the door at the end of the corridor swing open as though it's been kicked hard. The force makes it bounce back against the doorjamb.

I push Raven back into the room, grab my cut, my boots, and her trainers in one hand, and with the other I grab hers.

"Run!"

Chapter Six

DWARF

It might not be my finest hour, and in normal circumstances, a Marine doesn't flee. But tonight, there's no doubt I've been faced with evidence of the supernatural. There's just no other explanation, or none I can immediately think of.

Voices and sounds might not do me any harm, but if this is a ghost and they can influence the physical as evidenced by the violent opening of that door, I'm not sticking around to see what else they can do.

Raven's compliant, and matches my pace without complaint as I leap/hop down the stairs, still needing to favour my ankle, but anxious to put space between us and it, not allowing myself to think a phantom might not be bound by physical rules.

I head straight for the kitchen and raise that trapdoor.

"Not down there," Raven cries out, the first real words she's spoken since we were awoken.

For a reason I don't understand, I think we'll be safe underground. I come up with the only logical justification.

"Only one way in and out. Easy to defend."

"Ghosts can move through walls."

"Then the forest won't be a barrier," I counter. "At least down there I can work on the radio." I may not have had enough rest but now have even more reason to attempt to make contact with the outside world.

The words *tickety tock* are still echoing around us, increasing in volume, making my heart thump like it's about to leap out of my chest. I stab at the keypad with the number I committed to memory earlier, open the door, and push her inside. As I slam the door shut, the sound is mercifully cut off.

At least Grandaddy remembered soundproofing.

Leaning back against the door, I pull Raven into my arms. My heart is beating a furious dance, as is hers.

Breathing in through my nose and out through my mouth, I try to calm down. I'm a practical person. I've never believed in spirits or in an afterlife. When you die, you die. Much as I'd like to come back and haunt my enemies, I never thought I'd have a chance.

While the evidence my previous beliefs might have been wrong has just been left behind us, I'm unable to come to terms with the thought we've been chased by a ghost. Now I can hear it no longer, I think I must have been suffering from a hallucination. *Maybe there's some sort of poisonous gas leaking into the cabin.*

Raven's losing it completely, sobbing in my arms. Her body is shaking, and I think if I were to let go, her legs wouldn't support her. All my doubts are now gone along with any blame I attached to her, and questions about her sanity. Gas leak or not, no wonder she ran as if the demons of hell were after her.

It's exactly what I'd just done myself.

Was I right? When I can hear something other than the rushing of my blood through my veins, I strain my ears. No repetitions of tickety tock sound down here, and there are no footsteps descending the stairs. *Or not yet.*

Hallucination, that's what it must be.

"What did you hear?" I rasp at Raven, knowing she'd been

woken by something. Maybe it hadn't been the same thing. When she doesn't immediately respond, I shake her lightly.

"Tickety tock," she cries out. "Repeatedly. And footsteps." Her hand forms a fist and hits my chest lightly. "You know. You heard it the same as me."

Oh fuck I did. Is there such a thing as shared delusions? I shudder, not knowing what to believe. But just in case, I find myself hoping Grandaddy's prepping included some talisman protecting his bunker against spirits.

I might have muscles. I might carry a gun. Yet I'd felt fear the likes of which I've never known. Being up against a group of insurgents has nothing on what occurred upstairs. At least with a seen enemy, you've time to prepare, to understand which tools to use to come out the victor. Against something ethereal, you haven't a chance.

I no longer blame Raven for blindly running into my bike. I've experienced the same terror as she'd done. And worse, I can't imagine how dreadful hearing those chilling sounds on her own must have been.

Now, for the sake of my sanity, and hers, we've got to get out of here. There are only two reliable ways of doing that. One is to go down and wait by the road, hoping the right person would stop, assuming, of course, whatever the entity is, it's confined to the cabin. The other is to get that ancient radio working.

As the minutes have passed and nothing's disturbed the silence or come knocking at the door, Raven's sobs have stopped, and her violent shaking has turned to the occasional shiver. I admit to feeling steadier myself, and at least in a better frame of mind to get working.

"Know where your grandaddy kept his tools, sweetheart?"

She frowns. "I'm not sure. But don't all men have a man drawer?"

They do indeed. I grin. Taking her hand, maintaining the contact for myself as much as her, I head for the kitchen. After opening a couple of drawers, I see even a prepper can't avoid such a typical masculine habit. There in the midst of other "maybe useful to keep" shit, I find a couple of screwdrivers, an assortment of wires and some pliers. An electrical tester would be too much to ask for, and of course, I don't find one.

Taking my treasures, I make my way to the room at the end of the hallway and angle the flashlight to complement the dim overhead bulb. There I examine what I've got to work with. The battery's probably fucked. The terminals are corroded, so I strip the old wiring away and take the back of the radio apart.

"Your grandaddy have a storeroom?" I would think he would have.

Raven thinks for a moment. "He's got a place where he hoarded loads of shit."

"Could you go look and see whether he's got spare batteries?" In the event of an alien attack or World War Three, I suspect he would have been prepared. Knowing what's happening and keeping in contact would be the only lifeline he would have had. Therefore, having spares would have been vital.

When she hesitates, I place my hand over hers for a second. "I'll be right here. One shout and I'll be with you."

She straightens her shoulders and takes a step back. To give her confidence, I summon up a smile and a confident jerk of my head in the direction I want her to go.

While she's absent, I put my mind to the task ahead, replacing the chewed wires.

She doesn't take long. Soon she's back, and as I expected, Grandaddy did indeed stock up with spare batteries. Mindful these must be years old, I'm grateful she's carrying three of them. Fuck knows what charge they might hold, or whether they've got any at all. It would take a hell of a lot more work, but if this doesn't bear fruit, I might have to find a way to hook the radio up to the mains instead.

There may be better tools upstairs.

There might. I shudder at the thought. While I might not like

48

to think of myself as a coward, I don't want to wander about the cabin in the dead of night. Not when I can't identify who, or more accurately, what, is up there. Any searching will have to wait for daylight. But who'd blame me? Normally before facing any enemy, you have a good idea of the danger they present, and what weaponry you might be faced with. On this occasion, I have no fucking idea. My Marine training didn't teach shit about taking on something from hell, or at least, the spiritual world.

While rationally I can't accept it, I'm unable to come up with any other explanation as to the origin of the sounds we heard.

It takes an hour or so of fiddling about, but finally I'm ready to fasten the cleaned-up terminals to the battery. Holding my breath, I press the power button. A satisfied grin comes to my face when a steady red light glows.

"It's working." Behind me, Raven claps her hands, then her arms come around my neck. "You did it!"

Briefly I squeeze her hands with mine, sharing her pleasure. Step one is indeed complete. Now to see if this thing will work.

With my phone dead, the satellite one equally useless and lying forgotten upstairs, I've no way of knowing the time. *How long had we been sleeping before we awoke?* It can't have been long, it was still pitch-black outside. And now we've been down here for about an hour. Without being able to see whether the sun's risen, I can only go with my best estimation. Maybe it's five a.m. I grimace, knowing I'll probably be waking someone.

Reaching into the depths of my memory, I try to remember how this thing works. I pull the microphone toward me and begin twisting dials.

Thank fuck I dabbled with amateur radio in my younger days, and still remember my call sign. After tortuously having to go through the formal codes, I manage to make someone understand that I need help from my brothers. A quite simple message, *bike down, no cell signal.* And then the address which Raven had helpfully jotted down on a piece of paper.

That done, I replace the mic then push myself back from the

desk with a sense of satisfaction. Part one of our escape mission completed.

Raven goes from grinning to biting her nails in just a few seconds. "How long until help gets here?"

Putting my hands behind my head and interlocking my fingers, I grin. "Give Toad an hour or so to stop complaining about being woken at this bumfuck of an hour, then another half hour to get the brothers together. I'd say a good two to three hours before the cavalry arrives."

She grimaces and nibbles another nail.

Reaching for her hand, I squeeze it. "Hey, at least someone's coming. We know we'll be able to get out of here."

Her face twists again, and she glances up to the low ceiling. "I don't like staying down here, but I don't want to go up *there*."

I notice her breathing is shallow and realise she's struggling to keep herself from panicking. Stretching out my legs, I wince at the pull on my ankle. I regard her carefully and try to engage her in conversation. "That was some bullshit last night, wasn't it?" Now I've got a message out, I relax a bit and instead of focusing on the practicalities, analyse what happened instead.

I'd been unnerved enough, but Raven had been downright terrified, and I don't jump to the immediate conclusion that it's because I have a dick and she hasn't. While I doubt anyone but a committed ghost hunter would have been much enamoured by what happened during the night, it strikes me Raven's reaction was extreme. She'd run headlong into the woods without any shoes.

Taking her hands and pulling her in between my outstretched legs, I stare at her and remember what the horror had pushed out of my mind. Back down at the road, she'd said her daddy was after her. If that was who I heard, he wasn't being loving or friendly. While I'm no expert, from the little I know from horror films I've seen or books I've read, ghosts don't hang around haunting the living without reason.

"Raven," I say, still staring at her. "You said it was your father and that your father died." She also said she'd used to live here. I take a chance. "Does tickety tock mean something to you? Are you Mouse?"

Already I'm thinking there are reasons for some pent-up energy to remain here. Possibly enough for her to harbour terrible memories in her head. No wonder staying here would give her nightmares. But while that could explain why she's hearing these things, the question remains, why am I hearing them too?

From the expression on her face, I've hit a bullseye. She jerks as if she's a puppet and someone's just lifted her strings.

"Why are you here, sweetheart? What made you come?" The state of the cabin shows no one's lived here for years.

She straightens, tosses that glorious, though in need of a brush, hair back over her shoulders, and offers in a theatrically light tone, "Do you want me to see if I can rustle up some coffee?"

Hmm. She's evading my question. But coffee does sound good, particularly if it's going to loosen her tongue. I'm slightly wary of any that her grandaddy stored away all those years ago, but perhaps if we can find an unopened jar, it might not be completely unpalatable.

As I nod and watch her move to the door, I realise if she doesn't want to talk to me, there's nothing I can do. It's her business after all. Shouldn't be any skin off my nose, though I do have a bad case of curiosity, and her telling her story would be a good way of passing the time.

But she owes me no explanation. I already know *and understand* why she caused me to crash my bike. I attach no blame to her. If I'd been alone, it's possible I'd have done similar myself.

As her footsteps fade in the direction of the kitchen, I try to convince myself I don't care. When my brothers arrive, they'll load up my bike and then we'll take her to the nearest town and drop her off. She can go back to wherever she came from, and I'll get on with my life.

And make a point of staying out of haunted houses in the future. My own joke falls flat as I realise I'm deadly serious. This possible brush with the spiritual world has been enough to last me a lifetime.

As for this cabin? It can rot for all that I'm concerned.

Still, as I get to my feet to follow in the direction she'd disappeared, I know I'll always wonder what all this has been about if I can't get her to open up and tell me what she knows.

"Here, try this."

Taking the tin cup from her hand, I blow on it, then cautiously take a small sip. It's drinkable, just, with hopefully enough caffeine to start me feeling human again.

She too sips as though she also needs fortifying.

"So?" One last prompt to pry. If she doesn't want to tell me, I won't continue to pressure her. She owes me nothing.

But as if what passes for coffee has revitalised her, she props herself against a countertop, and words come out of her mouth.

"I was born here," she begins, her eyes going upward as if clarifying she doesn't mean in the bunker. "Lived here until I was eleven. My daddy had married my mom and moved her in to live with Grandaddy when my gramma had died. There was talk that he needed looking after, but I think that was just so Daddy could live in a free house." She grimaces. "I never knew my grandmother or my mother. There were complications after my birth, and she died. She had me here. I'm not sure what medical assistance they got, but it wasn't enough."

"Fuckin' sorry to hear that, darlin'."

Her lips press together. "It's hard to know what you've missed when you never had it from the start. I was brought up here," again she points above us, "with my brother, my daddy and my grandaddy."

The cabin was big, but austere. Had she noticed that as a child? For all the lack of facilities or female influence, it doesn't necessarily mean it wasn't idyllic. Not wanting to jump to assumptions, I ask, "You have a good childhood?"

She shrugs and shakes her head at the same time. "I knew nothing different. Neither my brother nor I went to school. Daddy wanted to keep us close. We were homeschooled by his pa."

"Not your dad?"

"He could barely read and write himself." She scoffs. "My grandaddy used to say he failed with him as a child." She smiles softly. "But really it was because he was allowed to run wild. Granddaddy knew the mistakes he'd made with his son and wanted to do right by me. He taught me all that he knew. He was good with letters and building stuff with his hands."

"What did your dad do?"

"Drank? Lazed around?"

I start to get the picture she's drawing, and it doesn't sound very enviable at all. "Seems a bit of a lonely life for a girl. Was your brother good to you?"

She snorts. "If by good you mean putting snakes in my bed and pulling my hair, then yeah." A flicker of pain comes over her face, and I get a feeling her brother wasn't particularly nice at all.

Not a good childhood then. I frown. "What happened when you were, what did you say, eleven? How come you moved away? Was that when your father died?"

"Grandaddy sent me away the same day. I went to live with his sister." She smiles for once at what appears to be a happier memory. "Aunt Agnes was great. I enjoyed living with her. As for this place?" She glances around her and the lightened tone when referring to her aunt disappears again as she gives a shudder. "I never came back until yesterday."

"Your brother go with you?"

Her sudden look shot my way shows she's surprised I asked. "No." The sharpness of her response suggests there's a story there. Particularly when she adds, "Grandaddy was going to straighten him out, but that's the last thing I knew. I don't know where he ended up." She pauses, then adds, "Or whether he's still alive."

A tingling in my spine suggests I'm not getting the full story, such as how exactly did her father die? Was her brother involved? Something had definitely happened that made her grandaddy decide this was no place for a young girl.

Without giving too much weight to my question, I casually ask, "How did your father die?"

She looks away sharply. For a moment, I don't think she'll answer, until she murmurs almost under her breath, "A gunshot wound."

My brow creases. That answer only raises more questions, like who pulled the trigger? Was it self-inflicted, accidental, or otherwise, or did Grandaddy end him, or possibly the brother she mentioned? Or, I narrow my eyes, could it have been Raven?

Nah. She was just eleven, I remember, and she's hardly a strapping girl even now. Something tells me not to push further. She's probably got enough to deal with, with the fact he died.

This place can't hold good memories. I gesture around me. "Why did you come back?"

Her eyes fill. "I loved my grandaddy, but I never saw him again after I moved out."

Guilt on his part? Because somehow he killed her father? Was it not accidental as I had thought, and perhaps a fit of uncontrolled anger perhaps over the waste of space son he'd brought up?

"Aunt Agnes told me he'd had a stroke and had been moved to a facility to care for him about five years back."

"You didn't visit?"

She gazes at nothing and her eyes glaze as though in regret. "Not at first. Aunt Agnes said he wouldn't have wanted me to remember him the way he was now. When my aunt died two years later, I wanted to reconnect with the only family I had." Her head shakes side to side, and she wipes her eye. "But then Alzheimer's had kicked his ass. He didn't recognise me. Worse, he became agitated when I walked in. I didn't visit again." A deep breath fills her lungs and is let out on a shuddering sigh. "Then, he died."

Christ, what this woman has been through. "When?"

"A few weeks back." She pauses and again her head shakes, this time as though in disbelief. "He left me this place in his will." Her eyes widen as she looks around. "I never expected it, but I suppose there was no one else to leave it to." She pulls back her shoulders and I see a glimpse of the spirit I'd seen before. "I thought I'd return, see what state the place was in, tidy it up, possibly keep it and rent it out, or sell it. I doubt it's worth much, but it's better than it rotting away."

Narrowing my eyes, I try to read what she's not telling me. Her reason for being here is practical enough and makes sense. Yet, unless she's strapped for cash and needs money, why would she return? The cabin doesn't seem to hold any happy memories for her. If it were me, I'd leave it to rot or burn it down.

Unless she's facing her fears from the past. "Raven," I start, cautiously. "What does 'tickety tock' mean to you?"

She recoils as though I've hit her. She pales so much I feel like a bastard for asking her. I'm about to backtrack and say it's none of my business, when she opens her mouth and blurts out, "It was a game my father played with me."

My jaw clenches as I wonder exactly who had the fun out of that particular game. It certainly doesn't sound like a fond memory. That voice didn't sound friendly.

Could the most unlikely culprit for the death of her father be Raven herself? Had somehow she been the cause of her father's death, and was that why he's come back to haunt her? Assuming I suspend my disbelief in ghosts, of course.

Was that the real reason she was sent away, and why her grandaddy wanted nothing more to do with her?

And where's her brother? Where does he figure in all this? Is he dead or alive? Could he have been killed at the same time as her father?

Am I holed up here with a killer?

Raven's shivering and hugging her arms around herself.

Knowing I've not lived a blameless life myself, and if she is responsible, then there probably has to be a good reason why she killed her father, I step forward, take her into my arms, and just hold her.

Chapter Seven

RAVEN

The woman who caused Dwarf to crash his bike, the scared, broken woman standing held in his arms, is not the woman I am, nor the one I'd want a man like him to see. But for now, I'll take the comfort of the silent support he's offering me.

While he could have probed further, and I'm sure there's a myriad of questions flying through his head, he's keeping silent. But what are we really but strangers? I'm not going to admit how, as a young child, my father abused me.

I'm not going to explain how he would wait until Grandaddy went down to his bunker, before he'd start looking for his little *mouse* as he called me. He'd walk through the cabin saying 'tickety tock, time's running out' as if it was a game of hide and seek. But it wasn't fun for me, and I didn't like what happened when he found me. In the end, it was better not to hide—that just made it worse—the hunt making him all the more excited.

He's dead. He's been gone fifteen years. I came through. I'm a survivor. I'd thought I was strong enough to return to the scene where it all happened.

But last night... Hearing *his* voice, *his* footsteps. Knowing I wasn't asleep, I was awake... Fear had flooded through me like never before. Instantly, I'd been thrown back into the persona of that abused little girl. All I could do was run, and not stop running, not stopping to look behind me.

During that rush through the forest, I'd been part-woman, part-child—half of me feeling like my flesh-and-blood daddy was after me, and half of me just as terrified by the thought of being chased by a ghost.

All my years of therapy, all the success of putting my abuse at the back of my brain, moving on, not letting it influence me, had been wasted it seemed. I hadn't been anywhere near strong enough. What a mistake returning here had proved to be.

Though coming back, all I thought I would be facing were residual memories not completely hidden away. I couldn't have expected that after all these years my father would be here waiting for me.

If Dwarf hadn't heard him as well, I'd put it down to the stress of returning here to the cabin which was all I'd known for the first eleven years of my life. While on one hand it's good to know I'm not going insane, that I wasn't the only one to hear, to *feel* his malevolent presence, the fact he *did* somehow seems worse to me. It confirms it's real.

Can he reach out from beyond the grave? Could he really hurt me?

He already has. I scoff at myself. Just look at me. I'm a shaking quivering wreck, not the confident businesswoman I've worked so hard to be.

Grandaddy had given me the chance by getting me out of this place. Going to stay with my aunt, my great-aunt to be correct, had been a lifesaver. She was a force of nature and quite direct. There was no hiding that I'd been abused nor that I'd had my important firsts taken away. She swept nothing under the rug, just dealt with it matter-of-factly. The very first thing she did was make sure I got therapy and had as much as I could ever need. Despite not having children of her own, she'd done every-thing she could to bring normality into my life.

The adjustment hadn't been all smooth sailing. It had taken

me time to adapt, to mix with others at school, to be accepted, to move from being an outcast, to having friends. But as time passed, I embraced the changes to my life, threw myself into the opportunities offered, adapted, and gradually almost forgot I'd ever led another life.

With Agnes's support, in time, the scared little girl grew into a confident teen. While therapy wasn't able to completely put my abuse back in its box, when I eventually had my "first" time, it was only about as awkward as most of my friends' reportedly had been. While I pride myself on being a woman who doesn't need a man to let her know her own worth, I've had a number of normal relationships with no hang-ups at all. Nothing serious, but then I had more important things on my mind.

I'm strong, independent, and after college, I began building my own business up from scratch. Though I'm not in the major leagues, I have enough commissions to keep a roof over my head and food on the table.

My first impulse when I'd heard I'd inherited this place was to have nothing to do with it. It could rot where it stood as far as I was concerned. But something irked at me. This had been my grandparents' place, the one they'd built and where they'd lived out their dreams. Though it had all gone wrong in the end, that needn't be the end to their fantasy. Maybe I could apply my magic to the place, turn it into an Airbnb or something? Grandaddy's basement could be advertised as a curiosity.

My designer brain had started to buzz with the possibilities, yet part of me knew coming back would be confronting my past, reliving moments I'd confined to history. *Was I brave enough to come back?* Or, alternatively, *how could I live with myself, knowing I lacked the courage to return?* That would be acceptance that I hadn't gotten over what my father had done to me. I refused to let him win. I refused to allow him one more moment of power over my life.

So, I'd cleared my calendar for a few days, packed my bags, booked a flight, and left.

When I arrived yesterday morning, the sun was out, the birds were singing, and I was hit by what a peaceful place this was. The cabin was in a worse state of repair then I'd remembered from growing up, but it wasn't unredeemable. It just needed more work before my designer hands could be applied to it.

I'd walked around, soaked up the atmosphere, tried to make myself remember the good times with my grandaddy. Him teaching me at the kitchen table, which was now lying on just three legs, him reading stories to me by the side of the fire, listening to the spitting of the flames. Him taking me fishing, and hunting. While I can admit to some squeamishness while he made the kill, I'd be excited at the thought of having fresh venison to eat.

Looking back now, I was forcing myself to only remember the pleasant things, ignoring my underlying sense of unease. Long before I spread out my sleeping bag on the one mostly usable bed, I'd been unnerved by the light dimming and the increasingly ominous rustling in the trees. I'd become a city girl, unnerved by nature's sounds, and I'd uneasily dropped off to sleep.

I hadn't been surprised to wake with a gasp, the nightmare still holding me in its thrall. Though I was shaking and scared, I'd told myself not to be so stupid, nothing from a dream could hurt me.

Until the sounds had come again, and this time, I wasn't asleep.

It was real. It was happening all over again.

That's when I'd instinctively grabbed my robe and run as if the hounds of hell were chasing me.

Straight into the man who's currently holding me tight in his arms.

"Raven, you okay?" He sounds concerned.

Swallowing hard, I try to pull myself together.

I'm not the girl I once was.

I'm a survivor.

I survived my father once. But how could I fight that monster now? *How can you kill a man who's already dead?*

"Raven?" Dwarf loosens his hold and runs his hands up and down my arms. "Talk to me."

Shuddering with effort, I try to lighten my voice. "I suppose no one would want to buy a cabin with a resident ghost. I better come up with a new plan."

Though the concern doesn't completely disappear, lines smooth away from his forehead as he snorts. "You could burn the house down. Sell the land."

And undo all of my grandaddy's hard work? It wasn't his fault his son had turned out bad. Or maybe it was. Maybe my grandad hadn't been the man I'd thought he was.

He'd left me a haunted house. That gives me an idea. "Or I could get an exorcist in."

Dwarf barks a laugh at my suggestion. "Right here, right now, I'd say I don't believe in ghosts. This place can't be haunted."

"So why are you here?" I challenge, raising my eyebrow and pointing above my head. "Why aren't you up in the cabin?"

He shakes his head and chuckles. "You've got me there." Then, a little uneasily, he adds, "But we've got to get up there soon. Else my brothers won't be able to find us."

I try to summon some of my normal confidence, knowing by now we'll be emerging into daylight. "I was here yesterday. The haunting only began in the night. Ghosts can't walk in daylight, can they?"

"How the fuck would I know?" He wipes his hand down his face. "I'd have said they don't exist and couldn't walk in the dark. I'd still say that, but..." His eyes move uneasily to the ceiling, then he visibly shakes himself like a dog coming in out of the rain. "Of course, I don't fuckin' believe in ghosts."

"Then what chased us out of our bed last night?" Replaying my words, I blush at the wording I'd used. Sneaking a sideways glance at him, I suspect he'd not be one that I, myself, would chase from my bed. The longer I'm with him, the more attractive he's becoming.

Dwarf's not a classically handsome man, but he's got a presence, a big personality which makes up for his lack of height. Despite me causing him to crash his bike, he's been nothing but kind to me.

His hands are huge. What would they feel like running over me?

We've got a couple of hours to kill.

What the fuck am I thinking about?

Blushing again, I chase such thoughts out of my head. This really isn't the right time or place.

Strangely enough, he too looks disconcerted when I catch him sneaking a glance at me.

He coughs to clear his throat. "How about we try some of those MREs and then brave the day and go upstairs?"

"I'd brought some food with me," I tell him, then frown as I realise cooking breakfast means starting a fire in the wood-burning stove. While as a child all that was quite normal to me, as a city-dwelling adult, I like my life easy. "But MREs would probably be quicker."

Standing, he goes to the cupboard where he'd found them before and gets a couple out. He waves them at me. One's a chicken dish, one beef. When I indicate the chicken, he heats them and passes over the one I'd chosen.

Despite its age and my suspicion, it's palatable at least. It's only when I start eating that I realise how hungry I am, and to my surprise, I finish everything.

We eat in silence, reminding me we're two strangers not friends. We would probably have walked past each other had we met in the street. Feeling awkward, I brew some more of what passes for coffee, then, when we've drunk that, Dwarf stands.

"Come on. Let's go upstairs."

I'm about to protest when I realise he's just as nervous as me, if that gun in his hand is anything to go by. "You think that will work?"

His mouth twists as he takes my question seriously. "Haven't gone up against the supernatural before, but never yet faced an adversary that didn't run from lead." He closes his eyes briefly and then opens them again. "You know, it was just noises. There's probably no threat."

"The slamming of the door?" I remind him. "That was physical. What if—"

"What if nothing," he snarls, suddenly angry. "I know what we fuckin' heard, but I still can't believe. Maybe a breeze blew the door shut. What I do know is that if we don't get upstairs, my brothers won't be able to find me."

Breeze be damned. I know a door being slammed in anger. The sound's etched on my brain. But I do understand Dwarf's fight against the belief in the supernatural, even with the facts right in front of his face. I've never believed in an afterlife either. I've never wanted to.

But how else can I explain the voice of my father in the night, using the words he used to use to torment me? That exact tone, the phrasing… it was *his* intonation. There's nothing else that I can believe, other than my father's returned to haunt me.

Reluctantly, though, I have to agree. We can't stay here. Even if rescue wasn't on its way, we'd have to emerge at some point into the light of the day. It must be Dwarf's calming presence, as I've already stayed down here longer than I normally stay. Even with Grandaddy here, by now, panic would be gnawing at me.

I follow Dwarf to the stairs, fisting my hands to stop them from grabbing onto his leather vest like I had in the middle of the night.

I'm a strong, brave woman, I remind myself. *I don't need a man to lean on.*

But right now, maybe I'm wrong.

Yesterday, I thought the cabin lit by sunlight was a pleasant place to be, the only mark against it, the memories it held. Today, when we exit the trapdoor in the kitchen, even the air seems oppressive, and rather than finding it easier, I find it hard to breathe.

I tense, tilt my head, and listen carefully, but all I can hear is the wind blowing through the trees.

Dwarf puts his hand on my arm. "There's no need to be worried."

"Says the man who ran to the basement last night."

He snorts. "There's time for valour and time for retreat. Even I can't fight things I can't see."

"You wouldn't be able to see a ghost anyway," I mumble.

"Hey, woman, are you fuckin' with me?" His hand twists in my hair, and he turns me around to face him. He's grinning at me. "Now let's go get your stuff together so we'll be ready to leave."

When he releases me, I step back. "We?"

His brow creases. "Yeah. We. You didn't expect me to leave you here, did you?"

I hoped he wouldn't, but I'd thought the most they would do is call me a cab.

He misunderstands me. "Fuck, woman. After all this, you want to stay?"

Shuddering, I shake my head. "No. But it seems such a waste. I didn't have a chance to do anything I wanted to do."

"Just sell the fuckin' place." He pinches his nostrils.

"With the resident ghost?"

He shrugs. "Maybe your dad won't bother anyone else."

Could that be? Could I, in all conscience, just walk away, knowing someone else was going to be living with the evil spirit of my dad?

Yesterday, I would have said ghosts didn't exist. But now? My eyes go to the stairs, and I shudder.

Seeing my unease, Dwarf takes hold of my hand. "I'll come upstairs to get your stuff with you, okay?"

Oh, how I long to be able to tell him I can look after myself, but just the thought scares me. Instead of standing up for myself, I give a weak little nod of my head.

Dwarf's ankle seems to be bothering him less today, I notice, as I walk with him up the stairs. The air seems even thicker as I enter the room where last night we'd tried to get some sleep. When I remember something and step back out to look up the hallway, the door at the end, *the one to my old room*, is firmly closed. Despite the sun blazing in through the windows, I shiver.

Entering the bedroom once again, I find Dwarf's already rolled up my sleeping bag for me. As I hadn't unpacked, it's a simple matter of collecting my useless satellite phone, and zipping my suitcase closed. A suitcase that he takes out of my hand and proceeds to carry down the stairs.

At the bottom, he eyes the phone I'm carrying, his head tilted to one side, and his eyes narrowed. But I have no idea what's going around in his head.

Chapter Eight

DWARF

I no longer think that Raven's insane, how could I, when last night, I too fled from a ghost? It was so not my finest moment, that I'll be inclined to omit that part of the story once my brothers arrive to pick us up.

But seeing the phone in her hand makes me think things don't add up.

Apart from her manic behaviour which can now be explained, Raven seems to have her head together. She's not crazy, just a normal woman pushed beyond her boundaries. I have absolutely no doubt that being as she had the forethought to purchase a means of communication to use in this back of beyond, that she also made sure to get a plan that would allow her to use it.

That she couldn't seems puzzlingly convenient to me. It might have stretched my imagination, but if it had broken due to something supernatural, like some poltergeist activity throwing the phone against the wall, given everything else, maybe I could accept it. But messing with a calling plan seems to be beyond the capabilities of any ghost. But then, what do I know? Everything that's happened in the last few hours has been outside my experience.

Apart from the whole haunting aspect, there is too much here I don't have answers for. Although it would be an admission of my weakness, and something that may well come to bite me in the ass, I start to think about involving my brothers. Rather than them just picking us up and taking me home, and her to the airport, maybe I should invite them in to take a look around? Pick their brains and see what their take on the situation is. At the very least, they'd be interested as fuck in that bunker underground.

Running my hands through my hair, I wonder whether I could concoct some story that doesn't lead them to suspect I fled from a bodiless voice in the night. Maybe I could still come out of this with my pride intact.

Maybe.

I eye Raven, wondering whether I could bribe her to keep her mouth shut? Then realise I'd look weaker than ever if I asked her to make out I'd been some fucking hero which I most certainly had not.

At least the strapping on my ankle is making it possible for me to walk without too much of a limp today. I must have just wrenched it rather than doing too much damage.

Which reminds me... "How are your feet?"

"A bit sore," she answers. "But as long as I avoid doing a marathon, I'll be fine."

My eyes narrow, suspecting they're more than just sore, but I admire her spirit. Again, I lift her suitcase and carry it out of the cabin. Putting it down on the porch, I walk a few more steps, then turn and look back, my hand shielding my eyes from the sun.

It's the first time I've seen the outside in daylight. Though rundown and neglected, in its heyday, this would have been an impressive place. Sure, there are a few tiles missing from the roof, but otherwise the exterior looks structurally sound and fairly sturdy. It looks like it was built by craftsmen and meant to last.

With the sun gleaming on it, it's hard to reimagine the terror I'd felt in the night. Frowning, I consider there must be some fucking explanation. Noises from animals outside and settlement sounds of the house perhaps, that my brain misinterpreted to form words and footsteps. Standing here now, with peace settling around me, it's hard to believe I'd reacted like I had.

I'm a Marine. I should have stayed to fight.

But fight what?

However much I try to rationalise it, I know what I heard. A physical enemy I'd have stood up to, but how do you take on an ethereal voice?

Raven has followed me out, as if she doesn't want to be left alone inside, and I really can't blame her. Without knowing all her history, I believe there's something she's omitted to tell me. That game her father played didn't sound like any normal shit to me, but I don't want to ask her the obvious. Some wounds go far too deep to be opened again. If, and when, she's ready, she'll tell me.

Could it be that her terror communicated itself to me, and influenced me to start hearing things? Was it not real but in both our imaginations instead? Could she have been talking in her sleep, and I heard and relived it in a dream?

But I'd been awake. I know it. As I purse my lips, I realise that wouldn't explain the phone not working.

Marine or not, as I cast another look toward the cabin, I realise I can't wait to see the back of this place and to leave its mystery behind. What on first glance looks like, if it were done up, an attractive abode, now only serves to send chills down my spine. Give me the explainable any day of my life. Tell me to go fight a physical enemy and I'll march into battle quite prepared to lose my life to save my brothers or my country. The unexplainable has proved another matter entirely.

Coward? Yeah. I suppose I am.

"I'm going to walk down to the road to check on my bike."

She broadens her shoulders and takes the handle of her suitcase. "I'm coming with you." She eyes the leg I'm still favouring, though not so much as before. "It's longer, but easier to walk down the track rather than try and take the direct route through the forest."

There's no denying she's got a good point. One more twist certainly wouldn't help my ankle. The track is at least paved or was. Disuse and neglect have caused grass and weeds to grow in the cracks. Still, it will be somewhat easier progress. Taking her suitcase back from her, hell, I'm a man, she's a woman, and that's what my extra muscles are for, I start heading in the only possible direction. Down—to the road, and what's left of my bike.

If it wasn't for the stubborn pain in my ankle, and that I have to tread carefully, analysing every step, this could be a pleasant morning stroll. While in the dark, the closely knit trees had seemed ominous. Now, birds flit from branch to branch, bees and other insects buzz around us, and the sun shining through the canopy above forms an ever-changing kaleidoscopic effect that could even be called enchanting. The air is filled with the scent of pine. A rabbit runs across our path. A squirrel scutters along a branch. And, if I'm not mistaken, I see the flash of white that looks suspiciously like the tail of the animal I originally thought responsible for crashing my bike.

Each step I take away from the cabin, I begin to doubt my sanity. Every yard gained makes me think I must have picked up on the hysteria of my companion. *Ghosts don't exist, do they?*

Then there's the matter of the satellite phone. Casting a sideways glance at the woman stoically walking along beside me, not one murmur of protest about her sore feet escaping, I wonder whether she's not as savvy as I previously thought, and that she'd just simply forgotten to get the phone connected.

There must be a logical explanation.

The trek back to the crash site is certainly longer this way, especially as of necessity, our progress is slow, both of us limping and moving carefully. We go down the track which must be a good half a mile, then back up the road to where she'd run out of the woods and into me.

Following the skid marks, I soon come upon my baby, and take a moment to stand, my jaw clenching as I take in the sorry vision. It looks no better, and maybe worse, in the daylight than in the glow of my phone yesterday.

"Oh, I'm so sorry." Raven's hand covers her mouth. "I didn't mean to—"

"Hey, no worries." Gingerly, I slide myself down into the ditch. At least the bike's lying on a bed of pine needles and hadn't slid across the road. The twisted front wheel and the suspect alignment of the handlebars is damage that can be fixed fairly easily. But until my brothers arrive to help hoist it up, I won't be able to access the damage properly.

"I'll pay for it to be fixed." Raven has come down beside me. She's crouching, and her hand moves to the wheel as if her touch could heal it.

It was her fault, but having experienced the terror she'd felt for myself, I can't blame her. She hadn't intended to run into me. "We'd be a piss poor club if we couldn't fix our own bikes," I tell her, dismissively. "Looks worse than it is, darlin'." Or, so I hope.

A car approaches, showing had we waited until daylight, we'd have been able to get help. In fact, he even slows down. "Need help there, buddy?"

I wave him off with a gesture that conveys my thanks. "Got assistance coming."

He gives me a chin jerk and speeds up again.

Only a few minutes later, I hear a welcome sound—multiple motorcycle engines. I broaden my shoulders and brace myself, as a huge fucking smile of relief comes to my face, which slowly turns to one of confusion.

I'd expected one or two to come, along with the prospect driving the crash truck. But as the bikes begin to appear around the bend, I start to count them off.

There's Toad, my prez, riding out front. Behind him is Raider, the VP, and next to him, Metalhead, our sergeant-at-arms. Hell, there's Stumpy, the enforcer. Scalpel—well that's great—our medic can look at my leg and Raven's feet. Then there's Bonkers, heaven help us, Midnight, and Cloud. Only Crumb and Cash seem to be missing.

At my gesticulations, they pull over onto the side. I wait until Toad's engine song ends, then step forward as he dismounts.

"Good to see you, Prez." I hold out my fist. He bumps it, then our arms pull each other in, and we slap each other's backs. "Didn't expect you to bring the whole crew."

Toad glances behind him as if only just noticing they're there, then looks back at me and grins. "Seems we all wanted to find out what happened to our resident chef."

"Yeah, Ruby all but poisoned us last night when you didn't make it back," Bonk yells out.

Ruby? My eyes go wide and my nostrils open. "You didn't fuckin' let her in my kitchen?" I thunder. Ruby, the prez's woman, was raised as a socialite and has never cooked in her life. Fuck knows the mess she'd left my domain in if they're not, as I expect, joking.

Toad snorts, knowing only too well the lack of culinary expertise of his wife. "As if. We ordered in pizza."

"Was worried about you, fucker." Stumpy steps forward, and I'm subjected to that back slapping thing again.

Metalhead is looking behind me. "Can see why you didn't contact us last night," he drawls. His eyes are clearly roaming over Raven's body.

Metalhead is the epitome of a tall handsome biker. I suppress my urge to see Raven's expression as the upturn to his mouth shows he, for his part, is appreciating what he sees. I swallow down my disappointment and prepare for this being yet another case of me being passed over for one of my brothers.

Yet, unusually, I don't feel like rolling over and taking it.

"Raven?" I hold out my hand and draw in a breath, only

71

releasing it when she approaches me, and her fingers close tightly on mine. My soul feels soothed at her touch.

Eyeing my brothers cautiously, not knowing whether this will be a mistake but only time will tell, I do the right thing and begin to make the introductions to my competition.

"Prez, this is Raven. Raven, Prez. That's Raider. This fucker," I narrow my eyes, "is Metalhead." I introduce the others. As I call their name, each throws her a chin lift.

As if she's overwhelmed, she presses closer against me.

Toad steps around me, and stares down into the ditch at my bike. "Shit, Brother. What happened? You take the turn too fast?"

In the bright sunshine with that cabin well behind me, I'm loathed to tell my brothers anything about things that go bump in the night. I'm just about to open my mouth and concoct some story which doesn't leave either Raven or I in a bad light, when she speaks up. "Er, that was my fault. I ran out in front of him. I caused the crash."

With narrowed eyes, Toad first glances at her, then back at me. He raises a brow.

I shrug. "Yeah."

"Her car damaged?" Toad's looking at me with narrowed eyes, as if questioning why there's no car in sight and why I'm so close to the woman who fucked up my ride.

"Um, I wasn't in a car. I was on foot."

As I'm thinking we should have spent some time getting an acceptable story straight, deceptively lazily Toad turns his eyes on her and asks perceptively, "You running from someone, sweetheart?"

I see Raider cracking his knuckles. Yeah, a little girl like her brings all our protective instincts to the forefront.

When Raven tugs at my hand, I glance at her. She raises her shoulders as if to ask what she should say. I clench my jaw and shake my head. When she frowns, I speak for her instead.

I had every intention of telling them she was spooked by a

bear, when other words come out of my mouth. "She was running from a ghost."

Cloud guffaws loudly, and Scalpel snorts. Raider puts his hands to his belly, and Metalhead rolls his eyes and shakes his head. Toad's frowning, and Stumpy, the asshole, is circling his forefinger by his brow.

"So, she what?" Bonk starts. "Thinks crashing your bike is better than being caught by a ghoul?" The fucker puts his hands up to his head, leers forward and makes a wailing *ooh* sound.

Midnight, ignoring everyone else, flicks back his long black hair and stares with interest into the forest behind. Taking a packet out of his cut, he extracts a cigarette. Cupping his hand around a lighter, he puts a flame to the end. After taking a lungful of smoke and exhaling, he regards Raven and jerks his head.

"What's up there?"

"A cabin," she answers him with a wary look toward me. I squeeze her hand in encouragement.

"That's where you saw this ghost?" Midnight presses her.

"You fuckin' believe her?" Raider snorts.

Midnight's dark eyes fall on his VP. "There's more to this world than you'd expect or can probably imagine." After that ominous pronouncement, he contemplates Raven. "How and when did it appear? In what form did it manifest itself?"

Stumpy's obviously still of the view she's got a screw loose, and his expression as it falls on Midnight suggests the Native American must be as crazy as she if he's buying into her story.

She pulls away from me slightly, still keeping hold of my hand, but giving Midnight, the only one not openly laughing, her attention. "I was sleeping. Woke up. Thought I was still dreaming, but I wasn't. I heard a voice." She shivers even though the sun is warm.

As Bonk snorts and rasps, "Fuckin' nightmare is all," I decide to back Raven up.

"It was the voice of her dead father. I, er..." Straightening my shoulders, I broaden my back, preparing for the ridicule to be heaped upon it. "I heard it myself."

"You heard it?" Toad stops his chuckling, but his mouth remains open.

Raising my free hand defensively, I state, "Look, I know what you're all going to think. After the accident, we went back to the cabin. No, I wasn't drunk or stoned, and what I heard scared the shit out of me, so take that how you want." I add a glare that threatens retribution to the next person who teases me.

Metalhead opens his mouth but shuts it at the look on my face.

"Takes guts to lay yourself open like that." Toad's giving me a thoughtful look.

Midnight's dark gaze flicks into the forest once more before returning to Raven. There's an obvious flare of interest in his eyes as he asks, "Mind if I take a look at this cabin of yours?"

Chapter Nine

RAVEN

I already knew Dwarf was part of a motorcycle club, and obviously it was the other members, or brothers as he referred to them, who were the ones he'd called on for help. But knowing and being faced with such a large group of bikers had come as a shock. Suddenly confronted by eight leather-clad men, led by their president with his scarred face, proved to be intimidating. All towered over Dwarf, and were so imposing, I'd moved closer to him as though he was my support.

Their interaction, though, was interesting, and if I hadn't known better, I might have thought they were siblings for real.

Of course, it wasn't surprising that they'd ridiculed the reason I'd caused Dwarf to crash his bike. Before yesterday, if I'd been told a similar story, I'd have wondered what the person had been smoking. But I did notice that one of their members, the man called Midnight, presumably because of his long dark hair, seems more intrigued than amused. That he's clearly of Native American heritage might explain why he's possibly more open to things that others would dismiss.

I'd hoped I'd seen the last of the cabin and had left all its terrors behind. My suitcase sits forlornly by the side of the road.

I'd hoped the bikers wouldn't want to linger, and would just load it, me, and Dwarf's poor stricken bike, and take us far away from here.

"I wouldn't mind seeing this haunted house myself," Toad drawls, lazily. He turns to one of the men who's standing aside from the rest, and who'd arrived in a truck and not on a bike. "Punchbag, get her suitcase and Dwarf's bike loaded."

"Prez..." The man, younger than the rest and seeming to be not so sure of himself, steps forward and examines the position of the bike. "Er..."

"Too much for you to handle, Prospect?" Said prospect lurches forward when his back is slapped. "Well, I don't mind sitting this one out. I'll stay and help you."

"You scared of ghosts too, Bonk?" the one introduced as Scalpel challenges, his lips curving in mirth.

Bonk mock punches him. "Nah, just can't be bothered to go on a wild goose chase."

"Yeah, yeah. Fuckin' coward." The massive man standing with arms folded rolls his eyes.

"You shut your face, Metal," Bonk warns.

Their president shakes his head, looks up at the sky, and I'm certain mouths something like *give me strength*. He instructs, "Okay, Bonk and Stumpy both stay and help with the bike—"

"Hey, Prez. I want to go ghost hunting," Stumpy whines, then his mouth snaps shut at a glare from the man he'd addressed.

Scalpel, rather than joining in the altercation, has been watching Dwarf carefully. When Dwarf shifts, moving weight from his bad leg to good, he asks, "How badly are you hurt, Brother?"

"Just twisted my damn ankle when I dropped the bike, but it's not too bad."

Scalpel raises his chin, but still frowns as he looks down at Dwarf's boot which is unlaced to accommodate the swelling.

"I'll take a look at that in a moment." I gather from his name and his interest that he's a medic of some sort.

My attention snaps back to where Stumpy is complaining and mumbling something unintelligible to me, a phrase about when he was a prospect, he was expected to do *all* the work by himself, and if he didn't, he wouldn't get his patch. For a second, my lips twitch as I wonder whether he's talking about something like a scouts' badge of merit for rescuing a bike.

I notice the scarred man pinching the brow of his nose, then saying tiredly, "Change of plans. We'll *all* get the bike loaded then we'll *all* go up to the fuckin' haunted house." I also don't miss how his snap decision has the men jumping into action.

Ropes appear, muscles are used, and soon the bike's out of the ditch and onto the road. They then have to manoeuvre it onto the back of the crash truck which, with its twisted front wheel, takes a lot of grunting and more than a few uttered and snarled fucks to get it loaded. But eventually it's done and is strapped down.

My suitcase is also lifted into the back, then before I realise what he's doing, Dwarf has picked me up and I'm now sitting in the front of the truck with him easing himself in beside me.

Before I can so much as huff in indignation, Dwarf's opened the window and is shouting out, "Down here, hang a left at the turning and then it's about half a mile up."

As if they'd practised the choreography, with their prez in the lead, the bikes are mounted, engines started and then roar off. The prospect driving the truck follows more sedately.

My heart rate speeds up when the cabin comes into sight. My intention when I'd left it had been to never go back. Now as we drive toward it, I start to feel apprehensive all over again. *It's daylight,* I remind myself. The walk through the forest, shown at its best with the sun filtering through the canopy of leaves, had done much to raise my spirits and chase the night's demons away, and the antics of Dwarf's brothers had helped to vanquish my remaining blues. But my heart grows heavy once again as the cabin appears in front of me, my brain filled with memories of the past and the ghost who'd resurrected them in the night.

Tickety tock.

My palms start to sweat, and instead of a confident woman, I shrink until I feel I'm just a shell of myself. That haunting had successfully stripped away the protective layers that I'd acquired through therapy. Memories swamp me of how weak I once was, and how my daddy had so easily overpowered the much younger me.

"Hey, you're okay." Dwarf takes my hand and I know he can feel me shaking. "You can stay out here in the truck if you don't want to go in."

But that would be weakness and letting my daddy win all over again. I've broken the hold he had over me before, and now I need to do it again. The only way to do that is face my fears, and whatever remains in that cabin.

I'm not alone, I tell myself. I've got Dwarf and his brothers beside me. *Nothing can hurt me.* The worst I'll need after this is perhaps a little more therapy to put the past back into the box where it belongs.

"I'm coming in." My words are said with as much determination as I can summon, and I'm proud when my voice doesn't shake.

Bravely, I take the hand Dwarf offers to me, and exit the truck. He doesn't let go as he gently encourages me forward to where the men have already dismounted their bikes.

With a jerk of his head, Toad acknowledges our approach. "Nice place," he states admiringly.

"If you hadn't told us where the track was, I'd have ridden straight past," Metalhead comments admiringly.

"Bit of a dump." The man with the letters *VP* on his patch, whose name I think is Raider, gives us his view. "But I suppose it has potential."

Dwarf grins as he slaps his VP's back. "You're not seeing the best part of it either. It's got a hidden secret."

"The ghost?" Bonk rolls his eyes.

"More than that. And something you'll like." Obviously, I know what he's talking about, but note how Dwarf teases them by not offering more explanation.

"I want to go in first alone. Get a sense of the place," Midnight demands, frowning at the others.

"Go on," Toad offers, magnanimously. "Go do your voodoo shit."

"Ain't fuckin' voodoo shit," the Native American complains, as he glares at his prez then steps toward the doorway.

I hadn't stopped to lock the door, so it pushes open easily. When Midnight disappears inside, one of the men takes out a packet of cigarettes and passes them around—there are only a couple of takers. I step away, moving upwind of the smoke, and wrap my arms around myself.

A voice whose owner I didn't hear approach makes me jump. "So, what's the history of this place?"

Willing my heart rate to slow, as being back here has unsettled me, I give Toad the Readers' Digest version. "My grandaddy and Gramma built the place after the war. Stayed and raised their family. Their surviving son, my dad, stayed with them and brought his wife, my mom, here. I was born. She died at my birth. I lived here with my brother, my dad and my grandaddy until I was eleven."

I glance at Toad who's looking at me curiously. "Your dad move you away?"

"He died." My words are clipped, giving nothing away.

"Sorry to hear that, darlin'." Compassion flits across his face. He lets a respectful moment pass, before picking up his enquiries again. "So, you and your brother—"

"Just me," I interrupt. "Jack stayed here. I never came back until yesterday. Grandaddy died recently, and it turns out he left the place to me."

Toad's eyes soften. "Aw fuck, darlin'." He turns back to the cabin. "It's rundown, needs a fuck load of work, but could be a good place. You planning on living in it?"

Shivers run down my spine at the idea. Even if last night hadn't happened, the cabin holds too many bad memories for me. "No, I could never live here again." I straighten my shoulders. "For a start, I have a business in San Francisco. I just came here to see the state it was in." Shading my eyes from the sun, I give the cabin a closer examination. "I'm an interior designer. I thought maybe I could modernise it, do it up." *It was a pipe dream, even without the resident it already has.* "But it's in a worse state than I remember. Too much structural work for me to do. I'll probably sell it as-is. That's if anyone wants it."

"When Midnight's finished whatever the fuck he's doing, I'd like to see inside," Toad confirms.

Chills run down my spine at the thought of going back in. But surely, I can't have much to worry about with Dwarf and his brothers with me. I suppose if the ghost does his thing again, at least it might make them believe. At the moment, I think all of them are convinced Dwarf and I are imagining things. And why shouldn't they be? I'd have been of the same mindset if I were them.

Turning, I find Dwarf no longer at my side. Instead, he's talking to another biker who hasn't been introduced as yet. As if in tune with me, he glances up and catches my eye, then he beckons me over.

"Raven, this is Cloud. He's our technical expert. Mind showing him your phone?" When I reach into my purse and start to take it out, he shakes his head. "No, not your cell, the satellite one."

Realising I'm being a bit slow, I reach back in and take the correct and useless one out. "I'm going to be asking for a refund."

Cloud, a man, who like all the others, stands a head taller than Dwarf, takes it from me. "Did you try and use it before you arrived at the cabin?"

Dwarf hadn't asked that question, and now he stills, appearing interested in the answer.

I roll my eyes, wanting to disavow him of the view I'm a stupid female. "Of course, I did. I knew there was no signal out here, and just in case, didn't want to be stranded. At the very least, I needed to call a cab to come pick me up and take me back to the airport."

"And you had no problem with it?" He turns it over in his hand, then passes it to me so I can unlock it.

"None. I only made the one call, but it worked alright."

He taps a few keys, then his brow creases. "You certain? There's no calling plan associated with it."

Dwarf shakes his head. "Already know that, Brother. Discovered that last night."

"But there was," I interrupt Dwarf. "I just told you, I used it." I place my hands on my hips and frown at them both just in case they suggest I'm making it up. If I hadn't made that call to try it, I'd doubt myself.

Cloud shares some kind of non-verbal communication with Dwarf, then uses words when he speaks to me. "Mind if I hang on to it for a bit?"

I shake my head. It's useless to me. "Not as long as I get it back so I can get a refund on it."

"You'll get it back," he assures me. He thinks for a moment then gets out his own phone. "You mind giving me some of your personal details so I can look into your calling plan? Like your full name, for example?"

"Raven Katerina Dempsey." I think for a moment and then decide I don't mind him knowing the rest. I give him my date of birth, guessing by the calculating look on Dwarf's face that he's estimating my age—*twenty-six years if he'd asked, I would have told him*—and also my registered address.

Perhaps I shouldn't be giving my information out to strangers, but something tells me Dwarf is trustworthy, and by extension, so are his friends. And anyway, I doubt they'd bother to follow me back to California.

Midnight reappears and approaches me and Dwarf, his lips pressed together and a frown on his face. "Can't sense shit in there. Where exactly did the apparition appear?"

"It was no apparition," Dwarf and I answer together, then both of us give an embarrassed chuckle. Dwarf continues, "It was a disembodied voice and footsteps. We heard it from the first bedroom on the right upstairs, and then the doorway at the end of the hall slammed open." Before Midnight can say anything, he adds, "And there wasn't a wind blowing."

Midnight shrugs. "Well, I'm no expert, but I got nothing." He grins, showing perfect white teeth. "But I might not be attuned to White man spirits."

Dwarf snorts and slaps his back.

"Can we go inside now?" a whiny voice sounds.

"Yeah, Bonk, I'll give you a guided tour," Dwarf calls out over his shoulder. He puts his hand to the small of my back and pushes me forward toward the door.

As soon as I step inside, I realise I needn't have been worried about returning. As the nine bikers stomp in behind me, the atmosphere is changed entirely. What previously looked large, now looks small with them all crowding around.

Presumably lured by the possibility of a ghost, five of them head straight for the stairs and the upper hallway.

Bonk knocks into Midnight's shoulder as he passes. "Let's see if this White man can sense things beyond your understanding, Brother."

Midnight shoots him the finger, but just says, "Be my fuckin' guest."

Toad watches his men ascending, then turns to me. He jerks his chin up to where they went, and asks, "How many bedrooms?"

"Four up, two down," I answer.

He nods, seeming satisfied with my answer. "Bathrooms?"

Dwarf snorts. "An outhouse outside."

Toad's eyes widen and he grimaces. "That would need to be fixed for a start."

I nod and gloomily agree. "It's a lot of work for anyone crazy enough to buy this place." I already know it's no nest egg. I'll be surprised to find any buyer to take it on.

"I think you said there was a surprise inside?" Now Toad raises an eyebrow at Dwarf.

Dwarf chuckles in response and his chest puffs out. "I did indeed."

Chapter Ten

DWARF

Having my brothers swarm over the cabin has changed the dynamics completely. I hadn't missed how Raven had shrunk into herself as we'd driven back to the cabin, clearly dreading returning to the place. But with my brothers assing about, the shadows which had seemed so menacing in the dead of night have now lost their mystery. I even notice the darkness around Raven's eyes start to disappear as she watches Bonk and Stumpy battle for first place as they ascend the stairs.

I'm intrigued by Prez's interest in the place and know what I'm going to show him next will enthral him further. If we can exorcise this place, then I've an embryonic idea which I suspect he's already starting to share even before I give voice to it.

Toad beckons to the VP and the sergeant-at-arms to accompany us as I lead the way into the kitchen, then stand back so Raven can have the privilege of the big reveal of the trapdoor leading to the basement.

Toad's brow creases, his eyes narrow and he tilts his head, then as I grin broadly and gesture he should follow Raven downward, he starts down the steps. Raider follows him.

Standing back, I let Metalhead go in front of me, then hurry on after them, eager to see their reaction.

I don't have to wait long.

"Well fuck me," Toad exclaims soon after he's through the now open door.

"What the fuck?" Raider's not far behind.

"Well, I'll be fucked." Metalhead turns and looks me in the eye. "This is something else, Brother."

I grin back. I already know.

I let Raven have the honour of showing them around the bunker and explaining what she can of the facilities.

It's not long before Toad comes stomping toward me. He lifts his chin. "This is one fuck of a find, Dwarf."

There's a spark of interest in his eyes, and his nostrils flare with anticipation. But before he gets too carried away, I have to remind him.

"If you're thinking what I think you are, Prez, got to remind you. This cabin's already got a resident."

His face twists, and his head moves side to side. With a furrowed brow, he leans in and asks disbelievingly, "You're not fuckin' telling me you believe that shit?" He lowers his voice. "Thought you were backing her up as you seem to like the girl."

I do like her, and enough to support her. I meet his eyes. "This time yesterday, I'd have laughed you out of the state had you suggested I'd be terrorised by the unnatural. But, Prez, however much I'd like to deny it, I was fuckin' spooked last night."

He doesn't mock me, just gives me a curious glance, then places his hand briefly on my shoulder before continuing up the stairs. Raider and Metalhead, in an animated discussion, follow in his wake. Almost as soon as they've disappeared, Bonk, Midnight, Scalpel, and Cloud take their place. I hear Raven starting her spiel all over again. When Stumpy's face appears peering through the doorway, I beckon him on through.

"Best catch up as she won't want to go through it all again," I warn him.

It's getting crowded down here so I just wait by the door for them to satisfy their curiosity. It's not long before Raven appears, wiping a hand over her eyes. She yawns and I'm hard put not to copy her. It reminds me how little sleep we got last night.

Offering a tired grin, she says, "I think I missed my calling as a tour guide."

"You're doing a great job." Raising my hand, I smooth a strand of hair back from her face. "How are you holding up?"

She bites her lip as though she's giving my question serious consideration. "I'm doing okay. I'm starting to think I imagined everything. With all these people around, it seems impossible that any of last night was real."

I know what she means, but facts are facts. "Pretty concrete you running into my bike. You could have been killed, Raven." And doesn't that thought leave a bad taste in my mouth? "Come on, let's leave them to poke around on their own." Again, taking her hand, it seems such a natural thing to do, I lead her up and out of the trapdoor. Looking out of the kitchen window, I see an overgrown area that was presumably a yard. There's a tree with a branch begging to have a swing swung from it.

"Take a walk with me?"

I don't have to ask her twice.

The air outside is fresh, unlike the musty smell that lingers in the cabin long locked up. As Raven walks beside me, I head for the tree that I saw.

"Hey, I was fuckin' right." I pump my fist in the air.

Giving me a strange look, she asks, "About what?"

I point upward to where the fraying ends of a rope are still knotted over the branch. "You had a swing there, right?"

Her eyes glaze as she looks up. For a moment she's quiet, then she speaks, "It was always there. Grandaddy redid the ropes from time to time. I used it a lot, except when Jack would come and push me." She rubs at her elbow.

I frown. "He pushed you too high?"

"He pushed me off. Broke my arm."

It's not the first time I don't get a good feeling about this brother of hers.

I turn at a sudden howling and wailing from inside. Rolling my eyes, I realise it's just one of my brothers fooling around, confirmed when I hear Toad yelling for them to stop behaving like five-year-olds. I snort softly. Par for the course.

Putting thoughts of my brothers to the back of my mind, I look at the yard again and notice some kind of stone bench. It's overgrown, but I can easily clear some of the ivy. After doing so, I pull Raven over to it, then sit her down. Crouching in front of her, I take both her hands.

"Will you tell me, Raven? Will you tell me what happened here, and how your father died?" I've got a suspicion that it was no accident. I'm starting to believe he was killed, and the most likely suspect in my mind is her brother, Jack, though it could have been by her grandaddy or Raven herself. Something happened that made them send her away.

She clutches at my hands, holding them tight as though she's anchoring herself. For a moment, I don't think she's going to say anything. She's quiet for so long that when she does start talking, her voice comes as a shock.

"I suppose it doesn't matter now that he's gone. It was my grandaddy. Grandaddy killed him."

Hmm. Well, I did have him on the list. He'd killed his son. I frown. "An accident?"

She shakes her head, and her face falls. Her voice drops to a whisper. "He shot him with his shotgun."

Well fuck me. I knew she's been battling with some childhood trauma. Perhaps I'm now getting to the bottom of what it could be. "Did you... were you there?"

She grimaces and turns her head. "He killed him in front of me." When she scrubs at her cheeks as if to wipe blood away, I start to realise exactly how bad this had been.

Christ. I rub my hands over my face. No wonder she was sent away. This cabin would hold nightmares for her. She's probably been seeing it happen all over again now she's back. Once again, I wonder whether I'd picked up on some strong emotion coming from her. I've heard how strong the power of suggestion could be. Maybe that's all it was.

How had she the guts to come back to the place where it happened? Hell, that just proved how strong Raven is.

My mind goes back over our previous conversations. While she hadn't maintained contact with her grandaddy after she'd left, she'd led me to believe that was more on his part than hers. She never speaks with anything but fondness for the old man. Surely, if he'd killed her beloved father, she'd have hated him.

Yet, all the implications are it's her father she'd not gotten along with. And that fucking game, *Tickety Tock*.

Reluctantly, hesitant to hear the details, I tentatively ask, "Why did he kill your father?"

Raven's face drops into her hands. She mumbles an answer which I don't quite catch. I ask her to repeat it. "Tell me, Raven. Help me understand." Pain fills her eyes, and my gut rolls. A man doesn't kill his only son without there being a very good reason. "Raven, you were eleven, just a child." I brush away a lock of hair that's fallen over her eyes. "Tell me, please."

She shudders, and when I think she's going to refuse to open up, she suddenly starts speaking, her voice chillingly void of emotion, and her eyes glazed. "Grandaddy used to disappear into his bunker for hours. Daddy knew while he was down there, he had time."

As she pauses, I suspect I might know the answer as to what the time was needed for, but hoping I'm wrong, I gently prompt her. "Time for what?"

She swallows a couple of times. "Time to abuse me."

In my head, I have an image of her grandaddy coming up out of his bunker to see his son on top of his beloved granddaughter. I feel his rage as though it was my own. Once would have been enough for him, but for her? I grit my teeth and ask for the answer, while hoping it was the first and only time, and that he'd been stopped before the damage had been done.

"Was it only the once?" I ask, struggling to get out the words as my jaw is so tense.

She disavows me of that hope immediately, her tone cold as though she was talking about someone else. "He started when I was nine."

My eyes close and I summon strength to stop myself from exploding, forcing myself to question her calmly. "You didn't tell your grandaddy?"

"Daddy said he was younger and stronger than him." A sob comes from her throat, and angrily she wipes tears from her eyes, as though ashamed they're betraying a weakness. "That if I said a word, he'd kill him." A sob escapes from her throat as emotion now starts to betray her. "That day, Grandaddy unexpectedly came up to get something, and he caught him." She grimaces and gives a half-grin. "Daddy was wrong. Grandaddy wasn't weak. He pulled him off me, threw him downstairs, then got his shotgun and blasted him then and there. There was so much blood…" She shakes her head. I reach out my hand to cover hers, but her eyes meet mine, and with a certain savagery she adds, "So much blood. I'd run after them fearing for Grandaddy." She brushes her hand against her cheek again. "My daddy's blood splattered over everything." Then she looks at me, saying fiercely, "But I was pleased. I knew he'd never be able to hurt me again. God help me, but I was happy he was dead." The set of her jaw challenges me to tell her, her reaction was wrong.

Without hesitation, I support her. "I don't fuckin' blame you." If he wasn't already dead, I'd have killed him myself.

Now the floodgates have opened, she carries on, "Grandaddy buried him up in the woods. Got Jack, my brother, to help him when he came home after school. Jack was furious at what had happened. Grandaddy tried to tell him why, but Jack already knew." She pushes her fist against her mouth. "He used to watch, Dwarf. Jack would watch."

Jesus Christ. This just keeps getting worse.

"How old was he?" I grit my teeth, thinking if he watched it was probably only a matter of time until he'd taken his turn too. At least she'd been saved from that.

"Jack was fourteen when Daddy was killed." Raven's sad eyes rise. "Dwarf, I thought I was over all this, but returning has brought it all back. I wish I'd kept away."

Fuck doing the cabin up to sell. I'd burn the place to the ground if I were her.

"Tickety tock?" My teeth grind together. "That wasn't some game, was it?"

She huffs. "For him, not for me. When Grandaddy went down to the bunker, that's when Daddy would start. He'd stalk the house, trying to find me, always calling out those words, that the clock was ticking, and my time was running out. I... I'd hide, but he always found me. The chase seemed to excite him more. The longer it took, well, it made what came after worse. In the end, it was better not to hide at all." Her whole body shudders. "Last night he was coming for me again—"

"He's dead. He can't hurt you now." Yet even without knowing the facts, those sounds had terrified even me.

Her eyes challenge mine. "It was *his* voice. *His* footsteps. Don't you think those sounds are imprinted on my brain? He's been waiting for me to return..."

Could it be true? Could a dead man have been lying in wait? And if so, what does he want? Revenge on his daughter as she got him killed? Christ, this is the stuff of horror movies, not something that happens in real life.

I get to my feet, pull her up and into my arms. Holding her close, I promise, "He's not going to hurt you, Raven. Never again."

She's trembling, and I hold her tighter. "Fuck, have you any idea how brave you are? Coming back here—"

"I didn't know a ghost would be waiting for me," she cries out.

It's like that question about whether there's a sound if a tree falls in the forest when there's no one there. "If there is a ghost, Raven, he's probably always been here. You returning, didn't awaken anything."

"That makes it worse." Her eyes widen and her hand clutches at her chest. "The idea of him always having been here, wandering the halls at night, calling out, searching for me—"

Placing my fingers to her lips, I stop the words coming from her mouth. She's right, that visual's no better than something lying dormant, waiting for her to come back.

Again, I pull her to me, giving her physical comfort as I seem to be better with that than anything verbal.

I'm hurting for her. Jesus. What a life she had as a child. Her time with her grandaddy might have been good, but her brother, well, if I ever find him, he'll feel my fists. He didn't do shit to protect her, and if I'm reading the situation correctly, it wouldn't have been long before he'd have taken a turn for himself. No wonder the grandfather sent her away.

Part of me wonders whether Jack met the same end as her father. The suspicion makes me ask, "You've never heard from Jack?"

"No. Never."

Hmm. I suspect there's more than one unmarked grave in this forest. Grandaddy survived, there's evidence of that. But if his grandson proved as bad as the man who sired him, I suspect the old man's justice would have been swift. I approve that he didn't wait to ask questions when dealing with her dad.

"This isn't me," she murmurs into my shirt. "I'm not this weak woman."

My lips press together. "I don't think you're fuckin' weak, Raven. I'm amazed by your strength. Fuckin' in awe that you came back to this place at all." I try to imbibe honesty into my statement, my tone suggesting these aren't just words, but that I truly mean them.

I must get through to her because her face turns up, her eyes creased as though she still doesn't believe me.

So I give her more. "You're a survivor, Raven. Coming back to a place with such bad memories would be challenging for anyone. But add on last night and what we went through? The fact you're walking, talking, and not curled up into a ball? Christ woman, you're so fuckin' strong, I admire you."

It must be coincidence, but her lips form a shape that give me a sudden yearn to kiss them. Like a moth being drawn to a flame, I'm unable to resist, even if that wasn't what she was offering.

Not being one hundred percent sure of what her reaction is going to be, I let my lips gently brush across hers. She inhales sharply as if that wasn't what she was expecting, but her fingers tighten their grip on my shirt.

Applying more pressure, I use a hand to angle her head better, and when she opens for me, I wonder what took me so long to get my first taste of her. Her body fits against me as if she was made to be there, with curves in all the right places. When I tease with my tongue, she opens for me.

Predictably, my cock hardens, and in light of the topics we were just discussing, I move my hips back so as not to alarm her. But she impedes my action, pulling me closer instead, showing she's all woman, and her childhood trauma hadn't traumatised her to the extent she's been put off men forever.

Thank fuck.

Christ. It's not the right place, certainly not the right time, but I'm determined to have her. As she writhes against me, I'm beginning to suspect that she would be up for some one-on-one action, but would she be thinking of a happily ever after, or would I just be someone to scratch an itch, to tide her over until she got a man she really wanted?

As I remember Metalhead's obvious interest in her, a growl

comes into my throat. The vibration and sound causes her to pull back a little.

I place a hand either side of her face. "Only me, okay? Only me. Not one of my brothers."

The skin around her eyes creases, and her eyebrows draw down. She gives a little shake of her head. "I don't understand."

Fuck. I don't either.

Chapter Eleven

RAVEN

I hadn't expected Dwarf to kiss me. Yet the instant his lips touched mine, I'm so pleased that he did, taking it as an indication he sees me as a woman, and not a victim.

His touch, his caress, the strength of his hold, helped me overcome any trauma from telling him the full truth about what had happened to me here. The press of his cock against my body, the outward display showing he desires me, isn't distressing at all. It's reciprocated by familiar feelings of arousal within me.

If I'd seen Dwarf on the street, I might have walked straight past without giving a second glance. He doesn't look like a model or have immediate appeal in ways that would get my heart throbbing. But his personality makes up in spades for what his height and looks may be lacking.

Apart from my initial fear of his justifiable anger when I'd run into his bike, he's done nothing to scare me. Perhaps it was our shared terror during the night, but he's become like a knight in armour, my protector, someone I feel I could trust to always be there. Looks alone aren't enough to select a partner, there's got to be something else.

His actions, his words, his presence, and the ways he's stood by me have made me warm to him. And even before he took me in his arms, I was attracted to him.

Dwarf's brothers, well, some of them at least, are undeniably handsome. But it's the whole package that is Dwarf that appeals to me. As we stand close, lips locked together, I realise how well we fit.

His taste, his smell, his patience and easy acceptance make me wonder whether I've at last found the right man. As I lose myself in his caress, wondering where this is going, reality crashes into me. I'm based in San Francisco, and he rides with a club in Arizona. Anything between us could be little more than a one-night stand.

But if I had the chance, how could I turn that down? Already I feel more connected to him than I have any previous lover. Maybe it's because with him, I don't need to hold myself back. With him, I'm hiding nothing.

Unbidden, I release a moan as I realise I wouldn't turn down anything he has to offer. Almost simultaneously, he growls. Disturbed, I pull back.

He places his hands against my cheeks. "Only me, okay? Only me. Not one of my brothers."

My eyes narrow, wondering what the hell he's talking about. "I don't understand."

But I don't get more time to ponder or tell him I'm not interested in anyone else, as we're interrupted by the clearing of a throat.

Face glowing red, I turn to see it's his prez. Toad's wearing a wide smirk, presumably because he's just caught us in this compromising position. To give Dwarf his due, he doesn't seem disconcerted. Before taking his hands away from my face, he leans in and meets my forehead with his lips.

"To be continued," he promises quietly, making my insides clench at the accompanying heated look in his eyes.

"Whatcha want, Prez?" He continues to look at me for

another second, before letting me go and turning to the man who's interrupted us.

"We got food inside. I came to tell you." His eyes settle on me. "After we've eaten, I'd like a word with Raven."

With me? When I try to step away from Dwarf, he pulls me to him, my back to his front, holding me possessively.

Toad's smirk reappears, but he makes no comment, just stands back and gestures back toward the cabin "You coming inside?"

"You okay with that?" Dwarf asks.

The logical side of me wants to scream of course I am, but the emotional side says I never want to step foot in the cabin again. Though it will be full of the members of the Wicked Warriors MC, and even my father's spirit would be hard pressed to win out against them.

So I take a deep breath, once again grab onto Dwarf's hand, and enter beside him.

It's the aroma that hits me first. Obviously, we'd been out in the yard much longer than I'd have thought as someone's had time to go to the nearest town and stock up with an enormous pile of pizzas.

My stomach growls. It's been a long time since I downed that MRE. Dwarf tightens his hand briefly then lets me go. He steps forward to examine what's on offer, then beckons me forward.

While I help myself to a slice, he takes a whole pizza for himself.

I'm offered a beer which I accept to wash the food down. It's not my beverage of choice but I doubt these men have a handy bottle of wine hanging around. For the next few minutes, there's no talking as everyone stuffs their mouths.

Taking a second slice, and then a third as I realise I'm hungrier than I believed, I've no other thought than filling my stomach. Gradually, though, as my tank goes from empty to topped off, I start looking around.

There's so much testosterone in this room at the moment, any ghost worth their salt is probably not hanging around. The windows have been opened, the musty air dissipated some, and it's hard to believe what I experienced in the night actually happened.

As the pizza boxes are robbed of their contents, and empty bottles of beer start piling up, voices grow louder. I notice Toad and a couple of the others have their heads together in the corner. As they keep giving me sideways glances, I gather that for some reason I'm the topic of conversation, and I shift on the decaying couch, feeling awkward. *Are they talking about the poor woman who hears apparitions?*

"You okay?" Dwarf asks me, his brow creasing. "You're very quiet. Is it too much, being in here?"

I lean into him and lower my voice to a whisper. "Are they talking about me?"

He raises his chin and stares toward his prez and must also notice the glances coming our way. "Maybe they are. Or maybe it's about me." His jaw tenses slightly.

Thinking it's far less likely that they're discussing the man at my side, unless it's to question his sanity, I push myself up. "I need some fresh air."

"Hey, Raven. Can we talk to you a minute?"

They were talking about me. Now on my feet, I turn to face Toad.

The Wicked Warriors prez, having gotten my attention, narrows his eyes. "How much were you going to market this place for?"

That was so not what I expected him to be asking, it takes me a couple of seconds to get my mind to change gear. "I don't know. My original plan was to do the place up before selling." And now I just want to leave and never come back here again.

"What would you take if we bought the cabin as-is?"

For an answer, I take the keys out of my pocket and hold them out. "Take it. It's yours."

His eyes widen, then he shakes his head. "No can do. This is your inheritance, Raven."

My inheritance be damned. "I wish I'd never come back," I cry out. "I've spent years trying to get over what happened to me here. I thought I was strong enough not to let the memories fuck with my head. But hey, they certainly fucked with me. I should have gone with my first inclination to let the place rot where it stood."

"Hey." Dwarf's arms come around me, pulling me into him.

"Why the fuck would we buy this place?" one of his brothers asks, his face looking perplexed.

"Think about it, Bonk," Metalhead answers him, his eyes gleaming. "Somewhere hidden away, off the grid, with a functioning bunker no one knows exists."

The skin around Bonk's eyes creases, then smooths out again. "Well, fuck me."

Metalhead slaps him on the shoulder. "While I'll pass on the kind offer, I think you've got it, Bro."

I'm not stupid. I can imagine why an MC would like a place out of the way and off the grid.

But they're forgetting one thing. "It's haunted, remember."

"Yeah, haunted." As Raider rolls his eyes at my reminder, I feel Dwarf behind me tense.

"Don't forget I heard it too, Brother," Dwarf's deep voice drawls.

"Then we'll get a fuckin' exorcism done." Raider seems to have an answer for everything.

Midnight sweeps his long black hair over his shoulders and eyes Dwarf. "You sure you weren't just picking up on Raven's distress?"

I wait for Dwarf's answer.

"Heard what I heard, Brother." His statement is said as though he's issuing a challenge to anyone to doubt him further.

Toad's still standing in front of me. His stare is making me uncomfortable. Suddenly, he raises his head. "One way to tell whether or not this place is fuckin' haunted." At last, he turns away from me and glances at the rest of his men in turn. "We stay the night here."

"Yeah!" Bonk fists the air. "Always wanted to see a ghost."

"Be careful what you wish for," Midnight warns him.

"Woooo, woooo." Raider looms over the Native American who bats away his hands.

Toad stomps his foot on the floor a couple of times. Gradually, the taunting and jokes die down. "We'll head back now. Take Dwarf's bike back to the shop, and you can pick up anything you need to sleep rough. Anyone who wants to will return at dusk."

"I'm fuckin' in." Again, Bonk high fives the air.

"Me too, Brother," Stumpy states.

"Not leaving me out," Scalpel states.

"Nor me."

Metalhead elbows Midnight. "You going to go all shaman on us, Brother?" He receives a rude gesture comprising of the raising of just one finger.

With a snort and a shake of his head, Toad turns back to me. "Appreciate that you'd rather be far away from here, Raven. So, I'll get you a ride into the city so you can get to the airport—"

"Give me a moment, Prez?" Dwarf interrupts.

When Toad gives him a piercing look and then shrugs, Dwarf takes me over into a corner. When we're away from the others, he takes a moment to look into my eyes.

"Raven, what do you really want to do?"

Get out of here is my initial response, but then I follow that through to its natural conclusion. I'll go back to San Francisco, leave this cabin behind. It hits me then, that I'll be leaving Dwarf too. Whatever promise we were making to each other outside in the yard would go unfulfilled. Something tells me I'd like just one time with him, to see where this attraction between us could go, despite our lives being so very different and the distance between them.

Rather than answering him, I turn away to give myself time to think. Maybe the cabin affected me in ways I hadn't expected, and it was my overactive imagination that made me summon my father last night. Could I have only thought I'd woken up, and my nightmare still continued making me believe things were real?

Is it possible that Dwarf picked up on my anxiety?

Doubtful. I may not know much about him, but he doesn't seem a likely empath.

Watching the men milling around, their presence overwhelming in the cabin, their playfulness and joking around with each other, starts to make me think what I heard in the night was ridiculous. And even if there was something there, with all these people around, surely it's unlikely to show itself.

It would be all too easy to accept that ride from Toad, to go back to San Francisco and eventually forget any of this ever happened. Easy, that is, were it not for my fledgling feelings about Dwarf, and worse, that my father would have won all over again.

Clenching my fists with anger that my father has regained any influence over me, I turn to look directly into Dwarf's eyes. "I refuse to be a victim. If you and your brothers are staying here tonight, I want to come back and stay as well."

He sucks in air, but the curve of his lips suggests approval. "You don't have to, Raven."

"Will you be here?" I challenge.

He snorts. "I'll never live it down if I'm not. And," he waves his hand indicating his brothers, "nothing stands a chance against them, whether breathing or not."

And that's the only reason I'm considering it. Safety in numbers and all that.

I'd never have the courage to stay on my own, and yet there's a big part of me that wants answers. Whether that be I've gone crazy, or we'll get proof that something beyond the realm we know does exist.

While I don't want to appear weak, I really don't want to be left alone while they take Dwarf's bike back and go and collect their stuff. But I don't need to say a word. Luckily, Dwarf understands without me having to ask him, and takes it for granted that I'll be going with them.

It's only a few minutes later when I'm again in the front of the truck, sandwiched between Dwarf and Punchbag, the driver. Idly I wonder how the poor prospect got his name. Dwarf's handle is easy—he's literally dwarfed by his brothers.

His brothers, who haven't bothered to hide their fascination with me, and not all of it is for the woman who's haunted by the ghost of her father. I've seen the assessing glances sent my way, the kind any female over the age of puberty can recognise. I appreciate that no one's made a move, not when I've shown nothing of a reciprocal interest.

I've only eyes for one member of the Wicked Warriors MC. It's the man by my side who intrigues me. He didn't get rid of me the moment he made contact with the outside world. He kept me by his side deliberately. That I might hold the same appeal for him as he does for me was confirmed by that kiss.

That kiss.

I turn and try to interest myself in the scenery as my blood becomes heated, wondering whether things would have progressed had we not been interrupted. Dwarf's mouth on mine had made me forget my worries, where exactly we were and almost my damn name. If he can do that with just a meeting of lips, what could he do if we went all the way?

"You okay?"

Dwarf's caught me fidgeting as I try to shift in my seat, the turn of my thoughts making my underwear decidedly damp. His knowing smirk and the slight bulge in his pants suggests I might not be the only one having inappropriate thoughts.

I avoid telling him I'm not fine, but that he could make it okay, and instead ask lightly, "How long before we get there?"

"'bout an hour between the cabin and the clubhouse, so not too far now."

Presumably there's another reason the club is interested in it, it's not very far away.

He misreads the flush on my face. "You nervous? Don't be. You've met almost all my brothers already." His lips quirk. "And definitely the worst of them."

I mumble something intelligible. It's safer for him to assume I'm wary rather than the truth that I'm horny. His large hand comes out to cover mine, the touch of his fingers doing nothing to help my raging libido.

When he moves our joined hands onto his thigh, I glance down, then tear my eyes away from the crotch to which they've been drawn, and again try to concentrate on the scenery outside the window.

Is it hot in here, or is it me?

Finally, after the remainder of the sixty minutes have ticked by, the bikes in front of us continue on as the truck comes to a halt outside an auto-shop. Taking it that we're dropping Dwarf's bike off here, I get out to stretch my legs and to watch Dwarf and the prospect unload it. With a few choice swear words, and, on Dwarf's part, some impressive flexing of muscles, they manage to get it squared away.

When it's safely secured and locked up, we all pile back into the truck again, this time for a shorter journey which ends at an ominous looking building with a big sign over the top, *Wicked Warriors MC Arizona.*

Although assured I've already met most of his brothers, I stay close to Dwarf's side as we enter a bar area. It's an alien environment, and one I'm not immediately comfortable in. I'm taking in the dingy clubroom, the dark nicotine-stained walls and ceiling, unable to stop my designer brain shuddering at all the mismatched chairs and tables when a yapping at my ankles causes me to look down.

My eyes widen. *I'm being attacked by a rat.* No, not a rat.

Inwardly I laugh at myself and bend myself in half to reach the tiny dog on the floor. The thing continues to leap, bark and growl.

"Rolo!" a cultured feminine voice calls out, then gets closer to me. "I'm so sorry. Rolo thinks she's a guard dog and twice her size."

Chuckling, I respond, "I think she's unlikely to do much damage." Then to the chihuahua, who on hind legs barely reaches up to my knees, I say, "You're a cute little thing, aren't you?" As I scratch behind her ears, she stops her fuss and pushes up against me.

"Princess," a loud voice bellows. "That mutt of yours terrorising visitors again?" An amused Toad comes up and surprises me when his large muscular arm circles the woman and pulls her into his side. He's older, rough looking, while she's the epitome of femininity, but as she looks up and their mouths fuse together, I see how well they fit.

My cheeks glow at the unexpected demonstration of love in front of me. But before it becomes awkward or rated anything other than PG, Toad releases her and addresses me.

Before he'd been the dour MC prez, but there's a more boyish look about him now, as if this woman balances him somehow.

"Raven, meet my princess. Princess, Raven."

The woman pushes at Toad's arm, but has no effect on making him move, and her eyes sparkle as they land on me. "I'm Ruby."

"My ol' lady," Toad confirms, with a look of pride on his face. Then he explains to his misnomered *old* lady, as she's anything but, "We're not staying. We've just returned to get sleeping bags and shit."

Ruby's eyes thin as she looks confused. "Because?"

Toad grins widely. "The brothers and I are going to be spending the night in a haunted house."

Raider chooses that point to raise his arms over his head and loom, looking like one of the walking dead. Toad thumps his fist into his stomach. "Can it, Raider, or I'll leave you behind."

"But Prez…" he moans. "Don't be mean."

Ruby's looking from Toad to his VP, her brow scrunched, her head shaking in disbelief. Again, her eyes become slits. "You're yanking my chain," she decides.

Toad hugs her to him. "Actually, Princess, I'm not. There's a real ghost and everything." He winks at Dwarf.

Ruby pulls away from him and swings around. "You're fucking with me." When Toad shakes his head, she looks at Dwarf and then me. "A real haunted house?"

"Well, it's actually a cabin," I tell her.

Dwarf chuckles and fills her in. "Yeah, Raven got chased out of there last night. Ran into the road and made me crash my bike."

Ruby's forehead creases as she looks from him to me, then her brows rise. "You have got to be kidding me."

Breathing in deeply, I tell her, "I wish I was. I'm convinced there was some kind of spirit." Here, so far removed from the place where it happened, even to me it sounds unlikely.

"I heard it too, Ruby." Dwarf backs me up.

With suspicion in her eyes, Ruby regards us again, then her gaze settles first on her man, then on some of the men who've come back with him. What she sees must convince her something of intrigue must be going on, because her eyes sparkle. "Well count me in. I've always wanted to go on a ghost hunt."

Toad's face goes blank for a moment as if he hadn't considered her coming along. Then, presumably convinced it's all noises and no real danger, pulls her to him again. "Why the fuck not? You can protect me."

"From a ghost?" She snorts, still disbelieving.

Equally of the view we're going to hear and see nothing at all, Toad grins widely. "Yeah, Princess. You can hold my hand and stop me from getting scared."

Ruby claps her hands together in delight. "I've always loved haunted houses at fairs." She turns and her stare encompasses the men looking on. "But don't you lot get any thoughts about jumping out to scare me." She points at Toad. "I've a man and I'm not afraid to use him."

"Wouldn't dream of it." Scalpel chuckles, raising his hands.

"Bonk?" Ruby's narrowed eyes land on him.

"What, me? Never." He looks suitably chastised as if such a thought would never enter his head.

"Nothing's going to scare you, Princess, except for a real ghost." Toad's stern face lets everyone know he won't be very forgiving and he clearly wouldn't have a problem delivering retribution on her behalf.

"Ooh," Ruby says delightedly. "A ghost hunt. This is going to be exciting."

Dwarf's hand touches my shoulder as if he can read my mind and knows that I need support. He knows as well as I do that what haunts that cabin isn't some Casper the Friendly Ghost. This is a malevolent presence, the man as evil now dead as he was in life.

I'm certainly not looking forward to experiencing the apparition again. But, as I look at the men around me, busy with their preparations for the night ahead, some now carrying rolled up sleeping bags, and all seemingly armed to the teeth, I wonder, if the ghost does make his presence felt, what danger we could actually be in?

My daddy won't know what's hit him.

Chapter Twelve

DWARF

Frowning, I watch the preparations going on around me. The action makes me want to scream, *this ain't no visit to Disneyland, Brothers. This is the real thing.* But I bite my tongue. Here, back in the familiar clubhouse, it's hard to believe the events of last night actually happened. But for my bike being in the shop, and that there's a pretty woman standing beside me, I'd have dismissed it all as a dream maybe brought on by fatigue.

And boy, I muse, as I yawn so widely I crack my jaw, am I tired. It's looking like there'll be a fuckin' party going on in the cabin tonight, and it's doubtful I'll be able to catch up on my sleep.

Glancing sideways, I see Raven rubbing her eyes, though she's trying to keep a smile on her face—the type a visitor feels they need to wear when they're in a strange place. While this is home to me, it's probably far out of the realms of her experience.

While she talks to Ruby, I check in with Toad, getting the estimate for heading back to the cabin will be at least a couple of hours. Then I return to her side.

"Raven?" I speak quietly when Ruby turns away. "I'm done

in. Thinking of getting my head down for a while. You want to come with me?"

She pretends to fan herself. "You asking me to go to bed with you, Dwarf?"

If I was asking that, I'd phrase it differently, like suggesting we get naked together. But fuck me, for some reason, her teasing has made me blush. It's showing me a lighthearted side of her I hadn't seen before. Probably because we're out of that hellhole of a situation and all the memories it brought back.

Leaning closer, I growl into her ear, "I'm asking you to sleep with me, darlin'. That better?" I accompany that statement with an exaggerated wink.

She lets out a tinkling laugh. Some women reveal their mirth raucously, some have a grating sound, but Raven's is like the happy burbling of a brook on a summer's day and just makes me want to hear it more. The sound has even attracted attention. I see both Metalhead and Scalpel turn, and the sergeant-at-arms gives an all-too-interested look in her direction.

The risk of losing her makes me take action, picking up her suitcase in one hand, and placing the other on her arm, steering her toward the stairs.

Bonk's voice reaches me. "Hey, Dwarf. Can we raid the kitchen for shit to take with us?"

Uncharacteristically, I shout back, "Knock yourselves out." Normally I like to keep a good inventory of the stock that we've got, but right now, getting Raven and me some alone time matters far more.

My response gets Bonkers looking at me as if I've gone crazy. *He can talk.* Ignoring them, I continue to push Raven in front of me.

"Ooh, looks like Dwarf's going to get himself some," Cloud yells out.

Pausing, I turn to shoot him the finger. "We're getting some sleep. Some of us were up all night."

Raider, the asshole, yells, "Good for you, Dwarf. Didn't think you could keep going that long."

Raven blushes a deep red as snorts of laughter follow us.

"Ignore them," I tell her, encouraging her up the stairs. "The fuckers just like to yank my chain."

Raven's steps falter. "We... we are just going to get some shut-eye, aren't we?"

I'm not completely certain whether she sounds disappointed or relieved. Cupping my hand to her face, I reassure her, "They've no idea what the coming night might hold for us. I need to recharge my batteries before going back there again. While babe, I admit, I'd love to take things further, right now, I'm dead on my feet."

Tortured eyes meet mine. "I don't even want to go back there."

"Then stay here. There's no need for you to go."

Her shoulders pull back. "It's my cabin. *My* problem. I'm not staying behind."

She's so fucking brave. What happened last night scared the shit out of a strong man like me. Momentarily, I remember the panic I'd felt, acknowledging it was greater than any I'd experienced when serving overseas, faced by armed-and-dangerous insurgents.

I twist the handle and push open the door to my room, quickly scanning to make sure I hadn't left it in a mess yesterday. Luckily, old habits die hard, and my bed's squared away, just like it had to have been when I was a serving Marine. Realising the sheets hadn't been changed from the last time Easy, one of the sweet butts, was in my room, I decide the safest option for more than one reason is not to get undressed or under the bedclothes.

Raven yawns widely and stretches her arms over her head. She rolls her neck as though to get the kinks out of it, then her eyes fall on the pillows.

"Bathroom's through there if you need it." I point to the door off to the side.

With a grateful nod, she gracefully sinks to her knees, opens the suitcase I'd placed down by the door, and takes out a small toiletry bag. With that in her hand, she disappears in the direction I'd indicated.

Within a few moments, she's come back out, and I go and take care of business myself. By the time I've returned, she's curled up in the fetal position with one arm under the pillow, cradling it to her head. As she doesn't move when I slip into bed behind her, I gather she's gone out like a light.

Totally worn out, I slow my breathing, and soon drop off myself.

It seems like no time at all before a voice awakens me.

"Dwarf? We're leaving shortly. You coming?"

What the fuck? My time with the Marines means I've retained the ability to go from zero to full speed in the blink of an eye. As I sit up, shaking the vestiges of sleep off, I inwardly swear at the fuckers who've only given me a few minutes of rest, only to see by my phone we've been sleeping just over two hours.

Seeing that being woken so we don't miss out is a plus rather than a negative, I'm mostly polite when I yell back, "We'll be fuckin' there. Give us a minute."

Raven, less able to go from sleep to wake quite so quickly, wipes sleep from her bleary eyes and looks up wearily. She stretches like a cat, first arching her back then rounding it. Finally, she sits up.

"We going to do this then?" Sleep must have done her good. She sounds more confident than earlier. When I jerk my chin, she grimaces. "Nothing will probably happen with everyone there. Then I won't be able to prove if I was hallucinating or not."

Reaching out my hand, I place my knuckles under her chin. "Whatever you were doing, babe, I was right there with you."

"Projecting my terrors?"

I shrug, not knowing whether that's even possible. Or

whether, on the spectrum of what's most likely, sharing her illusion or hearing ghosts comes out on top.

She swings her legs over the bed, takes some fresh clothes from her suitcase, then disappears into the bathroom. While waiting, I lean back on the bed, link my hands behind my head and wonder whether the voices proving they're real would be for the best or not. Does she really need proof that her long-dead father hasn't forgotten her?

In that instance, we should burn the cabin down, no matter how much of an asset Toad thinks it would be to the club.

But if my brothers felt the same terror that I had, I doubt if too many would object. I decide to take along some matches just in case.

Raven appears. She's wearing form-hugging jeans that cling to her ass, and a t-shirt that shows off her small but firm breasts. I wince when she puts on a sweatshirt that hides her assets, but agree that the night will be cool, and it's best to be appropriately dressed.

Though hidden, the imprint of what her clothes are hiding is seared into my mind. I stand, grab my own fresh clothing, then approach her.

Regarding her for a moment, I notice how fucking gorgeous she is, and wonder if I'm crazy to think that I have a chance. My doubts don't stop me from testing the waters. "What about after? You coming back here with me, babe?"

She startles. I move closer. With my free hand, I brush a stray lock of her hair back behind her ear. Then I just watch her.

She nibbles her lip, then her mouth purses. I take the risk of pulling her close to me, cradling her head against my neck. Being almost the same height, she fits as though she was made just for me. When she doesn't object, I nuzzle her skin, my lips finding her pulse point.

"Mmm. You don't play fair, Dwarf."

I'm not playing fair. I want her to promise to come back, not just to lie beside me in bed, but to allow me full access to her. I want to touch those firm-looking tits, and I want to slide my cock into her body.

If she commits to me, maybe she'll be less likely to take one of my brothers up on their inevitable offer instead.

"I want you," I murmur directly into her ear. "We've no time now, but later…" To persuade her, I turn her slightly and move my lips so they can come down on hers.

She opens for me. I may have only kissed her once, but I get a sense of coming home, a familiarity with her flavour, a feeling this is right, right down to my bones. Her head angles perfectly for me. I don't need to crane my head like I do when a woman—as happens so often—is taller. I breathe in the scent that I already associate with her.

As our tongues glide together, I apply more pressure. Holding her tighter, I'm rewarded when she clasps and holds on as if the last thing on her mind is letting me go. Like a cat, she rubs herself against me, making me wish we had nowhere to be. I can't hide the reaction she has on me.

"Dwarf! Get your ass out here now!" A loud thump on the door shows Stumpy's impatience.

I have an overwhelming desire to tell them all to go fuck themselves but remember in time that club business comes first.

Reluctantly I pull back, leaving my lips lingering on hers for just a second more. "To be continued later?"

Slightly breathless and with glazed eyes, she waits for a second then responds, "To be continued."

Thank fuck. My eyes fall on something at the side of her bed, making me decide I'll be holding her suitcase hostage until we get back.

We'd gotten dressed in record time but we needn't have hurried. It's bedlam when we descend the stairs. You'd think they were preparing for a picnic in the park rather than a camping trip to a cabin. Fuck knows whether they left any food in the kitchen. They've got carriers full of meat—and just what the fuck is Scalpel carrying? *It's a whole fucking tub of salt.*

"Hey, bro. You should know that's not good for your health." My arm shoots out and stops the medic. "We won't need all that."

Jerking his hand away, he rolls his eyes. "It's for a protective fuckin' circle, dummy."

Raven snorts softly from beside me, attracting his attention.

"See?" Scalpel addresses her directly, "You can depend on me for protection."

Oh no she fucking won't. She's got me to protect her.

Like I did it so well last time, turning tail and running as I remember.

I shake those thoughts out of my head and settle for possessively putting my arm around her.

Metalhead walks past, staring down at something in his hand, so engrossed he knocks into my shoulder.

"Watch it," I growl, then catch sight of what he's holding. "Your GPS not working?"

He glances up and grins. "If the compass has trouble finding true north, then it's a sign of a supernatural presence."

"Hey, I've got you covered." Cloud staggers past, juggling an array of electronics in his hands.

"What the fuck you got there?" I bark.

Cloud looks down as if he's cataloguing the items himself. "EVP and EMF meters. Of course, I'd have liked to get my hands on a Ghost Box, but didn't know anyone who had one."

And he had the other shit just lying around? I don't bother asking him to explain himself or ask what the acronyms stand for. I doubt I'd understand the explanation, so leave him to carry off the toys which are obviously bringing him a level of satisfaction.

"I got it!" Punchbag runs in through the front door, holding up a bottle in his hands.

"Good job, kid!" Bonk calls out as he goes over to take it. He waves his acquisition in the air and shouts loudly, "Prospect's got us some holy water."

Narrowing my eyes, I frown at the prospect, wondering whether he'd really gone to a church or whether he'd just filled it up at the closest tap. Not that I expect we'd notice any difference. But Bonkers seems to be taking it seriously, proving we named him accurately. I shake my head and pull a bemused Raven closer.

"Flashlight and candles," Midnight announces before I can ask what he's carrying. "I went out and got them while you two were... well, doing whatever you were doing."

"Sleeping," I snap. Then realise if I want to hang on to Raven, it might have been better to confirm his assumption about what we'd been up to. If I'd claimed her, the brothers would stay back.

But I haven't claimed her. And, except for what's in my head, she's a free woman.

"I can understand flashlights if the generator quits, but why candles?" It's Raven who asks him.

"If candles flicker when there's no breeze, it can mean a spirit's present," Midnight answers her quite seriously.

Raider's obviously got it as badly as the rest as he comes along holding what I recognise as a digital thermometer.

Raven leans in close and speaks into my ear, "They have no idea what they're going to come across. If it goes like last night, there'll be no need for all this fancy equipment."

"Equipment, my ass," I murmur back. "All this would do is frighten any self-respecting spirit off."

Nevertheless, I'm going to be glad to have my brothers around me. Now dusk is falling outside, I realise, tough Marine that I am, I wouldn't go back to the cabin alone, no matter what you paid me.

Chapter Thirteen

RAVEN

The poor prospect looks upset to be left behind, the only one apart from two strangely underdressed girls, who have been given instructions to remain in the clubhouse.

Our departure had been delayed—while Dwarf and I had earlier descended the stairs looking well put together if though tired, Toad and Ruby now bundled down, her face flushed, her eyes sparkling, and Toad with such a cocky look on his face, leaving no one in any doubt of what they'd been up to.

For a second, I envied her, wondering if I, too, would have appeared with such a satisfied smile had Dwarf and I been allowed more time together.

I could feel he was hard when he'd held me close, and with those nibbles to my neck, he'd found my weakness, and my panties had grown wet. If he'd asked, I wouldn't have turned him down, even though I've no thought this will lead to anything further than just one night. I've got to return to San Francisco, and he's wedded to his club.

But when this visit to the cabin is over, I will come back like he'd asked and for more than to collect my suitcase if I get the chance. There's just something about Dwarf that I find attractive, maybe even to describe it as irresistible wouldn't be going too far. If I go home without experiencing what he can offer me, then I think I will have missed out.

I just hope he won't turn out to be addictive, as that could get complicated.

He might not turn heads, but my God, when he smiles... It lights up his face and does something to me, bringing things to the forefront I haven't thought of for a while. I've been concentrating on building my business and along the way have forgotten to have fun. So yes, I'll return with him later, and for once indulge myself.

Again, I'm seated in the truck, but this time it's only Dwarf beside me in the driver's seat. Protocol obviously dictates we wait until all the bikes have pulled out before slotting into our place behind them.

As the miles pass, my thoughts turn away from expectations of later, and think more on what will come first. Strangely, Dwarf seems to understand, and his hand reaches out to cover mine.

"It's going to be alright," he tells me with certainty.

"I think it's going to be a bust," I tell him, while hoping that I'm right.

"You could be right. All the ghost hunting programs I've watched aren't treated as a fuckin' party." Even in the darkness that now surrounds us, I can see him shaking his head, and can't miss his chuckle. "You can't expect any decorum from my brothers."

"At least I'll be able to say my goodbyes." I'm speaking my thoughts aloud. "I had some good times with my grandaddy before..." Before Daddy saw me as something other than his baby girl.

I push such thoughts behind me. It had taken years of therapy for me to accept that nothing that had happened had been my fault. That I'd been the victim of a depraved man. Of course, the therapist hadn't known Daddy was dead, just that I didn't see him anymore. The vision of those shots punching through his body, splattering me with his blood, was something I'd had to come to terms with by myself.

I just kept reminding myself that Grandaddy's actions had meant my nightmare had stopped.

"You needn't have come," Dwarf reminds me. "I don't want you to upset yourself."

"It's my fault for wanting to come to see the place I should have left relegated to my nightmares." I stare out of the windshield, thinking what a fool I was. "I think I had something to prove, that what happened couldn't affect me anymore. But by coming back, I haven't had closure. I've started it all up again." Now I'll have to pay for my own therapy, now I've no aunt to pick up the tab for me. "But I need to be here. I can't explain it, but it's my fault." I cast a glance over to him, seeing his jaw is set. "I've got a feeling that I'm the catalyst, and if I don't go back, the ghost won't appear."

"Maybe that would be better," he states, curtly.

"But it wouldn't mean he's gone away. I couldn't sell the cabin to your club, or anyone, not knowing that he was there."

"Thinking he was there," Dwarf corrects me.

"You heard him too," I counter.

He bangs the steering wheel in frustration. "Fuck knows what I heard or didn't, Raven. I'm starting to doubt myself."

I don't blame him. It's hard now to recollect the terror I'd heard in the night. On my own, I'd probably have put it all down to a hyperactive mind and an all-too-real-feeling nightmare if he hadn't heard the sounds himself.

Could he have picked up on my hysteria?

If we return now en masse, and as I expect, the ghost stays quiet, does that mean he wasn't there in the first place, or that he's too overwhelmed to show himself? My daddy would never be some benign spirit, and if he still haunts the world, I'd be afraid that someday, somehow, he'd cause harm.

By the time we're on the quiet road through the forest and approaching the turn, I'm a bag of nerves, unsure which outcome I'm most fearing. That this will prove to be a wild goose chase, or that the apparition will indeed make its presence felt?

I might be concerned the effect the latter would have on me mentally, but one thing I'm not worried about is my physical safety. Dwarf won't leave me alone, and surrounded by his brothers, nothing will get close enough to hurt me. As well as all the paraphernalia they've brought along to which I admit being sceptical about, they're armed to the teeth. Not that bullets will have any effect on a spectre, but there's just something comforting, knowing anything substantial won't stand a chance.

Toad beckons me forward when I step out of the truck. I take out the keys he'd refused to take earlier, and hand them to him. I've no inclination to be the first through the door. Actually, I'm sorely tempted to spend the night in the truck outside. I'm already a mess after last night, another exposure could put me back years. Even now I wonder whether I'll survive as the same person.

Night has fully fallen. I stand with my arms wrapped around me. The moon is out like it was the night before, and now that the sound of the engines has faded to the odd ticking, the hooting of owls and screeches of night creatures can clearly be heard. The cabin in front of me looks so dark and foreboding, I'm not sure how I'd had the nerve to walk inside when I'd arrived yesterday.

The sun had been shining through the leaves, making patterns proliferate on the roof, turning it into something almost idyllic. I'd paid the cab driver then turned with an actual smile on my face as I looked up at the place that held so many memories.

The painful ones I put right to the back of my mind, and instead forced myself to remember only my grandfather. He'd been my mom, my dad, my sibling growing up. Sure, Dad and Jack were around, but it had been him that I'd bonded with, and who'd taken me under his arm and treated me like a treasured daughter.

And now, courtesy of him, the deed to the cabin is in my name. He wanted me to have it. While it's too far out of the way and a long distance from the place I now call home, I'd never think of living here. But making the cabin into something that reflects nothing of its darker days is what I could do in his memory. Then I could sell it, as he would have wanted, and leave some other family living here, hopefully, happily.

So tied up in my visions for how to brighten the place, knowing I'd need help to make it habitable, I'd walked around with an expert eye, successfully keeping bad memories buried. I was more disappointed than I thought I would be to find how much damage time had ravished on my childhood home. By the time I was tired and mentally worn out, I'd gone to bed with no thoughts other than whether it was financially viable to do the work here, or whether I should just move on and pass it off to someone else to deal with.

By avoiding my childhood bedroom, the one at the end of the hall, I'd kept at bay my worst recollections, and managed to close my eyes to thoughts of my grandfather, pushing everything else out of my head. I started to dream of the time he'd taken me fishing, and I'd fallen in, making him bellow with his distinctive laugh. Or when he'd fixed the swing for the umpteenth time.

Until I'd heard my father's voice…

"Raven? You okay?"

Realising I'd zoned out, I give myself a mental shake and return to the present. While I'd been reminiscing about yesterday, the bikers have all passed me and have gone inside. All apart from Dwarf who's standing close, his brow creased in concern.

To answer, I first turn back to the cabin again. "I wasn't scared yesterday," I tell him, my own forehead furrowing. "Not when I arrived. There was nothing ominous, no sense that anything was waiting. Surely I should have felt something?"

Dwarf's shoulders rise and fall as if he hasn't a clue how to answer that question. I'm not even sure myself.

In movies, you always know when you shouldn't enter a particular building. From the outside, it would look abandoned and haunted. This cabin, although heading toward the very definition of derelict, displays nothing to suggest that any spectre of the afterlife lives in the interior.

Metalhead puts his head around the door to the cabin. "We're lighting a grill out back. Getting the steaks ready to go."

Dwarf shakes his head. "Food, I swear that's all they think about." Then he takes my hand. "Ready?"

My fingers cling to his, trying to send a non-verbal message that I don't want him to leave my side. I summon a nod from somewhere and enter with him.

Several of the men are hovering around. Cloud's looking seriously down at the devices he brought with him. Raider's walking around with his thermometer as if it were some kind of divining rod. Midnight's got a bunch of candles in his hand and seems to be testing where he can put them where a draft won't make the flame flicker.

While Ruby's not in sight, Scalpel is carrying Rolo around, and keeps asking the dog whether she can sense anything. With a curve to my lips, I wonder what he thinks he's going to find when her only response seems to be a lick on his hand.

The two men who hadn't been here earlier are studiously looking around.

"Where's this bunker then?" one of them calls out to Dwarf.

"Trapdoor in the kitchen," Dwarf yells back. He then moves his mouth to my ear. "Cash is our treasurer. He'll be looking into whether this would be a good investment."

Another man, new to the place, quickly follows Cash.

"That's Crumb," Dwarf informs me.

I catalogue the two new names, hoping I'll be able to keep everyone straight.

Looking around, I wouldn't say that anyone knows what they're doing, but if there's a chance of scientifically proving a ghost's presence, I'd be surprised if their equipment finds it. At the moment though, it seems everyone is disappointed. When the time ticks on to midnight though, I have a suspicion things might be different.

"Where the fuck's Dwarf?" a voice yells from outside.

Dwarf exaggeratedly rolls his eyes at the impatient shout and pulls me along with him through the cabin and out to the backyard. The men who are not currently engaged on the ghost hunt have come outside and have certainly been busy. An ancient grill made from half an oil drum that I can remember my grandaddy using is already glowing with red coals and orange flames dancing.

Dwarf huffs as he pulls me forward. "Can't you fuckers do anything without me?" He steps up to the grill, opens a cooler and takes some steaks out. He slaps them down and turns to glare at Metalhead and Midnight.

"You're the fuckin' chef." Metalhead shrugs.

I turn wide eyes on the man who's just spoken. "You've disappointed me. Call yourself men?"

Metalhead's back straightens, he narrows his eyes, and growls, "I'm a fuckin' man and I'm ready to prove it to you any fuckin' time you want."

Dwarf stiffens, but ignoring him, I make an exaggerated shrug. "Thought men possessed the barbeque gene." I nod to where Dwarf is working. "If you can't, then it follows, you're not a real man, but Dwarf, here, certainly is."

Dwarf snorts. Metalhead sucks in air, and Midnight bellows a laugh.

Chapter Fourteen

DWARF

As I use my expertise flipping steaks and burgers on the grill while brothers wait hungrily around me, I muse how different the forest seems to be.

While last night it was eerie, tonight it seems like the location of a frat party. The generator is rumbling courtesy of us bringing spare gas, and all the cabin's lights are blazing. Even the air I breathe is different, tinged with nicotine and weed.

Ruby has reclaimed Rolo from Scalpel and now has her on a lead, presumably so she doesn't run off and get lost in the forest. Toad, as expected, seems glued to her side, both seem to be enjoying the outing.

Catching me looking at her, Ruby waves her hand. "Hope you're making sure you're counting my calories and that steak's nutritious for me."

"Of course, Princess," I call back with a laugh.

"What was that all about?"

I chuckle at Raven. "Ask Ruby where she came from someday. Let's just say, she expects more from me than I'm prepared to give."

"You're not giving my ol' lady anything." Toad's loud voice

at my back makes me jump. "When will the fuckin' steaks be ready?"

"Rare coming up shortly." Toad likes them bloody.

Raven, I notice, is staying close to me. Even when Stumpy tries to draw her into conversation, she contributes politely, but doesn't succumb to his attempt to get her to step away. It makes me wonder whether at last I might have found the right woman.

Oh, I've not stood back and taken it lightly when one of my brothers has stolen a woman from under my nose. I'm a man, I have fists, and I'm not afraid to use them. I have bloodied many a face in my time. But I know when I'm fighting a losing battle, and when the woman shows a preference for another, I grit my teeth and clear the way.

But Raven? She's given me no incentive to actively warn my brothers away. Her eyes seem only for me, and while on the surface it's warming, my history makes me question whether it's only because I know her secrets and understand her fears.

If she really likes me, well, I've won the fucking lottery. She's beautiful, intelligent and takes no shit from anybody.

Already tuned in to me, she's there loading plates as the meat is cooked perfectly. Bit by bit, all the food disappears, except for what I saved for Raven and myself.

"Mmm. Perfect," she tells me as she bites into her steak. I watch entranced as she licks her fingers. While eating, her eyes are flicking around the yard.

"What you thinking?"

"Do they intend to party all night?"

I shrug. Knowing my brothers, they might well be.

"I'm thinking no self-respecting ghost is going to appear while you're all here."

I, for one, would be happy if just our presence exorcised any spirit without us having to do more. I lead Raven over to the bench we'd sat on earlier, and once we're seated, take hold of her hand. For a moment, we just sit in silence.

"I meant what I said earlier," I tell her. "Want you to come back with me to the club. Want you in my bed. And want to fuck you this time."

She gives a snort. "That's your pickup line?"

Raising my shoulders to ear level, I grin. "We've already slept together. Why waste time on cheesy lines?"

She gives that tinkling laugh again, the one that goes straight to my groin, then stares out over the yard, her eyes narrowing as she spies Stumpy rolling a blunt. But the curve of her lips shows she's amused rather than disgusted. "I want you too, Dwarf," she admits, making my heart leap. "But I couldn't give you more than one night."

My brothers would jump at the chance, would think she was speaking their language. But I've had enough of one-night stands, and I've always hoped to find a woman that was mine. My yearning to have her at any cost wars with my desire for more.

"You might find me irresistible." I turn it into a joke, while hoping I'm right. I'm already sure one taste of her wouldn't be enough.

"I live in San Francisco," she reminds me. "It's been a long time since I left Arizona behind."

I won't be leaving the Wicked Warriors MC, and this chapter is my home. They were here for me when I needed them. They've become more than a club, they're my family. I couldn't move away and leave them behind.

"What's waiting for you in California?" Belatedly, I realise I really mean who. I've never asked if there was a husband or partner in the wings. Though, I think as I frown, if there is, then why was she kissing me, and what kind of man would let her come here alone?

She shakes her head. "There's nothing. Just work."

"No man?" I want to be clear on that.

Her eyes widen in a *what do you take me for?* look. Yeah, I should have known she wouldn't have been a cheater.

"Look," I turn to face her. "I like you, Raven. I want to get to know you. But I met you less than twenty-four hours ago. I've no idea where the road we're on might take us, but I just know I'd like to get out of neutral and into first gear. Maybe that's where we'll land, or maybe we'll go further."

Biting her lip, she moves her gaze away from me. After only a short time, she looks back. "I like you too, Dwarf. Probably too much. Maybe it's best if I just grab my bag once we get back to your club." When she looks at me, the disappointment is clear in her eyes. "I hadn't thought this through and got carried away. A one-night stand is one thing, but it couldn't be more."

"Not what I'm offering." Now I take both her hands. "But that's where we can start. Hell, I can ride to California, or you can come here. There are phones, email."

"A long-distance relationship?"

How can I admit I've never really had a relationship before, either close or one separated by miles? "I'm just asking for a chance, Raven."

An owl hoots loudly above us, making us both jump. "Fuck." I rub my hand over my eyes.

She's looking up into the trees accusingly, as if nature's given her an unwelcome reminder of why she's here. "I just want to get through this night." Her eyes have that haunted look in them again as she glances uneasily toward the cabin.

"Wondered where you two had gotten to," a gruff voice interrupts.

My focus so set on Raven, I hadn't noticed Toad approaching. My Marine skills had let me down.

Leaning one foot against the stone bench, he leans over his knee. "I'm gonna get this party wound down. Get people settled where they need to be."

"We going in now?" With difficulty, I pull my eyes and thoughts away from Raven, and settle them on the prez.

Toad grins. "Almost midnight, the witching hour. If things are going to go bump in the night, they'll probably start around now."

Suppressing a shudder and the thought *he doesn't know what he's in for,* I stand and help Raven to her feet. I feel her reluctance and don't blame her. Only a quick glance at her face is required to show her nerves have returned to the forefront.

In my short chat with Toad earlier, I'd agreed to replicate last night's actions, which mean Raven and I would be sharing the same room as we had before. While I'd otherwise appreciate some alone time with her, I can't guarantee that a repeat of the activity won't see me making another ignominious flight from the building, and this time to be witnessed by my brothers. The only comforting thought is if so, I probably wouldn't be by myself.

Raven drags her heels, but we get to the door just as Toad puts his fingers to his mouth and lets out a piercing whistle, garnering everyone's attention. He then walks into the midst of the impromptu party which ceases like a switch being thrown. Beer bottles are put down, and men stand at the ready.

"Time to get settled in, fuckers," he states, his strong voice carrying clearly.

"Where d'you want us, Prez?" Midnight calls out.

The VP steps forward, consulting some notes he holds in his hand. "Dwarf and Raven are staying in the first room at the top of the stairs. Bonkers, you and Stumpy will be in the room opposite—"

"Bonk fuckin' snores!" the enforcer exclaims.

"The fuck I do." Bonk raises his fists.

"Calm the fuck down," Toad roars. "Bonk, sleep on your side or something. Stump's right, your fuckin' snores can wake the dead, and we don't want to scare them off."

Cloud snorts with laughter but settles down when Prez levels his death stare at him. He jerks his head back to Raider.

"Scalpel and Cash, you'll take the last bedrooms on the second floor." He too levels his gaze at the men he's mentioned, but they have the sense to stay dumb.

"Metalhead, me, Midnight, Crumb and Cloud will stay on

125

the first floor, alternating between the downstairs beds and the main room." Raider pauses and looks around. From the nods and chin lifts he's getting, it seems everyone knows their places.

"Where will you be, Prez?" Bonk calls out.

"We'll be wherever the action's going on," Toad responds.

"They'll be fuckin'!" Scalpel shouts, getting a laugh from everyone except Prez, who shows him his middle finger, and Ruby, who grins sheepishly.

"We'll have recording shit set up." Cloud steps up. "I want to hear the fuckin' spirits not you lot assing around."

"You'll just get Bonk's snoring—"

"And Ruby scream—"

"Shut the fuck up!" Crumb backs away from Toad's menacing glare.

"I do not fuckin' snore." Ignoring the others, Bonk approaches Stumpy, but the enforcer blocks his half-hearted punch.

"If you do, it will be on tape, so you won't be able to deny it." Midnight chuckles, and this time it's Bonk giving a one-fingered salute.

"No one's going to fuckin' snore, burp or fart." Toad steps to the forefront again. "One of you will stay awake while the other gets their head down for a while. We're here to investigate anything that might be walking around the cabin at night. That means we need people to stay awake and alert."

"Except for Raven." Midnight jerks his head toward the woman at my side.

She starts. "Me?" Her voice is a squeak.

Toad looks at her with compassion. "We think you're the trigger. So that means you've got to be asleep."

Her eyes widen as she repeats his words. "You want me to sleep?"

"Hey, get Dwarf to relax you. I'm sure he'll find a way." Scalpel's accompanying wink leaves no one in any doubt what he's talking about.

Bonk snorts and as if I hadn't already gotten the point, he demonstrates using his hands in a very childish way.

Noticing Raven's flushed face, I growl at them. "Ain't going to be knocking uglies with evil spirits hanging around."

"I don't know if I can sleep." Ignoring the lewd comments, Raven looks apologetically at Toad.

Prez's eyes soften in sympathy. "Just do your best. That's all we can ask for."

If there's really a ghost here, we'd already thought Raven was the magnet. And after what she'd told me outside, I believe there can be no doubt of it. I might not like effectively using her as bait, but while she had the chance to stay away, she chose to come here instead.

Am I really expecting a repeat of last night's drama? Rationally, I can't see how. Whenever I've watched a ghost hunter program on television, they've walked around reverently, speaking in hushed whispers—a million miles away from my brothers who are incapable to move without making a sound or keeping their mouths shut. Any self-respecting ghost would probably keep their distance tonight. The only people likely to see spirits are Midnight and Crumb, who are currently sharing a joint.

Nevertheless, as I glance around the cabin, a shiver goes down my spine. When we'd arrived in the daylight, the place had appeared innocent and innocuous. Now, lit by the ineffective lights that draw emphasis to the shadows, it reeks of foreboding. Unlike my brothers who are regarding this as a free trip to an attraction, I really am not looking forward to the night ahead.

"We'll be switching off the generator," Raider's speaking again, "to make sure we copy exactly how it was last night. Make sure you have your flashlights close by."

"I'm scared." Stumpy widens his eyes theatrically, and whines, "Can't I have a night-light, Mommy?"

"I'll stuff a fuckin' night-light up your ass," Metalhead threatens him.

"I'm considering getting a new enforcer," Toad states, his seriousness belied by the twinkle in his eyes. "Thought you weren't scared of anything."

Stumpy raises his hands. "Just fuckin' with you, man."

"Hey, Stump? Just check under the bed when you lie down and keep your feet under the covers."

There are roars of laughter at Ruby's advice, so much so, Rolo joins in, yapping along with everybody.

Metalhead takes out his gun and deliberately chambers a round, the sound loud as the laughter fades. He looks around with no mirth in his expression as he warns, "Any of you fuckers start running around, making silly sounds or pretending to be a ghost? Well, I've got a fuckin' bullet with your name on it."

Cash shakes his head at the sergeant-at-arms. "You don't seriously believe there'll be any real ghosts, do you?"

"Fuck no," Metalhead barks. "But I don't want to be chasing my ass while some of you fuckers pretend that there are."

"Got it?" Toad growls, his dark eyes settling on each of us in turn. "Anyone wearing anything that makes them look like a member of the fuckin' Ku Klux Klan is going to get full of lead. If Metal doesn't put a bullet in you, I assure you I will."

Ruby steps up and puts her arms around her man. "I do love it when you get all fierce," she says, in a stage whisper.

While Toad's face reddens, there's another burst of laughter.

Raider grins widely. "You're fuckin' fucked, Brother." He mimes shooting a gun at Prez's face.

"Fuck women." Scalpel rolls his eyes. "I ain't never getting tied down."

While other comments are uttered about how hen-pecked Toad's become, I notice the man himself looks unperturbed. The way he turns and takes Ruby's mouth is an indication he's got no regrets, even if the start of their relationship wasn't idyllic. I recall they'd hated each other at the start, Toad sacrificing himself to get five million dollars for the club. But the forced marriage turned into anything but, and against all odds, they're perfectly happy.

Glancing down to the woman at my side, I wonder if there's any chance I can persuade her not to return to San Francisco. If Toad and Ruby could work their shit out, maybe there's a chance for us. Their situation was even more unlikely.

"Positions everybody!" Metalhead claps his hands then starts making shooing motions, and gradually the room empties as brothers go to where they've been assigned.

Turning, I face Raven. "Are you ready?"

Taking a deep fortifying breath, she replies, "As much as I ever will be."

"Hey, wait up." Ruby, having torn herself away from Toad, approaches us. She looks at Raven with concern, and glances briefly at me. "If you'd prefer female company, just say the word."

I stiffen, not wanting her to take up Ruby's offer, and bracing myself for the answer.

"Princess!" Toad sounds annoyed. "You're staying right beside me. Raven's got a part to play."

Raven doesn't even think about it. "Dwarf's fine," she impresses on her. "Just, be careful. Look after yourself, Ruby."

I see Toad's woman's brow creases at Raven's instruction. Like everyone else, I don't think she for a moment thinks there really could be any danger.

For a second or two, she seems stunned, then she comes back to herself, and scoffs gently. "I don't believe in ghosts, honey."

Neither do I. But one's belief in them or not seems to matter not one iota to the ones doing the haunting.

Chapter Fifteen

RAVEN

I don't know whether I'm more worried about the ghost of my father putting in an appearance tonight, or if he doesn't.

If he doesn't, I don't know what Dwarf's friends are going to think of him or me—probably that we were smoking something yesterday. If he does... Well, even surrounded by the multitude of armed men, I'll still be scared and know it will fuck with my head.

I've worked hard to close the wounds that my father left raw. Knowing he could never hurt me again was part of the healing process. I'd rather find out that I have a tumour in my head that's giving me hallucinations, than believe he still exists on some plane.

I hate that at times today I've felt myself reverting to that scared little girl, particularly when I was confessing to Dwarf exactly what had happened to me. And, like now, when I obediently allow him to take my hand, and to lead me up the stairs.

It was a mistake coming back at all, and especially given what had happened, and I'm just compounding that error by being here tonight. If it was all in my head, it was an extreme reaction, showing just how much horror this cabin holds for me.

I'd wanted closure, but after all these years, I'm not entirely sure what resolution I'd been looking for. Maybe confirmation I was strong enough to survive my past. If I knew where my father's grave was, one outcome might have been that maybe I'd have spat on it.

But instead of closing the book on my childhood, coming home has just started a new chapter. I have no idea where this will end or whether I'll survive it. Already the damage has been done. Real or not, if my psyche believes my father will haunt me, I'll have resurrected my past and will have allowed it to taunt me. I'll never be free of the man ever again.

Already feeling defeated, I precede Dwarf into the room, and eye the bed cautiously.

Sounds of laughter and shouts are still filtering through the walls, along with the heavy stomping of men's feet on the wooden stairs. With everything going on around me, even if he exists outside of my imagination, I can't see how a ghost would put in an appearance tonight.

Don't ghosts prefer to haunt in the quiet?

Then, suddenly, the light goes out. As Raider had threatened, the generator must have been turned off. Immediately, Dwarf switches on the flashlight he's carried in with him, flicks the setting that turns it into a camping light, and settles it next to the bed. As if it was a signal, the cabin goes quiet, men hushed by the onset of darkness.

I shiver and wrap my hands around myself.

"Babe?" Dwarf notices and walks over.

"I can't get it out of my head." As I speak, a chill runs down my spine. "That Daddy's always been here. That he never left."

"Babe," he repeats, pulling me closer.

"Was that why Grandaddy never asked me to return?" The thought that that kind old man might have had to live with his son walking the cabin fills me with horror. "Or is it me? Was he waiting for me to come home?" I turn to face him. "What's going to happen even if he comes back tonight? You can't kill a ghost!"

Then I voice the horror I'd been thinking about. "What if it follows me home? What if he never leaves me alone?" By coming back, have I ruined my life forever?

Dwarf shrugs and shakes his head, as if having none of the answers to the questions I've fired at him. Instead, he decides on action. His hands rise and cup my face. I have a moment to read the intention in his eyes before he's lowering his lips and they land on mine.

We shouldn't be doing this. I need to talk things out. Work through the problems even if there aren't solutions. I need to focus on keeping myself together tonight, but... *God, can this man kiss.*

As his tongue sweeps into my mouth, his scent, his taste, the touch of his hands now moving to better position my head, fill my senses. Despite everything, I lose myself in his caress, the cabin and its intangible horrors fading in comparison with the physical presence of the man who seems to represent safety, and who's fast ramping up my desire. He's dominating my mouth—there's no other word for it—and hell if I don't relish the results.

Breathing him in, my world shrinks until there's only the two of us in it.

My fear, which was an emotion with no safety valve, begins to transform into arousal. God knows this is the wrong place, wrong time, but whether it's my brain seeking sanity or my body relief, I want to feel something other than the terror that's eating at me.

It's as though Dwarf's consuming the air that I breathe, and the circumstances I'm in, making me forget anything but the feel of him. Like a fish dangled on a hook, he reels me in. My panties grow damp as my arousal increases. It's probably the emotional rush from being back at the cabin, but as I can feel his hard length pushed against me and know I'm having the same effect on him as he has on me, I'm tempted to throw caution to the wind.

Last night I was so scared I thought my heart would stop

beating. I could have been killed had Dwarf not swerved before hitting me. If my father appears again, I might not survive.

If this is my one chance with Dwarf, I'm going to take it. I'm also not blind to it as being the biggest finger I could raise to my daddy who took my innocence from me, to be with another man in the cabin where he'd so cruelly taken me for himself and abused me.

I'm no virgin, no shrinking violet, and if I want something, I go after it.

I don't allow myself time to think, just act purely on instinct. Taking him unawares, I push against him with my hands, wrenching myself away, but only far enough to have enough distance to voice my request. "Fuck me, Dwarf."

His eyes sharpen, and he draws in a deep breath. His hands let me go and hover in the air. "Fuck, Raven." He runs his fingers back through his hair as if needing to find something to keep them occupied. "This cabin is full of my fuckin' brothers."

I don't give a damn. "I'll be fucking you, not them." Feeling bold, I place my palms flat against his chest. "I can be quiet, can you?"

"Why, Raven?" He still hesitates, the lines of his face, the way his hands hover, shows his torture. "Fuck knows I want you, but now doesn't seem the time or the place."

"I think it's exactly the right place," I refute. "I want to make new memories to chase the old ones away. And," I toy with the material of his shirt, wondering what I can say to persuade him, "maybe an orgasm will help me to sleep."

"Sleep?" He eyes me cautiously. "Raven, you want me to help you sleep? In that case, maybe I can go score a blunt from Stump."

My breath falters. *Oh God, have I read him wrong?* My skin burns as I wonder whether I've been misreading the signs. *He doesn't want me.*

But he kissed me. I can't understand. "I'll, er..." I turn away, wondering if I've got the courage to tell him I can sleep on my own. Have I mistaken pity for something more? But the thought of being alone while the ghost of my father comes calling is scarier than swallowing my pride and accepting I've made a fool of myself.

"Raven." His raspy voice, his tone, almost desperate, makes my eyes flick back to him. His jaw is clenched and his body tense. "Fuck, Raven, I want nothing more than to sink inside you." He takes a step closer, and as his voice deepens, it catches, full of emotion. "If you think I don't want you, you're fuckin' crazy." As I inhale sharply, he shakes his head, and at the same time stares at me intently. "But if we do this, you're mine. You've got to be fuckin' certain." His hand reaches out and caresses my face. "I'm not sure of your motive, but you need to know mine. I don't give a damn where or when, but when I take you, there's no going back."

How can I be sure? My life, my work, is in another state. If he wants me to promise forever, I can't give that to him. I need him. Need this. It's becoming so I want him more than my next breath. My breasts ache for his touch. My pussy feels so empty. But I can't make the commitment he's asking.

He seems to be able to read me. "Christ, Raven. Not going to tie you down. I know there's a fuckin' lot of hurdles before we can make a decision to be together. But I ain't being used to get close to my brothers. You take this step, you're telling me you want me and not one of them."

That thought had never crossed my mind. *What the hell does he think of me?*

Taking a step backward, I raise my hands. "If you think I'm here to collect trophies, then you've not learned anything about me."

Closing the gap between us, he cups my chin in his palm. "You want me, not Metalhead, not Raider—"

My eyes widen and blaze. "What the fuck are you talking about, Dwarf?"

His voice goes hoarse. "You're fuckin' gorgeous, Raven. Of

course, I fuckin' doubt it's me that you want. What can I offer that my brothers can't give you more of?"

It suddenly hits me. This man standing in front of me is so unsure of himself. For all his cockiness that comes along with being a biker, at his core, he's insecure. Sure, his brothers are taller, but it's not the outside that's been calling to me. It's his personality and what he's shown to be of the man beneath the exterior.

Something tells me he's been bitten before, hurt by a woman who used him. How can I persuade him it's him that I want?

Realising it's not me that's putting him off, but his own insecurities, makes me bold. I stab my finger in his chest. "How could I know what you can offer unless you show me? If you want me to spell it out, it's only you that I want. I don't give a damn about any of your brothers."

As fast as a snake striking, his hand moves from my chin and curls around my neck, pulling me to him as he plasters his lips upon mine. He thrusts his hips against me, leaving me in no doubt how much he wants me. My body automatically writhes against him.

I've unleashed a beast and we really are going to do this,

Dwarf's impatience shows as he tears my shirt over my head, then pauses, allowing his eyes to feast on my bra-covered breasts. When my hands go to remove it, he bats them away, and expertly flicks open the clasp. He sucks in air. Words are not needed to show his appreciation as his eyes flare.

This isn't going to be some gentle seduction routine. It doesn't need to be. I'm wet, willing and ready. When he pushes me back onto the sleeping bag covering the mouldy mattress, I help him instead of resisting, unbuttoning my pants and pushing them down my legs.

As he unzips his jeans and slides them down around his hips, taking his boxers with him and his perfectly proportioned cock bobs free, my mouth waters in anticipation.

Then worries flood through me. *I don't know what kind of lover he is. Will he just take me, chasing his own release? Has he protection, as heaven knows I'm not prepared. Will I regret this?*

One worry is immediately pushed aside as he fishes a condom out of his wallet and throws it on the bed beside me. Then roughly he takes my legs and forces them apart. For a moment, he just stares down at me.

Suddenly embarrassed, I turn my head to the side. I'm groomed but not bare.

"Fuckin' beautiful," he comments. "Love that the carpet matches the curtains." Then, my second doubts disappear when he lowers his head, and his tongue laps my clit without any warning, making me suck in a sharp breath.

Concerns I might have had about any talent he might be lacking fade into mist as he applies expertise I've never felt before. He gauges my reaction to everything he does and then reapplies the technique that has my muscles contracting. His hands aren't idle. His fingers probe into my depths, causing me to raise my hips and try to take more.

In a faster time then I've ever achieved with my vibrator, I'm tensing. My hands clasp at the sleeping bag, as I desperately suck in air.

"Come for me," he rumbles against my clit.

And God help me, I can't stop myself. Remembering at the last moment to stuff one of my fists into my mouth, I still can't completely smother my cries. It was all I could have hoped for and so much more.

He keeps licking me through the aftershocks, but as soon as I wince and pull away, he raises himself on his arms. Without wasting time, he's sheathing himself in latex.

Somehow, my legs are over his shoulders and my ass is on his thighs as he lines himself up, positioning me where he wants me.

I'm wet but there's still a slight burn as it's been a while, a delicious stretch as his wide cock breeches me. As his face contorts with his obvious effort to control himself, he advances inside me, fully seating himself after a few good strokes, strokes which have me gasping and writhing as he manages to hit that special spot.

When he's in completely, I realise he's perfect—not too long, but his girth makes me feel so full.

When he starts to move, any lingering qualms about whether he knows what he's doing are cast to the wind. He might not have an athlete's build, but the way he moves his hips...

"Fuck, babe. You feel so tight." His voice is jerky, his breathing hitched. "You feel fuckin' amazing."

"Oh God," I groan, remembering just in time to keep my voice low. "Dwarf..." I don't bother to waste any more words. There is no instruction he's needing, other than to keep doing what he's doing.

He speeds up, his thrusts moving me up to the top of the mattress. His lungs heave, his face contorts. For a second, I think he's going to leave me behind him, but his fingers find my clit and start rubbing furiously.

It works. I'm right there with him as his mouth slams down on mine, muting our joint exclamations. He kisses me hard as his pelvis still rocks against me. When he gentles the movement of his lips, I'm just about returning from my out-of-body experience.

"Best ever," I tell him when he gives me the room to speak.

His face transforms as a cocky grin covers it. "Back at cha, babe."

Chapter Sixteen

DWARF

I'd questioned it when Raven had first thrown herself at me. For starters, this is a fucked-up situation to be the setting for our first lovemaking session. Then there's the thought that's been growing, that she could be someone special for me.

Raven could do serious damage if she left me for one of my brothers. I don't want to be used as a substitute for another man. Her genuine shock that I thought she'd use me had done much to assuage my doubts, and it all came down to at last, I had a woman who only wanted me.

I hadn't wined or dined her, hadn't sent her flowers. Christ, I hadn't even gotten my pants down as far as my knees. But she was everything that I dreamed she would be—the perfect fit, the ideal woman. I'm no choirboy, she's far from my first, so I applied all that I'd learned. Her reactions showed how much she'd liked my repertoire.

And that accolade? *Best ever.* What man wouldn't preen after such praise?

Grinning down at her now, seeing the fucked flush on her face, I realise if her aim was to help us both sleep, she's achieved that on my part at least. I want nothing more than to pull her into my arms, hold her tight, get some rest, then wake her up and fuck her all over again.

Then I remember why we're here. It's like a bucket of cold water being thrown over me.

While I'd prefer small talk to come out of my mouth, I force myself to think of practicalities. "We better get our clothes on before we go to sleep." If anything happens during the night, I want to be prepared and not caught with my dick hanging out.

Her nod shows she agrees. As I slide off the bed, pulling up my jeans and boxers, and retrieving her clothes from the floor, giving them a good shake as I do so, she whispers to me, "Do you think anyone heard us?"

I think it's highly unlikely anyone remains in ignorance of what we'd been doing. They may not have heard her muffled screams, but they'd have heard the bed banging against the wall and the ancient floorboards creaking. Personally, I don't give a damn that they'll all know I've been claiming my woman, but I give her the assurance that she needs.

"I doubt it."

She gives a small snort of disbelief as she struggles back into her clothes. But if she's bothered, she doesn't show it. As she's dressing, I lie down, and when she's ready, I stretch out my hand. When she takes it, a little tug positions her beside me.

"This isn't the end," I tell her. "Not letting you go after you blew my mind like that."

"My home—"

"Don't give a damn about the obstacles," I cut her off. "Where there's a will, there's a way."

Her eyes meet mine before I turn the flashlight off, plunging us into darkness. Snuggling closer into my side, she whispers softly, "I've never met anyone like you before."

Me neither, Raven. But instead of speaking out loud, I just pull her to me. "Try to sleep, okay?"

"Tomorrow—"

"Can look after itself," I tell her firmly.

Not taking the hint that this conversation is over, she nuzzles against my chest. "I cleared my diary for a week."

Well, now, that's something I can work with. She's mine for a few more days at least. With a smile planted on my face, I close my eyes, trying to forget why we're here and anything other than the feel of the woman in my arms as I attempt to sleep.

Surprisingly, it's her whose breath evens out first, allowing me to feel a glimmer of pride in that she must feel safe in my arms—either that or the orgasms I gave her wore her out.

The cabin is silent except for the occasional sound of footsteps as somebody does a check around and the odd cough or clearing of a throat. It's comforting to have the sound of my brothers close by. I grin as I hear a loud snore, then an exclamation, which I think comes from the room opposite ours.

Apart from the examples of human occupation, I can hear nothing else. No *tickety tock*, no ethereal voices. Last night I must have been out of my mind. While I can't grasp what, how or why, there must be an explanation, Ghosts don't exist. I scoff at myself, knowing how stupid I must have sounded when I related what I'd heard to my prez. Toad must wonder what I'd been smoking.

Nah, nothing's going to disturb any of us tonight. And tomorrow, my brothers won't hesitate in yanking my chain and telling me what an ass I was.

In the darkness, I grin, holding Raven tighter. They can joke with me all they want. I've got Raven, and she's more than enough to make up for any deserved ribaldry.

My eyelids feel heavy, they shutter, then close completely. I turn on my side, spooning the woman who's come to mean so much to me. My lungs take in air in time with hers, and with a feeling of complete contentment, I feel myself drifting...

CRASH

My heart rate goes from fifty to two hundred beats a minute in a split second, and I'm on my feet, flashlight in one hand, gun in the other.

"What?" Raven's scared voice cries out beside me, and she reaches out to grasp my t-shirt.

In the light's beam I can see the door to the room is open and still quivering as though it's been kicked in.

"What the fuck's going on?"

"Who kicked my fuckin' door in?"

As well as the indignant shouts, footsteps are thundering up the stairs. Moving out into the hallway, I suddenly realise the crash I heard wasn't just this door, every door was simultaneously kicked in.

Raven's clutching at me, Scalpel, Midnight, Stumpy, Bonk, and Cash are standing looking bemused.

Toad's appeared, gun also in hand. "What the hell—"

"*Tickety tock!*"

The voice is ten times louder than it was last night. We all jump and gaze around, but there's nothing to be seen.

"*Tickety, tickety tock. Time's running out, little girl.*"

"Jesus."

"Where the fuck's that coming from?"

At the whimpered sound from my side, I holster my gun. All my brothers are armed and ready to shoot, and right now, Raven's a fucking mess and she needs me. I clasp her to me tightly.

"*Tickety tock. Come out, Mouse.*"

"The sound's coming from everywhere." Raider, panting as though he's run up the stairs, is staring at me with his eyes wide.

"*Tickety, tickety tock.*"

As the volume increases, I see Metalhead's eyes spinning around him. He backs himself up to a wall and holds his weapon ready to fire.

"*You can't hide, little mouse.*"

"*Tickety tock. Tickety tock. Tickety tock.*"

Footsteps sound, coming from the room at the end of the hallway, the room from which Midnight and Crumb have just emerged. The heavy thump of boots on wood sound like they're slowly approaching.

Raven's clasping at me, but she's not the only one grabbing at someone. Scalpel's hanging onto Crumb's arm, his eyes open wide.

Thump.

They're coming closer.

Midnight takes a look behind him and then moves fast. "Get out," he yells. "You can't fuck with something like that."

Another crunch of a foot stomping on the floor toward where we're standing and none of us need to be told twice.

Toad, Raider, Bonkers, Stumpy, Midnight, Crumb, Scalpel, Cash, I, and Raven belt down the stairs, almost falling over each other in an effort to get down first. Forget having your brother's back. At this moment, it's every man for himself.

In the main room we pause. Toad races over to where Ruby's been waiting, Rolo held tightly against her. Unless I'm mistaken, this self-professed lover of haunted houses is physically shaking. Once he's satisfied his woman is safe, Toad looks at us as if ensuring we're all accounted for, then his eyes return to the stairs where there's the clear sound of footsteps descending, but no body attached to them.

"Tickety fuckin' tickety tock. Where the fuck are you, girl?"

Crashing sounds make us all turn to see plates smashed to the floor in the kitchen. Books fly off one of the shelves, one narrowly missing Ruby's head. Rolo yelps from his position in her arms.

Toad's jaw clenches. "Everyone, outside. Now."

He won't be getting any argument from me or anyone by the look of it. The doorway gets momentarily blocked by people struggling to get out. Toad fists his hand in Bonker's cut, pulling him backward so Ruby and Rolo can escape. Metalhead holds back Scalpel to let Raven go through.

It's only seconds later when I'm able to join her, and behind me, the remaining brothers run out.

Emerging into the night, I half expect there to be thunder and lightning, or a thick fog swirling, but there's no howling wind, just a gentle breeze, and a clear sky from which the moon is brightly shining.

Outside it seems peaceful, not so the interior of the cabin, where the banging, crashing and that fucking voice shouting is continuing. Raven throws herself into my arms and as I hold her body, she's shaking so hard I can almost hear her teeth rattling.

"We going to get out of here, Prez?"

I think that was Cash, but it's hard to tell as his voice isn't normally an octave above normal.

"Yeah, Prez. Why are we waiting?"

Still clutching Raven, I move her head so I can see around her. Toad, holding Ruby much like I'm holding Raven, is standing, staring at the cabin. While lit only by moonlight, his features look taut.

We're all leaving a good few yards between us and the building.

Something, a heavy piece of furniture perhaps, causes another major noise and I swear I see the building shake.

"Jeez, it's like a freaking movie where the house is going to implode." Stumpy stares bemused.

"Or explode. Let's get the fuck back," Metalhead shouts.

I brought Raven in the crash truck which is parked a distance away. Other brothers run to their bikes and wheel them to a safer distance. Once they've moved them all out of range, uneasily they walk back.

The cabin is now eerily silent.

"You okay?" Urgently I turn Raven toward me.

Her hand's on her chest over her heart, her gaze fixed on the cabin. "Is it over?"

There's no way of knowing. I grunt which could mean one thing or another.

"At least I know it's not my imagination."

When I look down, I see she's biting her lip as if trying to be brave.

I don't know what to say. I know she's terrified that she's awakened something by coming back here, and that it will never leave her alone. And I can't comfort her one way or the other. This is nothing like I've ever known.

Fuck, I feel useless. I don't know what to do or what to say, so I settle for holding her tightly.

"I'm with you, Raven, okay?" And I mean forever if she'll have me. "We've got this."

All the answer I get is her trying to get even closer to me.

We wait. Brothers get out smokes and start passing them around. Scalpel's not the only one bouncing on his toes. I think we're all on tenterhooks, wondering what's going to happen next.

Five minutes passes, ten. Brothers start shuffling. Midnight sinks to his haunches to get his weight off his feet, and Bonk sits next to him on the ground.

I notice Ruby tugging at Toad. After a while, she hands Rolo's lead to Raider, and she and Toad disappear around the cabin and out of sight.

"Someone wants a piss," Crumb announces with a snort.

A piss and something else by the time they take. When they return with Ruby sporting a very satisfied smile on her face, which leads to a few raucous comments being thrown around and Toad showing more than one person his middle finger, it's been more than an hour since the last noises were heard from the cabin.

"We staying out here all night?" Scalpel stubs out yet another cigarette and smothers a yawn.

Toad turns away from Ruby and faces the cabin instead. I watch him as he widens his stance and places his fist under his chin. After a moment's study, he turns and beckons us all to move in close.

He stares down at Rolo who's completely unfazed and

licking her privates. His eyes move from the chihuahua and focus on Midnight.

"You're in tune with nature or shit like that. What did you pick up from inside the building?"

"Yeah, was this place built over some Native graveyard or something?" Bonk asks. When I raise an eyebrow at him, he splays his hands. "Well, that's the normal reason in films."

Midnight rolls his eyes and shakes his head. He brushes his long hair back. "I got nothing." He sounds almost apologetic.

"So, nothing to do with your ancestors then?"

Midnight snorts. "Hey, I'm not in tune with everything. I just heard what you heard, nothing more."

"Perhaps you haven't been smoking enough?" Cloud suggests.

Toad ignores everyone and refocuses his eyes on the dog. "Rolo jumped at the noises, but her hackles didn't rise." He lifts his gaze and settles on Raider. "Dogs sense the supernatural, don't they?"

"Maybe it's because she's not a real dog?"

Metalhead exaggeratedly oomphs as Ruby thumps him in the stomach.

As if to experiment, Toad takes the end of the lead from his old lady and walks across to the closed door to the cabin. He watches Rolo the whole time, but she doesn't hesitate and doesn't growl. But once they're in front of the doorway, she crouches and does a dump on the doorstep.

"So that's what she thinks of that!" Bonk roars with laughter.

"You okay?" I ask Raven again, this time quietly.

"I don't know."

Her reply is honest. I assess her, pleased she's not shaking quite so badly, but worried what damage has been done to her mind. It's too early to say. How the fuck can I make this better?

I motion to Ruby, waving her over to us. "Can you stay with Raven for a moment?"

"Sure."

As I remove my arm from Raven, Ruby puts hers around her. "Fuck, that was scary," she says softly.

When Raven responds with a nod, I feel she's in good hands. Stepping away, I walk over to join Toad, soon realising some of the others have the same idea.

Toad glances around, raises his chin, then stares back at the cabin.

"What's on your mind, Prez?"

He turns to me, then points back to Midnight. "Neither our resident spiritualist nor our fuckin' canine sensed anything out of the ordinary."

"You're saying we're seeing things that weren't there?" My eyes widen.

"Didn't see fuck all, just heard a whole load of noises," Raider states.

"And all the doors smashing open," Metalhead reminds us. "And don't forget the flying books and plates."

I give Toad a piercing look. "You saying we're all suffering from mass hysteria?" Maybe I could admit I'd picked up on Raven's fear yesterday, but it's too great a stretch to think we all could be similarly affected. I cooked the damn food, and there wasn't any hallucinogenic added into it.

"Still say we disturbed the resting place of the past residents." Bonk sounds quite sensible for once.

"This isn't a Stephen King novel." Toad rolls his eyes.

I grimace and take over. "And it's not residents, it's one. Tickety tock is personal for Raven. The only one doing the haunting is her father who abused her."

Toad's eyes come to mine quickly. "Fuck."

"He met his end here, didn't he?" Bonk continues. "So, it sounds likely he's the one behind it. We need to find an exorcist."

A hand rests on my back. Turning, I see Raven has come to join me. I wince, knowing I shared part of her story, but she doesn't seem upset.

"It's down to me. It's me being here."

"Nah." I pull her in front of me, and put my arms around her, crossing them over her stomach. "He's probably been haunting this place for ages."

"No, he hasn't," she states. As all eyes go to her, she explains, "When I arrived here yesterday, everything was in its place. There was no damage, no broken plates."

"Maybe he's upset because of what you and Dwarf were doing." The morning must have lightened with the advent of dawn as I can see Scalpel's eyes waggling, and I don't miss the blush on Raven's face.

"Waking the fuckin' dead, that's what they were doing." Cash doubles over at his own joke, but it's too close to the mark, and I, for one, am not laughing.

Toad cocks his head to where the sky is lightening. Although the forest-covered mountains block the sight, behind them obviously the sun is rising. Turning back, his eyes fall on the woman in front of me.

"I think we should go back inside," he says. "But Dwarf and Raven stay out here."

"Hey, I'll stay too. Make sure they have protection," Bonk's quick to volunteer.

"Nah, I'll stay. She might need medical attention."

"Fuckin' cowards." Raider rounds on them, then he turns to Prez. "Whatcha thinking?"

Toad shrugs, now moving his gaze away from Raven and back to the cabin. "Something doesn't add up."

"Well, of course, it fuckin' doesn't," Stumpy cries out. "The place is fuckin' haunted and needs to be burned down."

"You want it burned down?" Toad questions Raven.

Still holding her close, I hold my breath, waiting for her answer. The cabin belongs to her, and whatever happens now will be her decision.

She takes her time, straightening, which moves her away

from me. Her hands clench by her sides as she stares at the place that must have always featured in her nightmares.

Toad gives her the time, and eventually she raises her head with determination. "The cabin belongs to me now, not him. He got me sent away once before, I don't want him to do it again. If there's a way to evict him, I want to take it."

Toad's head snaps up. His eyes meet hers for a moment, then he turns to Midnight. "Any ideas of the next step? How do we get rid of a fuckin' ghost?"

Midnight shrugs. "Ain't a job for a shaman. Reckon you need a priest to perform an exorcism."

Metalhead tilts his head to the side. "Or maybe Raven sells the place to us and keeps away. He might not be back if she isn't here to tempt him."

"Not sure I want to take that chance." Cash is backing away as though washing his hands of the place.

Toad gives Metalhead an assessing glance, and slowly raises and dips his chin. "I still want to go back inside. Take a good look at everything."

"Oh no we don't." Crumb steps forward, and points in front of him. "You're not getting me to stay another night in there."

Raider jerks his head in the direction of the lightening sky. "It's not fuckin' night. Daybreak is coming."

"What? There's some kind of rule that ghosts only haunt in the dark?" Crumb doesn't seem comforted.

Midnight chuckles. "Seems that way, Brother. They prey on our fuckin' nerves. Dark, fog, anything where we haven't the full use of our senses."

Toad glances around consideringly. "We wait for an hour, then go back inside."

Raven stirs in my arms and I take it to mean the last place she wants to be is anywhere near the cabin, outside or not, if whatever's inside has a chance of being disturbed again. Despite her brave words, I know she's terrified of what she might have awoken by coming back. While I understand Toad not wanting to leave it alone, and I don't like leaving my brothers in the lurch, I make a decision on the spot.

"Raven doesn't have to be here for this. I'm taking her back to the clubhouse."

Toad shoots me a look, an assessing glance at Raven, then nods and is quick to agree. "I'll send Princess back with you."

Chapter Seventeen

RAVEN

My heart seems to take a long time getting back into a normal rhythm after having proof that things really do go bump in the night—or crash, bang, wallop in this particular case. This time it wasn't just me and Dwarf that heard the commotion and saw the aftereffects. It was his whole club.

And what a show it had been. Such an escalation from the previous evening, which had driven me crazy enough. If I'd have been alone, well, I think I'd have been more than scared out of my mind. I think my heart would have stopped beating on the spot.

After the ignominious exit from the building, I'd looked around at Dwarf's brothers, somewhat comforted to see at least some seemed as unnerved and as uneasy as myself. As I remember how they'd almost knocked each other over in the rush to get down the stairs, and the—now looking back on it, amusing—fight to be first out of the door, I know there's no reason to be embarrassed that my original reaction had been to flee. It's not just me being a typical weak and easily frightened woman. The experience had affected these men just as much.

I've a feeling these men wouldn't hesitate in front of any

physical enemy, and not an ounce of fear would they feel. But to be faced with the unknown, the inexplicable, that's a different matter completely.

Now though, as the sun is rising behind the mountains and beginning to filter through the trees, I want to again find the strong woman that's inside of me. The woman who overcame her childhood abuse and strived to put it behind her. The woman who learned to stand on her own two feet. The woman who didn't need any man to support her, financially or physically.

Dwarf wants to take me away, take the little woman somewhere safe, and without even asking me. I disentangle myself from him and take a step away.

I don't want to hurt him, nor reject his offer that comes from an obvious desire to protect me, but there's no way, if his brothers are staying, that I'm going to leave.

I approach Toad and speak firmly. "That cabin is mine." My eyes flick behind him, and I try to keep my voice and gaze steady. "And what we heard last night was all about me. It's my daddy who's haunting this place, and it's him who has to leave. I'm staying right here and I'm going back inside with you." When he crosses his arms over his chest and raises his chin, I know I've got to give him more to persuade him. "Someway, somehow, we've got to put my daddy to rest. Else, what's to say, now he's woken, he'll stay here." I gulp, voicing my nightmare. "What if he follows me when I go home?"

Dwarf's quickly by my side. "She's got a point, Prez."

"Still don't fuckin' believe in ghosts," Toad mumbles. "But if that's what she believes—"

"*She's* right here," I snap, not letting him get away with thinking Dwarf speaks for me. He might have had the shit scared out of him, but when I leave, he'll be able to forget anything ever happened. As for me, I'll always be unwilling to close my eyes in the dark.

Toad gives me a respectful chin lift, then tilts his head. I take it as a sign that I have a moment to plead my case.

I wave toward the cabin. "I concede he might always have been here and that my appearance, I don't know," I grimace, "increased his powers?" I shrug, showing I don't know what I'm talking about. "But that alone raises questions. Is a ghost tied to the place where it died, or have I now set him free?" Even though the warmth of the rising sun is hitting my back, shivers still run down my spine. I have to swallow a couple of times before I can regain strength in my voice. "I don't want to always be frightened of the dark or be scared to close my eyes. This has to end, somehow. Someway. Right here and now."

"Well enough put, but what solutions have we got?" Toad challenges me. "Seems like we're on the same side, darlin'. You want to be free of your past, and I want the cabin, but not with the current entity that's present in it. Sure, it might follow you and I'll be rid of it, but in the same way as you can't see how it's going to play out, I can't take the risk it might someday be back." He pauses and turns to Raider. "Am I really standing here discussing how to off a fuckin' ghost?"

His VP snorts, and it relieves the tension a little. "Seems, Prez, that's exactly what you're doing."

"Fuck my life." But Toad doesn't seem overly bothered. He looks like a man who eagerly rises to every challenge in life, and this is just one more hurdle to be surmounted.

It actually raises my spirits a little, knowing that we're on the same side. If anyone's going to put down my daddy for good, I reckon this man will at least give it a damn good try.

I notice I, and everyone else, are looking to him to take the lead. Instead of seeming fed up with being expected to have all the answers, Toad bows his head and rubs at his temple, looking deep in thought.

After a few seconds, he looks up. "Okay. We're going to go inside and see if there's any rational explanation for what happened during the night." He holds up his hand at the murmurs of protest. "At the end of the day, we may have to admit there's something supernatural going on, but I want to be sure of that before we take any next steps."

"Which might be?" Metalhead asks.

Toad shrugs. "There must be a fuckin' expert we can call on." He grins, contorting his scar. "There always is on TV."

While I've nothing to add to his plan, I go back to the original point. "I'm coming inside with you. You're not sending me away." My tone leaves no room for argument. Ruby, who's now moved behind Toad, winks at me. I gather she's giving me her approval.

"Yeah, stud." She pokes him in the arm. "You're not getting rid of me, either. I'm down for exiling a ghost."

"Princess." Toad turns to his woman. Placing his arms on hers, he gives her a gentle shake. "Ghost or not, you saw what happened in there. It could be dangerous. You almost got hit by a flying book for fuck's sake."

"A book, yeah, not a bullet." She sighs and rolls her eyes. "Welcome to the world of overprotective bikers, Raven."

Despite the situation, her exaggerated sympathy makes me give a small smile.

"Princess," Toad says in a warning tone.

Ignoring him, she takes the necessary steps to me and links her arm with mine. "I got your back, sister."

It's not an odd thing to say, but her casual words twist something inside me. I'd always wanted a female sibling, someone to have my back and not side with our father like Jack had done. It's been a long time since I had anything resembling family.

Toad stares at the two of us and then shakes his head. "Okay, but you wait out here while we go and check shit out and until we give you the all clear to come in."

"I'll stay with them," Bonk offers, magnanimously.

"Me too, Brother," Cash agrees.

"Er, I'm happy staying out here," Crumb admits.

"You go where you're fuckin' told to," Metalhead thunders.

"What the fuck are you, men or mice? You scared of a few noises?"

"I'm not waiting outside," I state firmly. "I've more right to enter than any of you." I notice how I can see all their faces more clearly as the sun's completely over the horizon now. "I was here all alone in daylight the day before yesterday, and nothing happened."

Dwarf steps up beside me and puts his hand on my shoulder. It seems he's not trying to divert the course I'm on, but instead, offering a tactile assurance he'll be right beside me.

Toad sighs heavily. "Anyone know what we're looking for? Apart from assessing the damage?"

"Evidence of a fucking ghost." Stumpy looks up to the heavens and then back down. "As if bookcases turned over and plates smashed aren't enough."

Midnight's looking thoughtful. He takes the few steps that brings him in front of me. "You know where your grandaddy buried your dad?"

Before I can answer, Raider asks, "What are you suggesting? That we put a fuckin' stake through his heart?"

"That's for vampires," Bonk puts in helpfully.

Before they can go off track, I disillusion them fast. "I have no idea, so that's a non-starter, whether stakes or silver bullets would even help."

"I still say burn the place down."

"Not useful, Bonk."

"Prez—"

"Nah." Toad steps forward, sparks flashing from his eyes. "You've seen this place. I want it. It would be fuckin' perfect for us. A self-contained bunker where we could hide off the grid."

"Perfect if we can evict its current resident," his VP reminds him drily.

"Ghosts often hang around because they have unfinished business. Give him what he wants, and he may go in peace," Midnight suggests.

"What he wants is me." I swallow down the anxiety that rises when I think about what my dear unloving daddy had done to me in the past. I want somehow for it to end here. I hate to think of the damage he's already done, undoing years of therapy. But this time I'm not a vulnerable child, I'm a woman. And I've got a motorcycle club beside me.

"Something else might be holding him here."

"Like what?" Toad looks interested, but in response, Midnight shrugs.

Bonk scuffs his foot over the dirt. "We need a fuckin' priest."

His suggestion is not immediately dismissed as Toad asks, "Anyone know one?"

It seems that they aren't a religious lot as no one does. And there's no point them asking me, I've never believed in any deity that refused to help to ease the suffering of a little kid however much I'd prayed.

With his hands on his hips, Toad turns back and looks at the cabin. After a moment, he exhales a sharp breath. "I don't know what the fuck we're looking for, but we're not getting closer standing outside. We'll go in. Search everywhere. See if you can find anything out of the ordinary. If we don't find anything..." he breaks off, shakes his head and scoffs. "Can't believe I'm actually saying this, but we'll go back to the clubhouse and Google someone who can perform a fuckin' exorcism." He glances over his shoulders as if to confirm everyone's with him. "I still think something doesn't add up. I've never believed in the fuckin' supernatural."

"Don't think you have to believe in it, Prez, if it believes in you." Midnight's words strike a chord with me. After the last couple of nights, I've been persuaded that something outside this physical sphere really exists.

As I shudder, Dwarf pulls me to him, and I allow him to draw me in. I lean against him and take a fortifying breath which seems full of the scent of oil and leather. I'm startled how much it already suggests home.

I can't lean on him. Not just because I never want to be beholden to anyone, but because my place is far away. Dwarf and I might be able to have a pleasant few days, but at the end of the week, my work will be calling to me.

As he runs his hands up and down my back in a comforting way, I remember how compatible we were in the middle of the night. The sex was out-of-this-world good, at least for me. Even now, I admit, it's going to be hard to walk away.

But before I can think further about whether there could ever be a me and him, I've got to deal with the reason I came to Arizona. The cabin that's been left to me.

"Let's do this."

Having pronounced his intention, Toad puts his hand on the doorknob. Before turning it, he looks back. "Don't know what the fuck we're looking for, Brothers, but anything that looks out of place, give a shout."

When Ruby steps up beside Toad, he enters. Raider and Metalhead are close on their heels. Ruby puts the tiny dog down and waits to see if there's a reaction. Rolo does nothing more exciting than chase her tail then sit and scratch her ear.

"Obviously her ghost radar isn't working," Dwarf whispers into my ear as he pulls me forward.

Making sure I don't step on the tiny four-legged creature, I take a breath and walk over the threshold. Already, beams of early morning sunlight are shining into the main room, completely transforming the atmosphere of last night. Dust motes dance in the rays of the sun, and apart from the visible damage, nothing seems disturbed or out of place.

Rather than being left behind, even the men who said they'd prefer to wait outside seem not to want to be outdone by women and follow us inside.

At first, the men around me just mill around, but slowly they seem to sort themselves out and decide on what they should be doing. Bonk tests the floorboards by stomping on them in turn, while Scalpel starts knocking on the walls. At first their movements are tentative as though expecting to get a response, but no ectoplasm makes an appearance, and no ghostly voice responds.

With most of them staying, for now, in the main room, I take a step toward the stairs. I'm determined to go into the room I've avoided up until now—my childhood bedroom at the end of the hall. The seat of my nightmares and where the damage to my body and soul was done.

Dwarf follows me as though he's going to stay glued to my side. Even with my independence raising its head, there's something comforting about not being alone.

He pauses outside the room we'd been sleeping in as something catches his attention. Taking out his phone, he clicks on the flashlight function and starts examining something on the door.

"Well I'll be fuckin' damned." The first words are said to himself, the next are shouted down the stairs, his voice bellowing so loudly it makes me jump. "Metal, get your ass up here."

In response, multiple footsteps thump up the stairs, more than just belonging to one man. But it's Metalhead who steps up to Dwarf and looks at what he's pointing at.

"Fuck me," he exclaims. Then he smartly does a one hundred and eighty turn, and steps to the door across the hallway. After he examines it, his hand comes up to smash into the wall, and when he swings around, fire flashes in his eyes. "We've been fuckin' had, Brothers."

"What is it?" Toad pushes through the brothers who've accompanied Metalhead upstairs.

Pushing myself closer, I want to see as well. From where I am, all I can see are a few splinters, and a hole where the latch used to fit into the door.

Metalhead draws his finger down the wood and shows his prez some black residue left behind.

Toad goes completely still, his face as dark as a thundercloud. Then suddenly he roars. "I knew something didn't make fuckin' sense. We're not dealing with the supernatural, we're dealing with a fuckin' prankster."

"A clever fuckin' bastard who knows what he's doing," Raider confirms, leaning in to study the evidence.

"What's going on?" Bonk shouts from the back of the crowd.

"Fuckin' doors must have been simultaneously blown open with an explosive. No ghost responsible at all."

My jaw has dropped to the floor. I squeeze Dwarf's hand as though to anchor myself. While I'm pleased there's an explanation for the horrors that chased me away, there are still questions to answer. Like who's behind it.

"What about the voice?" Midnight asks. "And the footsteps?"

I find myself nodding. What they've discovered doesn't explain that away.

Cloud seems to grow a foot taller as he takes charge. "We all heard the fuckin' voice and footsteps moving around. We're looking for speakers, Brothers."

As soon as he speaks, flashlights come out, and the men begin searching crevasses and crannies.

"Sorry about this, Raven," Raider shouts as he pulls off a piece of panelling. Then follows it up with, "Fuckin' got you."

I wince as he hits the adjacent dry wall, putting a massive hole in it.

"Hey," Dwarf starts, his tone angry.

Placing my hand on his arm, I stop him. "It's okay, Dwarf. I was almost persuaded to burn this place down. I want answers." As I stare at the small line of speakers that have been revealed, my teeth clench together.

"Got some under the floorboards too," Scalpel calls out.

Turning, I can see he's pulled a board up.

Stumpy runs up the stairs. He's breathing heavily when he gets to the top. "Miniature explosives brought down the bookcase and blew out the kitchen cupboard."

Cloud's standing with his chin in one hand, his other arm propping up his elbow. His eyes are narrowed. "This is some sophisticated set up." He pauses, then eyes me. "Elaborate and meant to chase you out. Someone certainly doesn't want you to have your inheritance."

"Someone who's either an explosive expert or one who has good connections." Toad shares a glance with Dwarf. "Any idea who that could be, Raven?"

Chapter Eighteen

DWARF

There's a certain relief in knowing I was neither going mad, nor that spirits inhabit the world which I know and love. But as Raven blanches in front of me and seems to need the strength of my arm to support her, I wonder for her what's worse.

Her father coming back from the dead to haunt her, or someone who's very much alive and wants to scare her out of her mind? Someone who doesn't want her to claim this cabin for herself. Not that there'll be much left of it by the time my brothers have finished with it from the way they're tearing it up.

Having disgraced themselves by fleeing into the night, they're taking out their vengeance on the building, trying to find all the evidence of the very human person responsible for pouring fuel on their fear. I don't actually blame them. If I didn't have Raven to watch out for, I might very well be tearing it apart for myself.

I'm enraged, but not that I was the victim of a plot to scare me out of my wits. No, I'm furious for Raven and worried about the person who'd go to such ends to hurt her. She'd blindly fled from the cabin so terrified she might have been killed had I not swerved the bike. My fists clench, wishing I had an enemy to take out my anger on.

Toad's been viewing the various discoveries. "No cameras?"

Cloud answers him, "No fuckin' Wi-Fi. No way of getting footage out."

"How did they fuckin' know she was here?" Toad raises his eyebrow at our technical expert.

Grimacing, Cloud's brow creases, then he shrugs. "He, she, they must have been able to estimate when she'd arrive. Set the first night up to scare her. The second was a failsafe in case the initial setup hadn't chased her off."

"But if she hadn't been here, then it all would have been for nothing."

Again, Cloud's shoulders rise and fall. "Fair bet she'd come back to the cabin once she knew she'd inherited it. Then it would have been a case of knowing when she'd arrive, presumably by checking the airports." He casts a glance at Raven, who isn't paying attention. She looks lost in her mind as she tries to cope with the idea someone wants the cabin so much, they set out to destroy her. "Either she's being followed or digitally stalked."

Either doesn't sit well with me. I catch Toad's eye, and know he's thinking the same thing as I. This isn't a case of just anyone. It's got to be someone close to her, someone who knows all about her past and what was necessary to trigger her. I'm chilled to think that if the intent had been to kill, they'd have blown the cabin up with her inside. Which means, whoever it is doesn't give a damn about how much damage, mental or physical that she sustains, they want the cabin intact.

"A word." Toad's request is formed as a statement. He jerks his head toward Raven, then to the stairs and doesn't check that she and I are following him down. We are, Raven seeming completely compliant and allowing me to steer her wherever I want her to go. He doesn't stop in the main room, just continues outside. Once there, he raises his head to the sun and breathes in deeply.

Raven, too, seems to appreciate the fresh air, and turns up her face to the warmth. It doesn't relax her though. Her forehead is lined, and her mouth is thinned. She seems lost in thought and while I'm standing next to her, very alone.

Toad only gives her a moment. "Who?" When she doesn't respond, he repeats his question more forcibly. "Who, Raven, who?"

Her eyes snap open as she looks at him. Crease lines deepen by her eyes as she answers in a plaintive cry, "I don't know."

There's something about her tone that suggests maybe she's got an inkling but doesn't want to admit it.

"Who stands to gain if you don't claim your inheritance?" Toad pushes her.

"I don't know," she repeats.

For some reason, I think she's lying. "What about your brother?"

A pained look crosses her face, and her words show she wasn't trying to mislead us. "If Jack was alive, Grandaddy would have made provision for him in his will. He wasn't mentioned, and everything came to me." She grimaces. "I thought that meant he was dead."

Maybe not. There could be another explanation for him being excluded from the inheritance. "Perhaps he turned out as rotten as your father and he didn't want to leave anything to him?"

As Raven shrugs, obviously not wanting to think a family member might care so little about her to go so far as try to scare her to death, Toad doesn't let up on her. "If not your brother, who else?" Raven jerks a little. Toad presses on, "Who else knows those details about your past? Who would know exactly how to trigger you? Who knows this cabin even exists?"

If I wasn't there to support her, I think Raven might have fallen at this point. That she's got no other answer is written all over her face.

Knowing he's got her, Toad gentles his voice and asks, "What do you know about your brother, Raven? Have you any info that we could use to track him down?"

Again, her shoulders rise and fall. "His name is Jack Dempsey. He'd be twenty-nine years old." After a moment's thought, she gives him his birthdate.

"When was the last time you saw him? Your grandaddy ever mention him at all?"

"She's had no contact with her grandad or brother since she was eleven years old," I answer for her, hoping Toad won't continue to probe, worried about how much Raven can take of this. Knowing a human was responsible is clearly not easier than when she thought it was a ghost.

But she suddenly becomes animated. "He's not behind this. He couldn't be. Grandaddy homeschooled him just as he homeschooled me, but Jack wasn't interested in lessons. By the time I left, he could barely read." She waves her hand back to the cabin. "It might have been fifteen years ago, but I can't see how he'd have developed the skills to work with explosives and set up such an elaborate trap."

Toad grimaces, conceding her point, but then his eyes widen as he realises something else. "That can't have been your daddy saying those things." Toad's eyes narrow, and as he stares back at the cabin, I wonder whether he's talking to us or himself. "But you recognised his voice?"

The last question is definitely directed toward Raven.

"It might have been fifteen years ago that I last heard it, but those words..." Her whole body shudders. "I'll never forget. I hear them in my nightmares."

"And the voice?" Toad presses again.

"Was Daddy's." Raven's firm response leaves no room for argument.

"Hmm." Toad looks thoughtful. "Was Jack's voice similar to your dad's?"

She gives a mirthless chuckle. "Jack's voice hadn't broken

when I left, so I don't know what he'd have sounded like as an adult."

"But he'd know." I exchange a glance with my prez. Whatever Raven thinks about the capabilities of her brother, or that she doesn't know whether he's alive or dead, the facts point to his involvement. Maybe if he didn't get it exactly, the words would be enough to trigger a reaction even if Jack didn't get his father's tone right. Just hearing the same threats might be enough to convince her she'd heard his voice.

"It can't be Jack." Raven shakes her head dismissively.

Toad props his leg up on the broken fence and leans over it. "You got any other enemies?"

Her eyes first widen, then again, her head moves side to side. "Firstly no, none that I know of. And even if I did a decorating job that had disappointed—not that any of my clients have told me I have—no one knows where I come from." She moves away from me, wrapping her arms around her as if she's thinking. "No one, except Jack, would know what my father did to me."

"Your aunt?" I'm grabbing at straws.

Raven's mouth drops. "She died. She would never have told anybody, even though we spoke about it. She didn't know all the details. I never told her about tickety tock."

"It's got to be Jack." If there's no other person, then however unlikely, that's who it has to be. I exchange a look with Toad.

She glances at me, then at my prez, then scrunches her brow and wraps her arms around her waist. When she speaks again, her voice catches as she obviously comes to the same conclusion. "If there's a human behind it, it has to be him, doesn't it?" There's such pain on her face that I ache to be able to smooth it away. Even though she's got no fond memories of him, it must sting to know your only kin wants to hurt you.

"It has." Toad doesn't spare any fake sympathy. That's him to a T. He's all business and doesn't waste time on emotion. Before he'd met Ruby, I'd have said he hadn't the capability, but she's changed him. Where she's concerned, he wears his heart on his sleeve. "Or at least someone he would have spoken about you too. The question is why." He raises an eyebrow in her direction.

Still hugging herself, Raven again takes a guess. Moving her gaze to the cabin behind us, she shrugs. "Because he thought Grandaddy should have left him this."

"A broken-down cabin in the middle of nowhere?" Toad's brows reach his hairline. "Darlin', even if you spent a fortune on it, it wouldn't be worth much. Certainly not worth going to all this bother for."

"What about the prepper shit underneath it?" I ask. Someone might want that for the same reasons we do. Somewhere to hide off the grid.

Toad raises and lowers his shoulders. "Perhaps, if Jack wanted to use it himself." He thinks for a moment. "Or maybe he got in with a crew who had a use for it."

"It was a pretty elaborate trick to get her running," I observe. "If it was someone else, they knew down to the last detail what would scare her. But if it was Jack, why didn't he just approach her and ask to buy it from her?"

"I'd have taken any offer." Raven bites her lip. "Hell, I'd probably have given it to him." She eyes the cabin again. "I only came back to face my memories, to bring back the good times and try to counteract the bad. I didn't ask for this, didn't want it. If Jack wanted it to be his, all he had to do was ask."

"He's still fuckin' with you," I suggest the answer. "Just like he did when you were a kid."

Toad places both feet on the ground. His brow furrows. "He went to a fuck load of bother." He casts his eyes back and then faces front. "And it's one hell of a trick for an uneducated kid." Pulling back his shoulders, he aims his feet for the door. "I'm going to get Cloud to try to look into his whereabouts. Seems we need to speak to him to get answers."

Raven moves so she stands in front of him. "You don't need to do this. I'll just leave and let Jack have this pile of shit if it means so much to him. You've already done enough for me."

She pauses and winces. "I really thought I was losing my mind until you discovered there was a rational explanation."

"Ain't nothing rational about any of this." Toad wipes his hands over his face, his eyes meeting mine briefly, signalling he thinks there's a deeper reason beneath. Knowing Prez, he won't rest until he gets to the bottom of it. "And I'm not doing it for you. I'm doing it for the club. I want this cabin. If I have to fight Jack for it, so be it." He walks off into the cabin.

"Come here." I hold out my hand to Raven. She walks into my arms as if she was born to be there. Not for the first time, I think how she fits so perfectly. I suspect she'd feel amazing, riding behind me on my bike—not that I've anything to compare it with. I've never had a woman ride behind me before. She'd looked good in my bed at the clubhouse.

I frown into her hair. Raven deserves her own house, somewhere we can start a family. My lips turn the other way around as I wonder why these strange thoughts are going through my brain.

It seems I'm not the only one who's been thinking. After taking a few minutes comfort from me, Raven pulls away. She walks off a few paces. When she speaks, she's facing away from me as though voicing her thoughts to the scenery.

"I can't believe it's Jack. Just asking me would have been so much simpler."

But not so much fun. I suppress my growl, hoping Cloud quickly finds Jack so I can have a few words with him. A conversation best done with my fists, and one from which I doubt he'd walk away.

"I wouldn't give him the fuckin' time of day," I tell her, my anger rising. "All he needed to do was approach you to see how things stood. Instead, he's played this elaborate game."

I glance back at the cabin. Fuck me, but he played it good. It wasn't an amateur job. Virtually undetectable. If we hadn't gone back to look, if I'd only given a cursory glance to the damage, he might have gotten away with the story of the ghost. From how she'd described him, Jack had to have help.

But, maybe, like myself, Jack had gone into the service and had learned a trade there. Still, setting up those contraptions and timing them so accurately had required some serious talent.

"I don't want it. He can have it." Raven turns away and walks off, as though sick of thinking about the cabin and the implications of her brother's involvement.

I stare after her. For once, I'm not focusing on her ass, nor the long hair that hangs down her back. I'm trying to put myself in her brother's shoes and wondering what his endgame is.

I start to wonder what would have happened if I hadn't come across her the night before last and wonder when her terror would have stopped her running. She could have tripped, fallen, still be lying out there in this godforsaken middle-of-nowhere spot. She could have gotten herself caught in a trap or run into a vehicle that hadn't been able to swerve or stop.

Jack had to have known how she'd be terrified out of her wits.

"You're not giving him fuck all," I shout after her, then close the gap between us so I can lower my voice. "My club wants to buy the cabin from you, so sell it to us."

Raven looks so sad it breaks my heart. "But if it's that important to him—"

"What he did was despicable, Raven. He tried to scare you to death."

Me putting it so bluntly seems to pull her up. She swings around to face me, her eyes wide and her jaw slack.

I press my advantage. "What would have happened to you if I hadn't been there that night?"

If I don't like to imagine the implications, it's clear she doesn't herself.

Again, I go to hold her, but this time, she steps back and again protectively wraps her arms around herself. Slowly shaking her head, she backs away from me.

When a shuttered look comes over her eyes, I realise she'd far rather be facing a ghost than the real-life spectre of her brother haunting her.

"Raven..." As she takes another step, putting more distance between us, I realise I'm losing her. She's no longer the woman who can summon up enough strength to return to confront the ghost. She's not the woman who begged me to fuck her in the middle of last night.

She's reverted to the girl who needed years of therapy to put the past behind her.

I don't know how to reach her.

"Raven..." I start again, knowing my pleas will fall on deaf ears.

"I... I need some time to myself, Dwarf. I need to think."

What man on earth wants to step away from his woman who's hurting? Definitely not a man like myself. And she is mine. She might not know it, but in giving herself to me, I've claimed her.

But though we've shared our bodies, we're still little more than strangers, and right now, I have no answers other than giving her what she wants.

Space to come to terms with this morning's revelations.

As I grimace and step away from her, something tells me I'm making a mistake.

Chapter Nineteen

RAVEN

Toad and Dwarf were right. There is only one explanation as to who is behind the despicable plot to chase me away from the cabin that I so unexpectedly inherited. While I might have told my therapist about the words my father had used, *Tickety Tock*, I'd never gone into the details with anyone else. The idea that my therapist would then talk to anyone else is something I immediately dismiss.

No. There's only one person presumably alive who'd know how those footsteps used to thump through the hallways as my daddy tried to find me. He wouldn't run, but he'd make his slow approach known by the heavy clump of his boots on the floor. He'd call me his mouse, and Jack's the only person who'd know that.

What happened to me hadn't been my fault. However much my father had blamed me for tempting him, it was his twisted nature and I'd done nothing to encourage him myself. I had the support and found the strength to move on, to embrace my new life without looking back.

Until I'd heard I'd been left the cabin in Grandaddy's will, I'd successfully managed to move on and put all the terrors behind me.

It's been years since I've had a full-bloodied nightmare. But arranging to return to the scene of the crime had obviously brought it all back. For days prior to my journey, I'd woken sweating with sheets tangled around me as I tried to fight an assailant off. But stupid me, instead of taking that as a warning, I took it as a challenge to face. In life, my daddy hadn't beaten me, and I wasn't going to allow him to do that when he was dead.

But despite my brave thoughts when I'd arrived at the cabin, I'd already been ill at ease, and it wouldn't have taken a lot for me to revert to that scared little girl. I'd tried to focus on the things that had reminded me of the good times that I'd had and ignored the small detail that I'd not been brave enough to open the door to the room I'd slept in as a child.

I accept now I was on edge from the moment I arrived and primed for the smallest thing to send me back to the time that I thought I'd buried so deep the memories of it couldn't be revived.

A visit from my dead father was no little matter, disturbing enough even if he hadn't been an abusive fuck. Just the sound of the cabin creaking would probably have been enough to keep me awake, but what I'd been subjected to had damn near sent me out of my mind. Who am I kidding? It sent me right over the edge.

To the extent I'd taken off into the night, wearing only a robe which ingrained habit had made me grab, and not even stopping to put shoes on my feet. If I hadn't crashed into Dwarf, heaven knows where I'd have ended up. Stuck in a hunter's trap or fallen over a drop-off. Even now I could be lying injured or dead.

Jack would have guessed the effect that it would have on me. He tormented me as a child, and clearly hasn't stopped now.

And that's what's seriously fucking with my head. That instead of reconnecting like any normal estranged member of a family, Jack had obviously deliberately stayed out of my life, though he'd known enough about me to predict my movements, possibly tracked me in some way to check when I'd arrive. And then put far too much energy into setting up this elaborate trap for me.

There had been little love lost between us when we were growing up, but I'd thought that was a typical sibling relationship, not having known any different. At school, I had seen other examples of sibling rivalry, so never thought it more than that. We'd never had a chance to get to know each other as adults, and if he ever crossed my mind, I wished him well and hoped Grandaddy had put him on the right path.

The evidence seems to suggest Jack strayed however he'd been steered.

Dwarf's question goes round my head. *What would have happened if he hadn't found me?*

Even if I survived my headlong flight through the forest at night, I'm not sure I would have returned to the cabin. Or maybe, in the light of day, I'd have come to my senses, knowing I'd have to return to at least collect my wallet and phone. At the very least, I'd have been a nervous wreck in need of some serious professional help.

If I'd survived, I'd have headed back to San Francisco, but what fears would I have carried home? Dread that my dead father would continue to haunt me, and that he might have followed me back? Would I have been facing a lifetime of nightmares, having resurrected my horrors from the past? I wouldn't have gotten by without more scarring or therapy. Jack must have known that.

Is that what Jack wants from me? To see me scared out of my mind, to upset my carefully ordered life? Has he achieved his objective, is this the end?

Or will he find some other way to taunt me?

Is it the cabin he wants, or me destroyed?

Toad said they'd try to find him, but if they do, I don't want to face him. I don't want to hear it confirmed from his own mouth. I'd rather live thinking there was a real ghost here, otherwise I'll be living with the knowledge my brother, my sole remaining family, wanted to scare me out of my mind.

More than anything, I want to be able to return to the woman who I was a few days ago—happy, fulfilled and moderately successful. Will I ever be that strong woman again, or will I always now be looking behind me?

One thing I know, if it hadn't been for Dwarf and his brothers, I'd still think I was being chased by a ghost. At least I know there's an answer and that my daddy hasn't risen from the dead. But I honestly don't know which I'd prefer. Jack must hate me, and that's a heavy burden to carry.

What do I do now?

I owe Dwarf, and I like him, probably a little too much. He wants me to stay with him. But if I stay, I'll use him as a crutch.

I've invested too much time in me to backslide now. I've got to retain control of my life, and there's only one way I can do that. My heart, and maybe Dwarf's feelings, will be collateral damage, but I'll just have to live with that. My goal will be to put this entire incident behind me, and move on, pick up the strings of my life and forget everything that is Arizona. Go to therapy and put it all into perspective. Jack's been dead to me for years. I'll just have to continue to imagine him like that.

Going home. Yes. That's where I should be. That's where I can re-discover who I really am. My business will keep me busy.

I'll hurt Dwarf.

I'll hurt myself.

There was never any guarantee that whatever was between us would go anywhere. Two souls brought together under extraordinary circumstances. Hell, we might find we hate each other when we have to cope with normality.

I might be walking out on the best sex I've ever had, but I have to protect my sanity.

If I run away, maybe I'll be able to forget. Forget Jack. Forget

Dwarf. Forget the cabin. Cleanse my mind and return to a time before any of this happened.

With my mind made up, I turn and walk stiffly back into the cabin. Dwarf moves as if to step into my path but shaking my head, I raise my hand to stop him. I see his jaw clench, but he stays where he is, as I enter in through the door.

While I've been outside, the men have started to tear this place apart. Floorboards have been lifted, and wall panelling removed. A selection of electronic equipment has been gathered in a pile.

On seeing me, Cloud beckons me over. Whether I'm interested or not, he seems determined to give me an update.

"It's sophisticated in many ways, in others it's not," he begins, pointing down at the paraphernalia sprawled on the table. "He clearly knew you were coming back, and when you were going to be in the cabin. The explosives, for example, were one-use only. The speakers and the sound system could have been reused many times."

Despite myself, I'm interested. "What does that mean?"

"I suggest he's been tracking you and knew when you were likely to put in an appearance. The recordings could play for a few nights in case he was wrong. But that his major plan was put into play last night suggests he knew you were back. That was the fanfare, the thing he thought would break you."

And it would have. If it hadn't been for the men here with me last night, I'm not sure my heart would have survived the doors all slamming open, and the other poltergeist effects.

"He knows I'm here?"

Cloud seems to be on my wavelength. "This cabin isn't on any grid, so he can't do anything electronically. I've had a few brothers scouting around, and they can't see any evidence of anyone having been here other than you and us. Nah, if you ask me, he's somehow watching the airport. Knew you'd arrived, and that you hadn't left."

I shudder thinking my brother, who I'd accepted I'd never see again, had somehow been tracking my movements. It's chilling. "Jack doesn't know me. His memories are just of me as a little kid." I point to the equipment. "This was aimed to frighten me. He couldn't know that it would scare me so much I'd have fled."

Cloud's eyes shutter almost sympathetically. "It would have been a fair bet," he says, half under his breath. "He obviously knows your triggers."

My eyes close. He's right. Jack certainly did. As a kid, he was happiest when he'd been hurting me. As an adult, it appears he hasn't much changed. I also recall the blocked-out memories of how he'd eagerly watched my father assaulting me.

"You alright, Raven?" Ruby's soft voice attracts my attention.

The answer is no, I'm not. I'm not sure I'll ever fit that definition again. I don't even have the energy to summon up the expected response for her. "Where's Toad?" I ask, instead.

She gives me an assessing look. "I'll get him for you. Here, hold her for a moment, will you?" As she speaks, she thrusts the little dog she's holding into my arms.

My hands reach out and I take her on autopilot. I make sure to hold her securely. Growing up, animals had a purpose, like hens for eggs, a cow for milk or a pig for meat. I'd never had pets, and as an adult, the idea hadn't occurred to me. I couldn't say whether I was a dog person or not, but when Rolo's eyes, which seem far too large for her tiny body, look up trustingly into mine, and her tongue comes out to lick my hand, I feel comfort in her presence and in her touch. *Ruby did this on purpose.*

Holding Rolo seems to calm my racing heartbeat down, but my impulse to return home just gains more clarity. My grandaddy sent me away once before as this place wasn't healthy for me. Nothing's changed now, and I'll just follow the same plan.

"You wanted me?" Toad appears, his arm resting on Ruby's shoulder.

I notice a small smile on Ruby's face as I hand her dog back to her. "I'd appreciate a lift to the airport, or at least to somewhere where I can get a signal to summon a cab." I voice the words I've been mentally practicing, coming firmly and decisively. "You make me an offer for the cabin," I wince, looking around at the damage that's only added to the decay, "and I'll happily sell the place to you. I'll transfer the deed, make it legal." I never want to see this place again. He could offer me ten dollars and I'd probably accept it, but the businesswoman inside me tells me Grandaddy would be disappointed if I just gave the place away.

Toad's eyes narrow. "You're welcome to come back to the clubhouse and stay for a few days." I don't miss the way his eyes warily move toward Dwarf, who's now entered and is having a conversation with Metalhead. His eyes keep coming this way, but he's not close enough to hear what we're saying.

Ignoring the twist in my gut as I realise how close I am to saying goodbye, I keep my voice strong. "Thank you, Toad. And thank your club for everything they've done for me. If you hadn't been here, I'd never have known..." My voice trails off. How can I complete the statement and say what a bastard my brother obviously is?

The Wicked Warriors' prez's eyes soften. He lowers his voice. "What about Dwarf?" As my eyes squeeze together, he continues in a quiet tone, "I know my brother, Raven. He's never looked at a woman the way he does you. He wants to claim you, make you his. Are you really just going to turn your back and walk away?"

What else can I do? My life's in San Francisco. Fighting back tears, knowing I've got to be strong as I've yet to explain myself to Dwarf, I practice on Toad. "My life's not here. Dwarf and I got caught up in something. Who knows how the two of us would gel in the real world? This," I wave my hand around the cabin, "isn't real life. And it's reality I've waiting on me. I've got clients who are expecting me back in San Francisco. Even if I thought it was the right thing to do, I wouldn't be able to stay."

Ruby looks like she's about to say something, but Toad turns and gives her a look. They must understand each other, as she raises and lowers her chin as she nods.

"Go talk to Dwarf." Toad looks tired as he runs his hand over his head. "After that, if you still want a lift to the airport, I'm sure he'll take you."

I wasn't going to walk away without saying a word, but I knew it wasn't going to be an easy conversation. I read Dwarf easily. He's a protective man, and he's come to think of me as his responsibility. I'm hurting and he sees it as his duty to make sure I'm okay. He doesn't understand my need to get completely away.

I can't adequately explain that the pull toward him isn't quite as strong as the urge to get back to everything I know.

The more I try to justify my reasoning, the more closed off he becomes. But I've got so much baggage in my mind, I'm hurting enough for myself, I can't hurt for him too. I keep to myself that when I go, I'll be leaving part of my heart behind with him.

I've never felt about anyone the way I have about Dwarf.

But that's not strong enough to battle with my desire to leave all this behind, to get back to the security of things that I know, and there's no room in my world for a biker.

We drive back to the clubhouse in silence. He unlocks his door, then leaves me alone in his room. I get clothes suitable for a flight out of my suitcase. Packing away my t-shirt and jeans and dressed as a businesswoman when I descend the stairs, his eyes narrow as if I'm someone he hasn't seen before.

It was all a dream, Dwarf. This is the real world, and there's no room for a me and you.

Dwarf waits until he has me seated back in the SUV and is headed toward the airport before he tries one last time.

"I thought we had something." His words are clipped.

I can't deny it. "We did, Dwarf."

176

His voice is full of emotion as he says, "I've been inside you, Raven. We've been as fuckin' close as two people can be. You weren't a fuckin' one-night stand for me."

"You weren't for me either." I can't keep the tears from filling my eyes, though I refuse to let them fall. "We were caught up in something, that's all."

"You used me." His tone suggests he doesn't like being used.

"If I did, you used me too," I counter. "But that wasn't it, Dwarf. I feel something for you. Last night wasn't something I did lightly. But my life's miles away. I can't stay in Arizona."

His lips press together.

For the two-hour drive, we're both silent. When we reach the drop-off point at the airport, he reaches out and grabs my hand. "Don't say goodbye forever."

I find I don't want to say goodbye at all. Being strong is so fucking hard. When he leaves, I know the tears will start, but I can't stay. I've got to rebuild, recover what I can from my life before I'm on solid ground. I want to return to the woman I was before I went to the cabin, and to do that, I've got to leave Dwarf behind.

I swallow hard to keep the catch out of my voice. "Toad's got my contact details."

His eyes blaze. "Toad's got your fucking details," he repeats, then thumps the steering wheel. "Give me your phone."

I pass it over—my cell, not the satellite one that I'd forgotten and left behind. Dwarf puts his number in. I take it back.

He sighs heavily. "I understand you've got shit to work through, but hell, Raven, if you need me, I'll be here for you. Call me, okay?"

He'd been my lifeline for forty-eight hours, but now it's time for me to stand on my own two feet.

But it's easier not to argue. Opening the door, I get out, take my suitcase off the back seat, then for a last time, lean in. My eyes soak up the last sight of the man who I never expect to see again. We come from two different worlds and it's time we got back into our own lanes.

I find I can't speak at all.

"I'll call you." His eyes look as suspiciously wet as my own.

I turn away before the tears blur my vision.

Chapter Twenty

RAVEN

I'm not normally someone who cries. Crying never stopped my father and since then, never solved any problem in my life. As I doubt it will help now, I angrily blot my tears on a tissue as I walk away from Dwarf. I'm not sure who I'm angriest with, him for making me fall for him, myself for letting him in, or my fucked-up family that have put me in this state in the first place. The one where I'm not sure which way is up and my world which I'd thought settled and sorted, turned upside down. What worries me most is whether I'll ever be able to move on.

A real haunting would have been bad enough in that it brought all my suppressed fears back to life. That Jack was behind it made it ten times worse. How can a blood relative hate you so much?

On autopilot, I go through the airport formalities. My suitcase is carry-on, so I don't have to check it in, and soon I'm through security and find a seat in the lounge as I wait for my flight to be called.

I feel numb. On the outward journey, I'd been mostly excited about seeing the cabin I'd left so long ago, though there had been an undercurrent of wariness that the good memories were overshadowed by what my father had done. But I'd been optimistic I could overcome the bad and concentrate on the years when I'd been younger and before I caught Daddy's eye. I wanted to go partly as a tribute to my grandaddy.

I'd been looking forward to it. Building my business, I hadn't allowed myself to take a break in years, so this was a mini vacation for me.

Instead of being something I could look back on positively, it had turned into a huge disaster, so much better if I'd never returned. I never dreamed that the actions of another male member of my family would chase me away.

And however much I want to disbelieve it, there's too many clues pointing Jack's way, and nobody else who could have known enough to have set me up.

On the short flight, I close my eyes and try to catch up on the sleep I've missed over the past couple of days. Each time I drop off, I jerk awake as I start to relive the events all over again. I wonder whether I'll ever be able to sleep without nightmares.

In the end, I give up and stare out at the clouds, simply trying to clear everything from my mind. It doesn't work. I keep thinking of Dwarf and the hurt in his eyes when I walked away, telling myself I did what I had to. I couldn't risk getting hurt again. But however hard I try, he seems like another ghost determined to haunt me.

I collect my car from the parking lot and drive the short distance to the rented apartment I call home. Blaming lack of sleep, I rub my sore eyes as I walk into my bedroom and place my small suitcase on the floor. I realise the backs of my fingers are wet. Surprised, I stare at the moisture, realising more tears are seeping out, too many for someone who never cries.

As something breaks inside me, the trickle becomes a torrent. Unsummoned, a shuddering breath goes through me, and I let out a sound I realise is a sob. As if unleashed, it's followed by more, and suddenly my legs are no longer holding me up.

As my body is racked by my cries, I bawl into my pillow. I

can't seem to stop wailing and I'm unaware of how much time passes as my semi-hysterical tears continue to flow. I weep until I must get dehydrated as eventually my tears dry up, turning to sniffles. Blindly, I reach out my hand for the box of tissues I leave on the bedside table and grab a handful.

As I hiccup, blow my nose and mop my eyes, I'm reminded of the reason why I don't cry. It's hardly beneficial. My eyes are puffy and sore, my nose is blocked, and my throat feels like it's been scratched by needles. And not one of my physical symptoms has done anything to ease the distress in my mind.

After snorting back a couple of final sniffles that despite my derision seem determined to have their say, I glance at the clock I have by my bedside and see that it's already eight p.m. Veering between taking a much-needed shower and then giving up for the day or feeding my stomach which has started to feel quite empty, the loud grumbling wins out the day.

Going into my kitchen, I catalogue what's quick and easy to cook, and come up with the solution of putting a frozen pizza in the oven. When I see the sorry flat unappetising item cooking, tears prick at my eyes once again as I remember eating pizza with the Wicked Warriors. Which, in turn, reminds me of Dwarf and how much I already miss him, and surprisingly his mismatched family as well. Ruby had been someone I could see me becoming friends with. The silence makes me feel lonely, but I try to shrug that thought off. I've done well enough over the years without anyone. Soon I'll get back into the swing of that again.

But was I wrong not to give Dwarf a chance?

I shake my head in denial. I'm a complete mess as my crying jag just proved, and certainly in no position to start a relationship. I've got to move on from the hideous setback those words of my father had summoned up, and furthermore, cope with whatever motive Jack had.

But I miss him.

What do I know of him though, except that he's supportive

and good in bed? If we'd met under normal circumstances, would we have even given each other a second glance?

Or, my traitorous mind puts forward an alternative view, *had the worst type of beginning made us learn things about each other that otherwise would have taken months to come to the forefront? Perhaps these feelings I have for him can be trusted after all.*

Problem is, I don't trust myself at the moment. I need to get myself back on an even keel—if that's even possible—before making decisions that will affect my life. If, when, I have achieved that, I still feel the same way, maybe then I can make contact with him.

That, of course, is, unless as far as he's concerned, out of sight is out of mind and he'll move on and forget me.

Telling myself that will be for the best, and in time I'll forget him, I eat my sad meal, treat myself to a couple of glasses of wine, and finally get showered, changed and ready for bed.

I've been yawning all evening, and when I lay my head on the pillow, it seems nothing will keep me awake. My eyes close of their own volition, and as my breathing slows, I think I'll sleep like the dead until morning.

Of course, I don't. I doubt I've been asleep more than a couple of hours before my father appears in my dreams. *Tickety fucking tickety tock* going around and around my head. I wake in a sweat with the bedclothes twisted around me. Even when I stare at the familiar items in my room, half of my brain tries to persuade me I'm still a kid back in that cabin, and I can't seem to stop the trembling, nor the fear of a visit from him.

Only able to eventually close my eyes with the bedside light on, I finally fall back to a restless sleep.

When morning comes, I'm tired and grumpy. As I drink my coffee, I leave behind the sadness of last night and become angry instead—partly at my own bad choices. I should never have returned to that cabin, knowing it would drag up bad memories. But most of all, I'm furious with Jack. If he hadn't set up those intricate plans to frighten me, I might have gotten the closure I'd been seeking.

Instead of returning cleansed, having closed the book on that part of my life, I'm dealing with the aftereffects of the resurrected abuse from my father, compounded by what Jack had done.

Why would my flesh and blood want to torture me?

I keep struggling to come up with an option that clears him, but there is nothing to be found. No one else, other than my therapist and grandaddy have any idea what happened to me. And only Jack would know the exact words my father had used, and the tone of voice in which he'd said them.

How could he hate me so badly? What does he want from me? Had he realised that what he'd done could have had dangerous ramifications? Had he wanted to kill me? At the very least, he didn't care.

If he wanted the cabin so much, he could have asked me. I would have given at least half to him. Maybe signed it over to him completely. It's not worth much in the state that it's in.

I'm considering how my second cup of coffee is no better at giving me answers than the first, when my phone rings. Glancing at the caller, I sigh with relief at the interruption to my thoughts and accept the call.

"Nat."

"Hey, Raven. I thought you'd be gone longer."

Standing, putting the phone on speaker, I go to refill my cup for the third time. "How did you know I was home?"

Natalie chuckles. "Saw a light on last night when I was passing. It was a fair guess unless you've been burgled."

She makes my lips curve. "No, you're right. I'm back."

"So, was it a wash out? I didn't expect you back so soon."

Suddenly I realise I want to talk face-to-face and not over the phone. Natalie has been my best friend forever, and there's not much I don't tell her. Talking over what happened, and what my brother had done, might make things clearer.

"You free later?"

She doesn't hesitate. "Lunch? Dinner?"

It's Sunday, no need to think of going into work. "All the above," I tell her, realising talking things out might help get my head back into the game.

"Hmm. Sounds like you've got shit to tell me. How about I come over in an hour?"

"Perfect," I breathe out.

We end the call. I shower, dress and make myself respectable. Sixty minutes later, she appears at my door. Half an hour after that, she's staring at me with her jaw almost touching the floor.

"So, let me get this straight. You thought there was a ghost, ran scared out of your wits, and knocked a man off his bike? Got together with said man—who happens to be a real-life biker—and after said ghost terrorised his whole club, found out about your brother," she pauses and frowns, "who I didn't even know you had, by the way," a shake of her head, then, "was behind it all the time?"

"That about sums it up." My last two days in a nutshell.

"Phew." She leans back on my sofa, resting her head against the cushions, then sits forward. "Look, friend, if this man was so hot you dropped your panties for him after just a few hours, why the fuck aren't you with him now?"

Trust her to home in on that point. "I can't get my head around what my brother's done."

She presses her lips together. I recognise the gesture. Unlike many people, Natalie likes to consider her words carefully, and doesn't often just blurt out the first thing she thinks of. It's why she makes a great sounding board.

"You've been upfront about your abuse," she eventually starts. "But only because you've put it behind you. I've always admired the way you've managed to move on."

"I was taken advantage of. It wasn't my fault." I parrot my therapist's words.

"But by a man who you should have been able to depend

on." I shrug. She's right. "And while you haven't seen Jack for years, because he's your brother, you think you should be able to trust him too." My shoulders rise and fall again.

She sips the coffee I'd just made. "You don't think you can trust Dwarf, because all the men in your life have let you down."

"Not everyone," I retort. "I've met other men—"

She cuts me off, "I've known you for years, Raven, since we shared a dorm room in college. You've had relationships sure, but none of them lasted. I don't think you like letting men get close."

I suck in air. "I've been busy building my business. I've been too busy to have a permanent fixture in my life." All she has to do is raise her eyebrow, and I look away from her examination. But then think of something with which to defend myself. "And sure, I couldn't trust Daddy, but Grandaddy had always been there. As for Jack? I didn't know what had happened to him."

She drums her fingers against the cup. "Man, men. The fact stands, you've been let down, Raven. And what Jack's now done has just compounded things and made them worse." Emitting a heavy sigh, she sits forward and puts her cup down. "Raven, your eyes light up when you talk about Dwarf. I've never seen you like this about a man before. He got to you. He got under the barriers that you set up. But you turned your back on him—"

"Alright," I cry out. "Dwarf could have been important to me, but then I found out about Jack. And you're right. Maybe Daddy started the damage, but what chance have I got to mend if my own brother could set me up like that? How can I trust anyone? Especially a man I've just met."

"Your brother's no more than a stranger to you. You haven't seen him for years. He never contacted you. You've never spoken about him to me." She fixes me with a stare. "Just because he's blood means fuck all. You have no idea whether you could trust him or not." Her face softens. "Dwarf isn't Jack." She huffs a mirthless laugh. "And with your experience with blood, I think you drew the short straw with your family."

"Grandaddy was alright." I go on the defensive.

"Grandaddy shot your father in front of you."

I grimace. Yes, there is that. "I didn't talk about Jack because growing up isn't something I like to remember," I admit. "And leaving aside whether Dwarf is trustworthy, it would never have worked. His home is in Arizona, and my life is here."

"Pah," she exclaims, throwing her hands in the air. "Raven, I love you like a sister, and I know you've put your heart and soul into your work, but it's not as if you couldn't do what you do anywhere."

Frowning, I consider her words. I make enough to survive, but it's not like I'm a major name in the business. "I don't even like Arizona," I tell her.

"Maybe he'd move here—"

I throw my hands up exasperated. "Nat, we only knew each other forty-eight hours, and it wasn't in a situation that could be called anything like normal. Who the fuck knows whether we could actually make it together? It's far too soon to think about upending one of our lives to suit the other."

"Hmm." She considers me for a moment. "So, you and Dwarf parted amicably? Ships that pass in the night type of thing?"

Biting my lip, I admit, "No. He seemed annoyed I was leaving. But, Nat, I couldn't stay. I've too much to work through."

"And he wouldn't have stayed by your side and helped you?"

I stand, my intention to go brew yet more coffee, but the resolve behind it is to get out of this conversation that's happening far too soon. I do have the feeling that Dwarf and his club would have stood by me. Though I try not to think on it, there's the unresolved situation with Jack. I'm sure they could have found him and discovered what he really wanted. Although I try to convince myself he just wanted to fuck with his little sister, a niggling doubt warns me it could be more than that, and this is far from over.

But I don't tell Natalie that. Here, back home, where everything is familiar, I think I'm more than capable to cope with anything life throws up. Maybe I've been alone far too long, but I don't like the thought of leaning on anyone. If I can't live life on my own, what kind of partner would I be for anyone else?

Nat follows me into the kitchen. "You're too damn independent," she tells me, lightening her words with a grin. "I'm surprised you let me in."

I bump her hip with mine. "You don't give me a choice."

After college, we'd shared an apartment together for a time, and there's not much about each other that we don't know. I mean, when you know enough about a person's habits to avoid the bathroom at certain hours, there's not much you keep to yourselves.

It's not surprising that she's figured out that it usually takes me ages to allow a man to get close, and that when they do, I cut and run. As I prepare the coffee, I stare out the window and tell her my thoughts.

"I was the one who pushed him to the next level. I don't usually jump on a man, Nat, you know that. That's why I'm worried I just got caught up in what was going on. It can't have been real."

"Why not?" she asks, drawing her fresh coffee closer to her. "There's no saying when Mr Right will come along."

But is Dwarf Mr Right? In many ways, he seems more likely to be Mr Wrong. The class of people he associates with for a start. I mean, bikers for heaven's sake. Then I realise how ungrateful my thoughts make me sound. Dwarf's friends had done nothing but help me.

Being a good friend, Nat knows when to push and when to leave things alone. Seeing I'm becoming closed off, she switches topic, and starts regaling some gossip about a mutual friend.

After a few gasps, a couple of "she didn'ts?" And a few "what the hells?" I'm laughing along with her. Arizona and Dwarf might not have been wiped from my mind, but by the time she leaves, they're not all I can think of.

When she finally leaves, I tidy my apartment and do chores, getting myself back in the swing of being home. When Monday comes around, I realise speaking to her had helped me put things into perspective.

Why should I expect anything from Jack, just because he's my brother?

I have a good life and I need to take back the reins. I need to forget about what happened in Arizona, and not let it overtake me. And that means making an effort to forget about Dwarf and all that he might mean to me.

I go into work refreshed and determined to move forward without looking back.

I don't call Dwarf.

But as I'd promised, after I'd appointed a real estate agent to act on my behalf, I contact Toad and agree on a price to sell the cabin to the Wicked Warriors MC. I hadn't haggled, and he'd gotten a bargain from me. The sooner it was all signed, sealed and off my hands, the better I'd feel.

It's one thing to make resolutions and promises to oneself, it's far harder to keep them. Like all the ways you decide to change your life when the new year comes, then end up doing the same old thing before January's even a week old.

As the days pass, however hard I try to put him out of my mind, memories of Dwarf haunt me. But instead of allowing myself to admit that maybe I'd walked away from the best thing I'd ever had, I force myself to look around me. There's no way he'd have fit into my life. The way we live is worlds apart. I do my best to convince myself leaving him was right.

And, if at night, when I feel weak and lonely, and thoughts of that one night with him fuel sessions with my vibrator, who can blame me?

Though myth says it should, time passing doesn't make it easier. Little things remind me of him—exhaust fumes, the scent rising from someone's leather bag, a masculine laugh that sounds too familiar. It's harder than I expect to forget about him.

When he enters my mind, I counter by trying to list all the reasons why we wouldn't work.

I also remind myself communication goes two ways and that, he too, could have picked up the phone and called. That he hasn't probably suggests I'm not on his mind as much as he is on mine.

No, it's me who's the lonely one not him. He'll have gone back to the women who swarm to bikers like groupies, and that thought hurts far more than it should.

I'd like to say I move on and put the last few days behind me, but that would be a lie. I battle with insecurity daily. I'd fought for years to overcome the feelings of fear and lack of control that my daddy had left me with, and now I'm back where I started. Not completely, but waves of desolation can suddenly creep up, making me question why me? At night, my dreams are haunted with a mix of the real horrors of my childhood and the repeats Jack had forced into my head.

Lack of sleep doesn't help me cope with my day, and I start to feel I'm hanging on by a thread.

It's then I admit I miss Dwarf dreadfully. But when I think of making contact, I picture him having already moved on. He hadn't taking me running away well, and that's what I'd done. I ran because I was too afraid of taking a chance with him.

I regret it now, but don't know how to make it up to him, or whether I'd just be setting myself up for rejection, should I call him.

Natalie thinks I'm a mess, and she keeps dropping hints that I should rectify the mistake I made by leaving him. She's made me realise what I have here in San Francisco is me existing, but not really living. I could do what I do anywhere if I were brave enough to take a chance and leap into the unknown.

But being Nat, she doesn't push. She doesn't come right out and tell me she told me so when I admit in leaving Dwarf, I'd been wrong. She does what she can to help me make the best of the position I've put myself in.

A week after I get home from Arizona, I'm on the phone to Natalie for one of her daily check-ins when there's a ring at my doorbell.

"Hold on, Nat. I think the books I ordered have just arrived. Yeah, I'm still listening. You can talk while I get this."

Because it's within the time frame the company had advised me the delivery would arrive, I open the door without checking who's there. But instead of a someone with a parcel, a stranger's standing outside.

"Oh!" I exclaim in surprise.

"You okay, Raven?"

"I'm good," I reassure my friend on the phone, then narrow my eyes as I focus on the man at my door. There's something about him that seems familiar, but I can't place where I've seen him before.

He's dressed in denim jeans and wears a blue denim jacket. His hair flops over his forehead. When he raises his hand to push it back, there's something about the gesture I recognise. Suddenly I realise he's no stranger, but someone I haven't seen for a very long time.

"Jack?" Can it be? Is this man the grown version of the teenager I remember? "I've got to go, Nat," I say into the phone.

"Wait," she says, her urgency coming down the line. "*Jack's* there? Your brother? Raven, hang on—"

"Yeah, I'll call you back." I end the call even though she's still speaking to me.

Chapter Twenty-One

RAVEN

"Raven." Jack's voice is an octave or so lower than I remember, and very reminiscent of my dad. "Well, look at you. You're all grown up."

My brain starts working at the speed of light. Unless I've been completely wrong and Jack wasn't behind what happened at the cabin, he must know I've not long returned from Arizona, and more than that, exactly what happened there.

But his casual approach and friendly opening statement doesn't suggest he suspects I know he's responsible for scaring me half to death.

After fifteen years with no approach or no word, it's too much of a coincidence why he's suddenly appeared. I try to keep my face impassive as inside I start to seethe, believing he thinks he's softened me up and is now going in for the kill.

I'm stumped how to handle this. What do you say to the brother you haven't seen since you were a kid, and when you know how little regard he has for your sanity and safety?

My hackles rise. Whatever he wants, he's now not going to get. He's right, I'm no longer the little girl he's used to dealing with. If he'd approached me rather than playing those tricks, I'd have played fair. Now? Well, my gloves are off.

And I hold the upper hand. I know more than he thinks I do.

"Jack," I answer when the silence stretches out too long. "To what do I owe this pleasure?"

Frown lines appear. "I was in the area, thought it was time we caught up."

Unless he's been stalking me, as the Wicked Warriors had suggested, he wouldn't know where to find me. But I ignore that little fact. Let him think I'm as dumb as the kid he probably remembers.

"Can I come in?" His eyebrow rises.

I'm blocking the entrance as I make up my mind, wondering how I would have greeted him if the events of last week hadn't happened. With pleasure at a long time coming reunion? Or with suspicion as to why he is here? I decide to play a mixture of both.

"It's been a long time, Jack. I didn't expect to see you. Why are you here?"

He shrugs and nonchalantly rests his hand on the doorframe, his position putting him closer to me. Jack's no longer the scrawny teenager I remember. He's all man, far taller and bulkier, and if the business at the cabin was any indication, doesn't have fond intentions toward me. I draw back into myself while still keeping hold of the door. He notices, and straightens, putting his hand back down to his side.

"Wasn't my fault we lost track of each other. Pops wouldn't tell me where you went."

"It wasn't my fault either," I defend myself. "I was eleven years old, Jack, and wasn't allowed to come back." Not that I wanted to. Apart from my Grandaddy who I missed like hell, the cabin held nothing for me. Even my grandfather's memory was tainted by the blood and the shotgun he'd held that last day. I'd been subjected to more than any child should be.

It had been with relief that my aunt had welcomed me into what I learned was a normal home. One where fathers didn't stalk children in the middle of the night wanting to do them harm, and where brothers didn't torment little sisters.

Jack seems unsure how to take me, so goes on the attack. "You didn't go to see Pops in the hospital."

I flinch at the accusation. "I did once, but he didn't recognise me."

Jack scowls. "Once?"

"I'd have gone more, but my presence upset him." I hate that he's putting me on the defensive.

"Of course, you upset him," Jack sneers. "You caused him to shoot his son."

It was my fault? No, Jack's not going to put that on me. Therapy had made me accept I was blameless, that my daddy had been sick in the head.

The tightening of my face must warn him he's gone a step too far. He holds out his hands placatingly, and asks again, "Can I come in, Raven? We need to talk."

Inside is Jack still the kid who bullied me at every opportunity he had? As a man, would he hurt me? What happened at the cabin suggests that he might, but I'm intrigued as to why he's come to see me, so curiosity wins out. While part of me screams to keep him out, I step back and allow him to enter.

He walks in and spends a moment looking around my comfortable, but not opulent, abode. Going over to a picture of my aunt and me on my graduation day, he picks it up, examines it, then puts it down with a sneer.

"What do you want, Jack?"

I suppose I should show an interest, ask what's happened to him in the intervening years, where he's been and what he's been doing, but I can't summon any sibling affection, not after knowing what he tried to do.

Suddenly he turns and focuses all his attention my way. "For some reason, Pops left you the cabin."

I tell him the truth. "I didn't know you were even alive, Jack. I thought either you'd died or upset Grandaddy in some way."

"Yeah?" His sharp eyes flare as they meet mine. "Well, I'm very much in the land of the living and that cabin belongs to me." Looking a bit shifty, as if he knows more than he's saying, he adds, "It can't hold happy memories for you."

No, and he knows they've recently been brought right back.

"You want the cabin?" I ask, as if I'm a bit slow.

"I sure do." He broadens his shoulders.

I suspected he did, which is why he tried to chase me away, but why is the question. I don't remember Jack as being sentimental, so there's got to be more he's not telling.

"It was left to me, Jack. It's mine." If last week hadn't happened, if the Wicked Warriors hadn't proved the "haunting" had to be down to him, I might have been more inclined to at least go halves with him.

He straightens and I don't miss the way his fists bunch at his sides. "You can't want to live there. It's a fuckin' shithole, Raven." He shakes his head and his eyes crease as if something doesn't make sense. "Have you even fuckin' seen it lately?"

He knows that I have. That's why he triggered his toys to work. He's fucking with me so I've every right to fuck with him right back.

"Yeah, I was there last week as it happens. It needs a ton of work but looks structurally sound."

He looks puzzled and bemused, then his jaw clenches as if suspecting what he set up must have gone wrong. I give no indication I'd found anything out of the ordinary. *Let him believe his plan hadn't worked.* I take some satisfaction from seeing his disappointment.

His eyes scrunch further, and his brow is completely creased. "Didn't your visit bring back bad memories?"

Oh yes, lots of them. I relived my nightmares all over again. But I make every effort not to show that on my face. "I have bad memories, but I also have good ones, Jack. I focused on the time I spent with Grandaddy. It was good to be there and say goodbye to him."

Jack's face glows red, and the muscles on his arm grow rigid. "You can't be thinking of keeping the cabin."

"Oh no," I reply airily. "I'm selling the place."

He looks like he's gritting his teeth. "Sell it to me."

While I don't want to enrage him, there's nothing I can do but tell him the truth. "I can't. A sale has already been arranged."

His eyes darken and lines appear on his forehead. "You can, and you will. Consider the sale you arranged off. Now you'll come with me, and we'll do what's necessary to get the deed changed into my name."

I stand my ground and shake my head. "I can't do that." He doesn't know who he's dealing with if he thinks he can demand things of me.

Unfortunately, though, I clearly don't know what I'm dealing with when it comes to him. Suddenly, I'm no longer standing in the middle of my living room. I'm pushed back against the wall and there's a hand held so tightly around my throat it's stopping me from taking in air.

Jack's eyes blaze. "You're a fuckin' bitch, Raven. You always want your own way. You tempted Daddy, and that's what got him killed. Well, you're not winning this time. You could have done this the easy way, now, it's going to be anything but for you. I'm going to have the cabin, and what Daddy promised to me."

As he pulls his hand away, I gasp in air to let out a scream, but before any sound can leave my mouth, I see his fist coming for me.

I WAKE with a throbbing in my head which makes me groan, and that's not the only part of me that hurts. When I try to stretch, I immediately know I'm not in my comfortable bed. There's no soft mattress under me. My limbs don't work, and it's dark all around, with cracks allowing some light to come in. I'm constricted as though in a coffin, but it's not the right shape, and there's a vibration which tells me I'm moving.

Slowly my brain kicks into gear and I remember Jack coming to see me. Remember him wanting the cabin, him making threats, and then him hitting me.

I try to lash out, but my hands and my feet seem to be bound. Scared out of my head, it takes me longer than it should to realise that my prison is actually the trunk of a car. As it hits a bump making me roll, tied up, I can't prevent bashing into the side, enlightening me as to why my whole body seems to hurt. The car makes a sudden turn and even though I brace myself, I roll once more.

The worst pain though is from my jaw, suggesting that's where Jack's fist had landed. I must have caught my tongue with my teeth as it's as sore on the inside as well as the outside, and when I try to move my mouth, it feels swollen.

My mouth feels dry and there's the metallic taste of blood.

Physically sore and mentally terrified, I realise Jack hasn't changed his ways. He's certainly developed no compassion for his little sister over the intervening years.

I should just have agreed to give him the cabin if he wants it so much.

But the stubborn part of me says he can take it over my dead body.

That's probably his plan.

Damn, what a fool I'd been. I'd come back from Arizona, knowing Jack had wanted to hurt me, but carried on as if he didn't exist in the world I'd built for myself. When I'd seen him at my door, I should have slammed it in his face, instead of letting him in.

Oh what I would give to redo things.

I've no way of knowing how long I've been unconscious. It could be minutes or hours. The way my bladder is screaming, adding to my discomfort, suggests it must have been a while.

My discomfort is increasing by the moment as I'm finding it

hard to breathe. I hadn't lied to Dwarf when I told him I was claustrophobic. This trunk is far too coffin-like for me, and I swear there's no oxygen coming in.

Ignoring the pain I'm already in, I thrust myself this way and that as I try to get free. There's a loud noise echoing around me, and it takes me a second to realise I'm listening to my own screams.

The car comes to an abrupt halt, rolling me forward once again. When the trunk opens, I take in a lungful of fresh air, sucking it down desperately. For a moment, the light of the sun blinds me until Jack's tall figure blocks it out.

"What the fuck are you doing?"

I'm hyperventilating, trying to get enough oxygen in. My lungs are heaving. My bound arms rise in supplication as right now I'm not capable of speaking. Huge shudders rack my body.

"You've got to shut the fuck up. You hear me?" His hand starts closing the trunk again.

From somewhere, I find my voice and hoarsely cry out, "Please no. I'm claustrophobic."

"Like I give a fuck." He eyes me with no sympathy. "Now be quiet."

"I can't," I shout. "I can't control it. I hate being closed in."

He glances around him at the cars going past. They're unable to see me, but I suspect he's worrying there might be a holdup or stop at traffic lights when people will be able to hear me scream.

He looks at me calculating, then sighs. "If I allow you to ride up front, do you promise you won't make a sound?"

I'd promise him anything right now if he'd just let me out of this trunk. "I'll be quiet."

Reaching in, he roughly turns me around so he can slice through the zip ties holding my legs together, then he rolls me right way up and cuts through the ones around my wrists. He pushes me back down as he studies the road, then, presumably, when it's clear, he reaches in and pulls me out. Stiff, I wobble, and he steadies me for a moment until some feeling comes back into my feet. When he releases me, I shake my aching arms out.

"Get in the car."

My body reminds me I've other problems. "I've got to go to the bathroom."

But we haven't stopped in a convenient rest stop. In fact, he's just pulled off the road. He rolls his eyes and swears under his breath, then indicates a couple of bushes. "Go there if you have to, but watch for snakes."

Oh yes, the bullying brother of my childhood definitely hasn't changed. He'd always taken every opportunity to unsettle his little sister. He remembers I hate snakes with a passion, that phobia caused by Jack himself.

"And don't run," he adds. "I'll catch you and you'll be back in the trunk."

He was always bigger and easily able to overpower me. I've little doubt anything's changed now. I don't doubt there's no chance of escape.

My bladder is insistent it needs relief. Trying to put the likelihood of coming across any slithering creatures aside, I hobble on still stiff legs and use the shelter of the bushes as he suggests. Then, with nothing to use as a wipe, drip dry for a second before awkwardly pulling my panties and shorts back up, telling myself this little discomfort is nothing compared to what else Jack's probably got in store.

I've got to get away from him, and sitting up front, I may have more of a chance. I'll not harbour qualms about breaking my promise if shouting gets me a route of escape.

As if being polite, he opens the door to the passenger side. As I slide into the seat, I get a glimpse of myself in the side mirror. My jaw is indeed swollen. My face is reddened and just as it feels, looks sore. My teeth clench despite the pain the action causes. Jack's got a lot to answer for.

And soon he has even more. Before closing the door, he zip ties my right hand to the oh-shit handle. I tell myself it's better than being in the trunk but have to acknowledge it won't make it easy to get free.

Looking around, I have no idea where we are. We could be anywhere. I don't want to make conversation, but knowledge is a weapon, or so they say, so I ask him. "Where are we going?"

Leaning forward to start the car, he responds, "Where do you think?" Then, with a leer adds, "Where we've got unfinished business."

There's only one place where he and I have any connection. "The cabin," I breathe out.

He neither confirms nor denies it. His desire to talk to me clearly no more than mine to discuss anything with him. We might have been separated for years, but neither of us seems interested in what the other has been doing.

I don't want him to take me there, not least because he'll find out I've been playing him. "If you want the cabin, we'll have to find a lawyer so I can get it signed over to you."

He snorts and gives me a sideways look. "If you'd said that earlier, I might have made that easier for you. But you chose the hard route, just like you always do. You've only yourself to blame, Raven."

"What are you going to do?" *Why hadn't I just given in?* What exactly am I going to blame myself for?

"The cabin's my inheritance, Raven."

And if I'm dead, he'll be able to claim it. That's what he means, I'm certain. But I'm too much of a coward to say it out loud.

Thoughts come into my head of Dwarf, as well as the regret I hadn't grabbed my chance with both hands and stayed with him. Instead of a possibility of a happy life, I'm now facing mine being cut short because of the madman beside me.

Dwarf. Oh, what I wouldn't give for him to be here holding me now.

If I ever get another chance, I won't throw it away.

But unless I escape from Jack, I won't have another chance to do anything.

Even if I wasn't suspecting I was being driven to my death, it would be a tedious journey. When I'd visited the cabin, I'd decided to fly precisely because I hadn't fancied an eleven-plus-hour drive. Nothing about this trip now makes me think I was wrong. When the silence wears too much on him, Jack puts the radio on to a station whose music I don't like, but I know it's not worth wasting my breath complaining. If I could summon up the energy, I'd tell him this was the stuff I really enjoyed which would probably result in him changing it. But in the grand scheme of things, it's a fairly minor inconvenience.

Worse is the pain in my jaw, my head, my legs, my arms and body where I'd been rolling around and bruised them. And top of the list is the fear that I feel, believing that Jack intends to kill me.

I know I have to get away from him.

But he makes that impossible. When inevitably we have to stop for gas, he uses a gas station where he can pay at the pump and makes sure to get into a lane where there are no other vehicles close by.

The car drones on, the pavement passing under the wheels. It's boring and monotonous and eventually I close my eyes. I jerk awake, but we're still moving.

Miles and miles go by as the clock slowly ticks up the hours. It's dark by the time we arrive at the cabin.

It might have been Jack's machinations and not a spirit haunting the cabin, but unease still trickles through me. If all Jack wants is the cabin, then he'd have taken me to a lawyer and gotten it transferred legally. Or, if he was going to kill me, he could have done that at any point over the last few hours and tossed out my body somewhere along the highway.

He wants me here, and for no good reason.

I'm not comforted when I see the gleam in Jack's eyes as he

undoes my arm—by now so dead it flops by my side—and drags me out of the car.

He looks at me for a moment, then at the cabin behind. Then he leans in close. "*Tickety tock,* little sister. Tickety fuckin' tock. Time's run out for you and tonight I won't just have to watch. Tonight, I'll get what Daddy always promised me."

Oh my God, no. It falls into place, exactly what Jack wants from me.

This isn't happening. I won't let it.

I eye the forest where I'd made my terrified flight all those days ago. At least this time, I'm wearing shoes. I know I can't let Jack take me inside. Anything's got to be better than that, so I lunge away from him and start running.

But he's no ghost. His legs are longer than mine and he's far stronger. When his hand lands on my shoulder and he wrenches me around, I'm helpless to do anything about it.

I do my best, kicking, punching, even using my teeth, but he overpowers me easily. Gripping both of my hands behind my back, he drives me in front of him, pushing me up through the trees and toward the cabin.

Chapter Twenty-Two

DWARF

I'm on one of the couches, nursing my third beer of the day when there's a scrabbling at my legs. Looking down, I see Rolo, then raising my eyes, am not surprised to see Ruby standing watching me.

"Siccing your dog on me now?" One side of my mouth quirks, but that's all I'm capable of.

She puts her hands on her hips. "If Rolo doesn't work, I'm getting Buster from my father's home." That might be more of a threat. Buster's her dad's rottweiler. I raise my eyebrow, and she doesn't disappoint. "I'm fed up with eating pizza."

I jerk my head toward the kitchen. "Then cook something different."

She snorts. "I'd happily do so, but no one wants me to."

I can understand that. Having no appetite, I'd avoided the stew she'd cooked the other night, but other brothers hadn't been so lucky. Many had ended up having the shits all night.

Toad doesn't call her his princess for nothing. Ruby was brought up in a wealthy home with a resident chef. It's been clear since the day she arrived that she can't even cook toast. Food, though, is the last thing on my mind right now, and I don't give a fucking damn about the state my domain, the kitchen, is left in.

Shrugging, I suggest another option. "Get the prospect to cook then. Or get Easy and Cilla to help." Might be a change for the club girls to earn their keep on their feet rather than their backs or their knees.

Ruby's face twists, showing what she thinks of my suggestions. She even goes so far as to stomp her foot to make sure she's got my attention. "What I want is for you to get off your ass and do something other than brooding." She nods at the phone lying on the arm of the sofa. "I take it she's still not called?"

I could act like a man and pretend I don't know what she's talking about, but I don't have the energy to play games. Instead, I raise my shoulders to ear level then let them drop, showing her assumption is correct. It's been over a week now and Raven's not reached out.

Ruby rolls her eyes. "You could always call her."

My jaw hardens. "She left me, remember?" Toad really ought to do more to control his old lady. It's not her place to give me the third degree. I glare, trying to portray I want to be left alone, but ignoring me, she shakes her head and sits down beside me.

"Don't you think she has a lot to be dealing with?" She raises her fingers to use inverted commas, "That 'haunting' must have brought terrible memories back. She was raped as a child, Dwarf. That she's even moved on from that is spectacular." She pauses, and her eyes stare into nowhere for a moment. "I can't even imagine how she did it. But she came through, then suddenly what happened got resurrected and became full front and centre, because of what her *brother* did. She'd already been treated in the worst of ways by family. Knowing her brother was the one behind it must have really messed with her head."

There's no must about it. It's certain it did. Setting my jaw, I tell her, "I'd have helped her work through it."

Ruby tosses her hair back over her shoulder. "When Raven

left, she was devastated by the betrayal. Even if she was able to think straight, what were you to her but another man who might let her down? Trust, once you've been let down so badly, must be so hard to give. She ran, Dwarf. She ran back to something that she could control, something and somewhere familiar. Where nothing could hurt her." She presses her lips together. "I got the impression she's an independent woman who leans on no one, because that's who she's had to become."

She's right in that Raven didn't trust me even to give me a chance to help her. She hadn't had to go back, but she'd fled as if those ghosts were still after her. Perhaps she's never let anyone in to get close to her.

"Despite what you think, Dwarf, I reckon she's hurting. She needs someone on her side."

"Then she could pick up the fuckin' phone." It's not fair to take my frustration out on Ruby, but she came to me.

She gives me a sad look. "Perhaps she's too embarrassed. Or, perhaps, by you not contacting her, you're confirming that there was nothing really between you." As I go to open my mouth, she doesn't give me a chance to speak. "Why don't you call her? What's the worst that can happen, Dwarf? She snubs you? At least you'd know where you stand and can stop sitting staring at your phone all the time."

"I'll stop," I growl. I just need a bit more time. For the first time in my life, I'd had a woman who for once saw me and not my brothers. Who I thought could be mine until she walked away, proving she'd never seen me at all.

She left me behind, and I've no doubt she doesn't even think about me. She certainly hasn't forgotten about the club. Only last night, Toad updated us in church that the sale of the cabin was proceeding with a very reasonable offer from the realtor Raven had appointed. Thanks to the millions Ruby had brought with her, the purchase wouldn't even be a blip on our financial radar.

We'd even been discussing what skills we've got to bring the cabin up to standard. I'd hidden that I'd done some building work in the past as the last place I wanted to be was there. It would just remind me of her.

Ruby nods down at my phone again. "Just call her, Dwarf. You might be surprised. At the least she'll know she has a friend who's thinking of her."

My hand twitches as if ready to obey, pick up the device and do exactly as Toad's woman had instructed, but my brain tells me I've had enough rejection in my life, and like always, the best course is to move on and forget her. Just as easily as she appears to have forgotten me.

I scoff at myself. I'm not moving on. I'm wallowing in my misery. I can't be bothered to do much of anything. My bike's been repaired but I can't summon the enthusiasm to ride it more than using it to get from A to B. Each time I ride, I feel her like a ghost up behind me. How can I miss what I've never had?

As for the kitchen, the place which usually I find therapeutic, I no longer want to be in there.

I'm a mess and Ruby's right to pull me up about it.

Something's got to give.

Signalling Punchbag to bring me another beer, I sit back on the couch as Ruby wanders off, Rolo trotting after her. I'll wait one more day, then if there's still radio silence, I'll... What? Fuck a sweet butt? Maybe, if my cock would rise to the occasion. How long will it be before it's interested in anyone that's not Raven?

I'm not sleeping well at night. I miss holding her, and if I do drop off, I wake with a fucking nightmare. *Tickety, tickety fucking tock.* While awake, I know the rational explanation, but in the dead of the night, my brain still conjures up the horror I heard. Maybe it's because I know Raven lived it, and that in years past, it wasn't a ghost and was far too real for her.

Another beer drunk, with the slight buzz, my weary brain turns off for a moment. I'm lying with my head back half asleep when someone kicks my feet.

"What the fuck?" I open bleary eyes to find my prez staring at me.

Toad flings a piece of paper into my lap. "Ring this number."

"What? Who?" I push myself up and wipe the sleep from my eyes, shaking my head to get some of the beer buzz out of it.

"Bitch called Natalie. She just rang the wrecking yard, asking to speak to a man called Dwarf."

I might be buzzed but I can't remember a woman called Natalie. "Don't know her—"

"I don't give a fuck whether you know her or not. She said it was urgent that she spoke to you. Said it was about Raven. Thinks she might be in trouble."

I sober up instantly. "What kind of trouble?"

"Got no fuckin' idea until you make that call."

I reach for my phone, miss and knock it onto the floor. Going to my knees, I retrieve it from where it slid under the sofa. Coming back up, I snatch up the paper he'd thrown at me, and carefully stab in the numbers. The phone rings once, twice, then a couple of times more. Just before I think it's going to ring out, a cautious voice answers.

"Yes?"

"This Natalie? I'm Dwarf." At Toad's gesture, I put it on speaker.

A panicked female voice blasts into my ear. "Dwarf, oh thank God. I didn't know who to call. I've been to the cops, but they don't seem to be very helpful—"

Cops? I exchange glances with Toad. "Spit it out, Natalie. What's happened to Raven?"

"I don't know," she cries out. "I was on the phone with her, and her brother Jack turned up at the door. She hung up as she was going to speak to him. She'd only mentioned she even had a brother a few days before..." Again, Toad and I look at each other. "I got worried. The tone of her voice suggested he wasn't welcome. So, after a few minutes, I tried to call her back and got no answer. I decided to go around and check for myself." As her voice breaks off and she sobs, I angrily want to snap at her just to get on with it, but I bite my tongue and allow her to tell me at the speed that suits herself. "The front door was open, a chair was turned over, and there was blood—"

"Raven?" I'm on my feet now, my heart in my mouth.

"Gone," Natalie wails.

Fuck it. I take a deep breath. *She might have left by herself.* "Her car still there?"

Natalie's voice rises an octave. "Her car, her purse, her phone. They were all left behind. I can only think that her brother has taken her."

Natalie's crying openly now, huge racking sobs, repeating over and over that someone's got to help her. She even suggested Jack might be part of a slave trafficking ring and that Raven might already be over the border. Her rambling isn't helping or doing anything other than riling me up.

Maybe it's the alcohol I've consumed, but my mind's a complete blank on where to go from here. I'm barely able to hold the phone in my hand.

"Leave it to us, Natalie. We'll take it from here. We'll find her." Toad's deep voice takes over.

Raven's friend doesn't even seem to notice the change in speaker. "Please, Dwarf, somebody's got to do something."

"We will," Toad repeats. "Leave it to us, darlin'." Reaching over, he takes my phone out of my hand, and repeating some platitudes, ends the call.

He gives me a shake of his head, and a comforting hand to my shoulder, then bellows at the prospect, "Round everyone up. We're having church." Then he points to me. "And you, you get yourself a pot of coffee and sober yourself up."

With determined steps, he walks away, leaving me there with my mouth hanging open and my phone which he'd given back in my hand. I'm trying to focus on what I need to do next as my overriding impulse is to find Raven. *There was blood.* Those words echo around my head.

My impulse is to jump on my bike, but I don't have a clue where to start looking for her. Then it dawns on me why Toad's calling church, showing my befuddled brain is far behind his. I'm not in this alone. I'll have my brothers at my back, and putting our heads together, we might just come up with some answers.

Now accepting Toad does know what he's talking about, I go over to the bar and fill up a cup. I down a black coffee, then have another. Punchbag, without being asked, passes some painkillers over. I swallow them down with a third cup.

By the time I've finished, Cloud and Metalhead have appeared, closely followed by Raider.

I detour to the heads to get rid of the beer and the coffee chasers, then, after splashing water on my face, feel a little more in control of myself and ready to think and not simply act in a blind panic.

Until I think of Raven in her brother's hands. Then my hands start shaking and I feel physically sick. He doesn't give a damn about her safety, or her mental health.

When I find him…

But that's the first hurdle. Finding where he's taken her.

By the time I walk into church, almost all my brothers are there. I'm amped up with so much energy it's hard for me to walk to my seat calmly and sit down. I don't want to talk. I want to be out there doing something. *Anything.* But logically I know I won't get anywhere by aimlessly riding around.

Prez bangs the gavel. "Raven's missing. Looks like she's been abducted by her brother."

I slam my fist down on the table. "We dropped the ball. We should have been out there looking for him. Should have known he wouldn't give up when his plan failed."

Toad half stands, looming threateningly over the table, his finger pointing at me. "For what fuckin' reason? Raven's just the bitch selling us the cabin."

I stand, my fists clenching. "You know she's far more than that to me."

"Yeah?" Prez challenges. "Well, why haven't you pulled your

head out of your ass?" He retakes his seat. "From where I'm sitting, you let her leave and did fuck all to go after her."

"Harsh," Metalhead says under his breath.

"But true," Stumpy supports Prez, with a pointed look in my direction.

"Come on, Dwarf," Raider says reasonably. "Sure, you gave us the impression you were claiming her, then when she walked away, you wanted nothing to do with her. Why waste resources on nothing to do with the club?"

I collapse back down, my head falling into my hands. Instead of appreciating how hard all this had been on her, that maybe she needed a friend, people on her side, I'd done my normal thing and indulged myself in brooding, thinking another one had gotten away instead of stepping up and fighting for what I wanted.

If I'd fought for her, for us, from the start, Raven might be here now and not in the hands of her asshole brother.

"She's mine." I say the words necessary to get my brothers backing, while meaning them with every fibre of my being. When, *when not if...* When we find her, I'm going to make things clear. We belong together, whatever that means. There will be some way to work it out. I'll let her know I live only for her, and I'll move heaven and earth to make her happy.

Prez raises and lowers his chin. "So that's clear, Brothers. Raven is one of ours." He pauses a moment, then asks, "What have you found out, Cloud?"

At Toad's words, Cloud sits forward, and I immediately know he's jumped into action even before Prez had got me riled enough to formally claim her.

"I've been doing some investigating on Jack Dempsey." As if to refresh his memory, he opens his laptop. "Jack's been in and out of prison for the past few years. Seems he doesn't much like earning money honestly. Not long after Raven was sent away, he ended up in juvie."

"For?" Toad snaps.

"Assault during a robbery." Cloud looks at his screen. "Being locked up didn't teach him anything. Once he was out, it wasn't long before he was back inside. The ultimate recidivist. The last stretch he had was five years, and he served every day of his sentence. He got out about six months back, and as far as the cops know, has since kept his nose clean."

"He's a man who wants money and doesn't want to work for it. He's after the cabin." Metalhead sums up what I'm thinking.

"Cabin's not worth much. Not with what we're paying," Cash butts in.

"But it's something," Scalpel says. "And he might just be incensed his sister ended up inheriting it."

My brow creases as I try to get my brain cells to work. "How the fuck did he know how to rig the cabin?" I'd been thinking he might have spent time in the military, and at least had picked up some skills. A man with no proper schooling and spending most of his time in jail is unlikely to have the smarts it took to rig the cabin. I doubt they have courses on explosives in prison.

As others murmur, obviously thinking along the same lines as me, Cloud clears his throat, drawing our attention.

"I think I've got the answer. For the last two years of his sentence, he shared a cell with a man called Carson Bland. Now Carson's an interesting character. He's got military experience, was booted out with a dishonourable discharge, and didn't do much to redeem himself after that. He got caught when he came up with an elaborate plan to kill his pregnant girlfriend."

"Nice guy," Stumpy comments drily.

Toad glares at him, then addresses Cloud. "And this plan involved?"

"Explosives and timers. He'd rigged her house, and her car. Just in case something didn't work."

Christ. "He get her?"

"Nah, Dwarf." Cloud looks at me now. "It was sheer fuckin' luck that she noticed something was off, and got the house checked out."

Raider taps his fingers in a drumming beat. "So, we know Jack was housed up with a felon who had the know-how."

Cloud nods. "Yes. What's more, Bland was coming to the end of his ten-year stretch. He got out the same time as Jack."

"And what do released felons want? Fuckin' money." I bang the table as it starts to make sense.

Cash shakes his head. "As I said, we're not paying much for the cabin. Certainly not enough to set two ex-felons up for life. The most it will do is put small change in their pockets."

"Maybe they see it as a place to hole up?"

Midnight shrugs. "That works. A base off the grid which they could flee to after committing a heist."

Crumb, not normally very vocal at meetings, waves his hand. "What I can't understand is why he didn't just approach Raven? She seemed like a reasonable woman. He could have offered to buy or rent the place from her."

"He probably thought she didn't have fond memories of him." I take it upon myself to respond. "He might have expected she'd tell him to get lost and put obstacles in his way once she knew he wanted the cabin."

Toad grimaces. "We know Bland has to be evil. Who plans to kill their pregnant girlfriend for fuck's sake? Maybe he suggested to Jack it was easier to get Raven out of the picture completely? Or at least, soften her up, so all she wanted was to get rid of the place."

While I hate the thought, I have to tell him, "Jack used to torment her when she was a child. It's just as likely he's just a cruel asshole who gets his kicks from seeing her suffer."

"She's been successful in her life while he's been in and out of jail," Metalhead puts in. "Fucker like that would be likely to blame anyone other than himself. He's probably jealous of her."

Interesting as this psychoanalysis of Jack is, it's getting us no closer to Raven, and every word is making dread settle in my heart. Every comment paints a picture of a man who wants to hurt her. Could I have lost her before I really have a chance to have her?

As my anger boils over, I repeat my earlier action, standing and slamming my fists on the table. "So where is this motherfucker now? Where's Raven? And what the fuck is he doing to her?" Silence reigns. Shaking my head, I spit out, "I'm going to San Francisco."

"What the fuck for?" Toad blasts at me. "Sit the fuck down, Dwarf. What the hell do you think you're going to do in the Golden City? We've got to get a bead on Jack before we tear off trying to find Raven."

That takes the wind out of my sails, and I do sit the fuck down. He's spoken the truth. All I know is that I can't just sit here doing nothing. My hands rake back through my short hair, my fingernails digging into my scalp. I can't stand the thought of Raven suffering.

Scalpel leans forward. "I'm a medic, not a psychiatrist, but there's one place he could take Raven too." My eyes shoot to him immediately. "The place that's so important to him. The cabin."

"That's if he's not killed her already," Stumpy unhelpfully puts in. "Be a lot easier just to get rid of her body then claim her inheritance."

My heart stops beating.

"Nah," Bonkers taps his head. "Maybe it takes crazy to know crazy, but if that's what he was going to do, why the fuck did he not just ambush her at the cabin? Why set it all up to drive her out of her mind? He wants to punish, torture her." His shoulders rise and fall. "Sure, in the end he'll probably off her, but first he'll want to have some fun."

"And what better fuckin' place than where it all started?" Raider slams his fist down.

Toad waves a hand. "Not sure about putting all our eggs in one basket, but I do think the cabin's the place we should start. Dwarf, you want to head out there with," he looks around, "Metalhead, Scalpel, Bonkers, Midnight and Crumb? At least check it out? Cloud, you and the rest of us will stay here and see if we can get more info on Jack."

I'm torn. One half of me wants to leap to my feet, get on my bike and ride there right now, but the other half asks, what if we're wrong and she's somewhere else?

"I'm in." Metalhead raises his chin toward me.

"Me too."

All the others Prez has named confirm they're game.

"Dwarf?"

It's got to be better doing something, but there's only flimsy evidence that's where he's taken her. She could be anywhere. *She could already be dead.*

Cloud raises his chin toward me. "We'll keep looking, Brother. We won't give up until we find her."

Not knowing what to do for the best, but knowing I'll go crazy if I do nothing at all, I throw up my hands. "Okay, I'll go to the cabin. At least we'll be able to cross that off the list if she's not there."

Chapter Twenty-Three

RAVEN

Though I try to struggle, Jack's got the upper hand, and he half pushes, half drags me through the door. As soon as we're over the threshold and into the cabin, Jack's fingers tighten on my shoulder, and he pulls me back.

"It fuckin' worked."

He sounds almost in awe as he views the bookcase lying smashed, and when he turns his body, I know he's spied the remnants of the crockery broken and scattered across the kitchen floor. He drags me over to one of the bedrooms and examines the door.

"It fuckin' worked," he repeats. Turning me to face him, he shakes me until my teeth rattle. "You fuckin' see this?"

"What?" I ask, innocently.

"The doors flying open, the bookcase falling..." He breaks off, examining my face, presumably wondering how the hell I witnessed what he'd set up, and kept my sanity.

Suddenly I don't want to give him the upper hand or give him the satisfaction of knowing just how much he scared me. I decide to play dumb. "It was like this when I arrived. I just thought an animal had gotten in or something."

His face blackens. I can almost read the thoughts going through his head. The only conclusion he can probably reach is that his arrangements had gone off prematurely.

He scowls. "You always did have the luck of the fuckin' Devil."

Suddenly rage goes through me. "Luck? *Luck?*" It gives me the strength to pull out of his arms. "You think my childhood was lucky? With you as a brother, and being raped by my father? Seeing my father shot at my grandaddy's hands?"

"You're the reason our dad died," he roars. "If you weren't such a stupid bitch, he'd still be alive. But you went running to Pops—"

I don't know why I have to correct him. "I didn't. He came in and saw. He saw what Daddy was doing and how wrong it was—"

"Wrong?" He looks apoplectic. "You were ours."

Ours?

His lungs are heaving with anger, and my own breaths are coming fast. I know he's going to hurt me. I'd tried running moments before, it hadn't worked.

I don't know what to do. I just want to survive. I know if I get out of here still breathing, I'm going to call Dwarf. Hell, I'll sell my business, move to be here with him. I was too cautious before. I should have taken what he was offering. I've been a fool, and in doing so, ended up in this predicament. Alone, in this cabin, with Jack.

As I try to mentally work through any of my very limited options, Jack's face transforms in front of me. His lips slowly part, and his eyes flare with something that's almost unnatural. His fists unclench, and he starts reaching for me just as he had before.

He looks just like my daddy.

Before fear can freeze me to the spot, I step back smartly.

"Tickety tock!" he suddenly shouts.

And oh God, those words, in that voice… It's exactly like my father's.

"Tickety tock. Tickety, tickety tock."

It's Jack, I tell myself. *My brother not my daddy.* But on some visceral level, I find it hard to believe.

Jack's face seems to morph again as he continues to repeat the words, his calculating look seeing exactly what he's doing to me.

Stand my ground.

I refuse to give in. But a whimper rises to my throat as he stalks toward me.

The next rendition of *tickety tock* gets my feet moving, but it's not with an adult's calculation of an attempt at an escape route. This time, it's a child's blind impulse to run. I flee, as I have so many times before, up the stairs toward the one place I should have been safe, but which had never offered me sanctuary. The room I'd avoided on my first visit.

Footsteps stomp behind me.

"Tickety tock. Tickety fuckin' tock. I'm coming for you, little mouse."

Blindly, I rush down the hallway and straight into my child-hood bedroom. For a moment, I'm stunned that nothing's here that I remember from my childhood. The room's been emptied, as if I'd never lived here. There's not even a bed nor a rotting carpet on the floor.

Belatedly, it snaps me into reality. I'm twenty-six, not a child anymore. And it's not my daddy running up behind me.

Like someone's suddenly slammed sense into me, fear turns into anger once more.

Jack might be bigger than me, but he expects me to be cowed and scared, and behave as I had with my daddy, as a young child who had no recourse but to submit to an adult's perverse desires.

My sudden onslaught takes him by surprise. I kick, punch, get in a hit to his stomach which has him bending over, and for a moment, have the upper hand as he didn't expect to be faced with a whirling dervish. I push him back down the hall, hoping my momentum will get him to the stairs. Already I'm sensing victory, seeing a vision of him toppling down them... planning to get his car keys and leave this place of horrors.

But even as my escape firms up in my mind, Jack turns the tables and launches himself, kicking out, sweeping my legs from under me, then taking advantage when I'm on the ground. His heavy body falls to cover me.

"Fight me," he says, grinding his hard cock into me. "Fight me. I think I like it better like this. I'm going to have you, Raven. Then I'm going to fuckin' kill you, you little bitch. Living the high life when I was left here to rot with that evil bastard."

My grandaddy might have been a lot of things, misguided perhaps, but those two words were things he definitely was not. As if I didn't have enough reasons to battle Jack for myself, his threats and insults fuel the flames.

I buck my hips, trying to dislodge him, hating it puts me closer to his dick. Unbalancing him, I manage to roll us over. I draw up my knee, hoping to have a shot at his balls, but he's too fast, too strong. Ripping my shirt in the process, he soon has me over on my back. With his knee, he pushes my legs apart and starts dry humping me, making vomit rise into my mouth.

His fetid breath doesn't help at all as he lowers his lips to my face. Doing the only thing I can, I bite him when he tries to force his tongue into my mouth.

"Bitch!" I get backhanded across my face. *Another bruise to add to my collection.*

I struggle, do what I can, but I'm going to lose this war, that's a certainty. Gradually, Jack's managing to counter any attack I make on him, overpowering me so I can't do it again. When he wraps his hand around my hair and pulls back on my scalp, his other hand encircling my wrists and his legs encasing mine, I'm trapped completely.

As if he realises, Jack chuckles quietly. "Tickety tock."

I'm not going to freeze. I'm not going to lie here and take it. I let myself relax, knowing Jack can't do what he wants to me while I'm still fully clothed, and to get access, he'll have to release me to remove my jeans. I'll bide my time. As soon as my hands are free, I'll gouge out his eyes. I'd rather he killed me than raped me.

"What the fuck's that?" Jack's head jerks up, his hand tightening in my hair, automatically making me wince.

But the pain is nothing to the sense of elation I feel hearing the sound of numerous motorcycles pulling up outside the cabin.

"That's the cabin's purchasers," I tell him, trying to keep the triumph from my voice, thanking God I carried on with selling the cabin. "They'll be here to do a survey or something."

"Fuckin' trespassers," he growls. "This place is mine. It's not for fuckin' sale." He starts getting to his feet, pulling me up by my hair.

Finding it a useful handle, he pulls me to the stairs and down them, my arms floundering to stop myself from falling. Once he's reached the bottom, he reaches into the bag he'd brought in with him and extracts a gun.

"Jack! Jack! Stop." I try to get through to him as he pulls me toward the door. "This is a motorcycle club, not a bunch of happy-go-lucky riders." I'm worried about becoming collateral damage in a hail of bullets. If Jack starts shooting, then the bikers are going to shoot back.

I think I've gotten through to him, but perhaps not in the way that I want, as he pushes me in front of him. "You open the door and tell them to get the fuck out of here. I've got a gun on you, Raven."

I hadn't thought through him using me as a human shield. For a second, doubt goes through me that I'm right about it being the Wicked Warriors. What if it's just a bunch of random bikers come to shoot the place up? Or even if it is Dwarf's club, it might be some I haven't met. As far as the bikers are concerned, the cabin as good as belongs to them.

With his gun pressed tight to my back, Jack slings his arm over my shoulder as he walks us both out. He keeps the door open behind him.

My eyes widen and I feel like fist pumping the air when I see it's not only Dwarf's club but Dwarf himself. He's off his bike and is checking out the car Jack drove us here in. I recognise the others that are with him.

Dwarf's attention is caught, and I catch the narrowing of his eyes when he spies first that my shirt is torn, then they become slits as he notices the bruises on my face.

"Hey, fellas," Jack calls out confidently. "This is private property."

After a glance toward me with narrowed eyes, Metalhead casually takes out a packet of cigarettes, taps one out and lights it. He steps up offering the pack to Dwarf, who I know doesn't smoke. I think it gives him the opportunity to say something under his breath.

Turning back to look in our direction, Metalhead exhales a plume of blue smoke. "Heard this place was for sale."

"It is," I say, jerking forward at the jab of the gun in my back.

"It is not," Jack snarls from behind me. "Get off my property before I call the cops."

"Your property?" Scalpel now swings his leg off his bike. "Strange that. The real estate agent said a woman was selling it."

Jack stiffens behind me, and whispers, "This is all your fault, bitch. Set them right. Tell them it's mine to do what I want with it."

I, of course, am going to do nothing of the sort. I keep my mouth shut. For a moment, it's a standoff until one of the bikers, Crumb, I remember his name, starts to walk around to the side of the cabin.

"Where's he going? Tell him to come back where I can see

him. No one's fuckin' walking around this place." Jack sounds panicked.

"He's going for a piss." Bonkers explains his absence, casually flicking ash off the end of his cigarette.

Dwarf looks surprised as if he was expecting me to run into his arms, but I can't tell him why I can't. Why I allow this beast of my brother to keep me anchored to him. I try to signal with my eyes that I'm trapped, but apparently, I'm not that good a mime artist.

Or so I believe. More attuned to me than I expected, Dwarf suddenly walks closer. Again, that gun gets stabbed into me, causing another bruise to add to the rest of my collection.

My man stares at me. Now, his act is worthy of an Oscar, as he looks dispassionately, and lifts his gaze to Jack over my shoulder.

"How much are you selling the place for?"

"Too much for you," Jack sneers. "And it's not for sale. It's my family home."

It's mine, not his, but I leave that thought in my head.

"Oh, come on, man. Anything's for sale at the right price." Metalhead steps forward and joins Dwarf.

"Where's the other one of you?" Jack appears agitated, and his head twists for a second in the direction Crumb had gone.

"Probably taking a crap," Bonkers calls out. "Man's got a sensitive ass if you get my meaning. Best you stay upwind of him when you go out back."

Scalpel snorts and fist bumps Bonk. They seem so relaxed, Jack's tension eases.

"How much?" Metalhead prompts again.

I might not be able to see Jack's smirk, but I can hear it in his voice as he replies, "Two million dollars."

Metalhead emits a sudden surprised bark. "What the fuck do you think this is? A fuckin' gold mine?"

Jack stumbles backward, taking me with him. "How the fuck

do you know?" he rasps, hoarsely. "Now get out of here."
Showing his hand, he adds, "Or I shoot the bitch."

Something in Metalhead's casual words have thrown a
switch in Jack. He was starting to relax and thought he was
going to get out of this.

Now I can feel his body quivering.

Chapter Twenty-Four

DWARF

When I turned to see Raven alive, I nearly collapsed to my knees with relief. It had taken all my acting ability to keep the rage off my face, and every ounce of my control not to charge in and rip her from the other man's hands, especially seeing the state of her. Her face is a mass of bruises, and her shirt is torn.

If she was free to move, I know she'd run to me. She looks strong, angry, not cowered and weak, so I assume that Jack, as that's who it has to be, has a weapon trained on her.

The thought of a bullet or knife doing damage to her is the only thing stopping me from throwing myself forward and tearing him apart with my bare hands.

Metalhead had made the same conjecture, as he'd imparted when he'd whispered to me.

Although I saw recognition and relief in her eyes when she'd noticed me, that she hadn't shouted my name wasn't a mystery. *Clever girl.* She's playing for time.

She's trusting me to get her out of this.

Jack seems perfectly content to hide behind a woman who he's obviously beaten and attacked, and I suspect that's because we're bikers. Most of the civilian world think we treat our woman like shit, and little better than animals. He's going to soon find out that neither I nor my brothers condone violence to the fairer sex, but for now it works in our favour and I'm not going to warn him.

I know two things he doesn't. One, despite Bonk's reference to Crumb's bathroom habits, he's not disappeared to empty his bowels. Nah, he'll first be calling Prez to update him, then will be looking for a back way into the cabin. The other is that my brothers are on board with handling this carefully, and nothing takes priority over Raven's safety. Hence, why Metalhead picked up on my cue to see if we could get Jack talking by offering him money for the cabin which we know he doesn't own.

But when he asks for two million, like my brother, I think that's fishy, but his reaction to the comment about it being a gold mine was what really got all my instincts to come online.

It's also made Jack trigger happy, revealing the weapon he's used to control Raven. As soon as he showed his, both Metal's and my guns are in our hands.

"Shoot her and you're dead," Metal says coldly.

Jack doesn't seem to know what to do. But then he's a failed felon, probably a failure at everything. He swings his gun from Raven and points it at Metal. The sergeant-at-arms, a seasoned veteran, just stares back at him coldly without shifting his aim.

"Down to whose bullet flies truer and faster," Metalhead tells him calmly and nonchalantly.

Whether it's due to my heightened senses of the standoff, I'm suddenly aware of everything. Have the birds all stopped singing, or was it so deadly silent before? Where has the cooling breeze gone? The air is now so still. It's ominous as if nature too is waiting for something. Maybe I'm just hyper focused as something has to give and have blanked everything from my senses except for the scene in front of me.

Jack shifts uneasily as if realising the fix he's in. Sure, he could shoot Raven, but he knows he won't survive her for longer than a few seconds. Or if he was foolish enough to shoot one of us, the same applies. He also doesn't know my relationship with Raven, or that any of us know her at all. Without that knowledge, she's not the bargaining piece she could have been.

I'd do anything to signal to her I won't let her be hurt, that I'd lay down my life before any harm comes to her, but if I show my hand, then it will make everything worse. Jack will know he's got the stronger position.

Instead, he's off-balanced and as his eyes flick from me to Metalhead and to the brothers standing behind, it looks like his mind's working a mile a minute.

Backup will already be on its way. Despite not a word having been spoken or instruction given, I know Crumb will have called the situation in. That's what it's like riding with seasoned brothers.

Jack's twitchy though, and we don't have time to wait for them to arrive. The situation could quickly deteriorate so it'll have to be resolved by the time they ride up the drive.

Jack might be off balance, but neither Metal nor I move an inch. Our weapons are held steadily. We've both been trained by the military and know how to face down an unfriendly.

If it wasn't for Raven, Jack would already be dead. But if it wasn't for her, we wouldn't be here in the first place.

I see the moment Jack makes a decision, and my finger tightens fractionally on the trigger. If I could, I'd yell at Raven to get down then take a shot, but he's holding onto her hair, and her dropping would be impossible.

Instead of using his gun, Jack sighs and begins to speak. "I've already got one fuckin' partner, but how about this? I'll let you in and you get a share of the profits. Say ten percent. How does that sound?"

My lips imperceptibly press together, wondering what the fuck he's on about. But luckily, Metalhead seems to be a step further ahead than me.

"The gold?" he asks, his tone optimistic.

What fucking gold? Risking a glance at Raven, I see she's equally perplexed.

Her brother suddenly looks sneaky. "You'd have to buy your way in with equipment."

Metalhead manages to both hold on to his gun and to light yet another cigarette. When he's put the flame to the tip, he focuses his eyes straight ahead. "What we talking about? Panning, drift or working deep?"

I try not to let any expression cross my face, but fuck it, is Jack, and now Metalhead, suggesting there could be a gold mine here? Had Raven's grandaddy staked a claim, or just discovered it and passed the knowledge on to Jack? And if there is gold to be found here, why hadn't they worked it before?

"We'd have to tunnel," Jack admits. "The lode's down deep. Pops discovered it when he was digging an extension to the bunker."

Metalhead sucks in smoke and breathes it out. "Have you had it surveyed?"

"Don't need to," Jack says. "I know what I'm talking about."

I suspect it's highly unlikely that there's an undiscovered gold mine waiting to be exploited under the cabin, but then again, there have been stranger things happen. My lips want to quirk. What were the chances that when Toad eventually settled down, his wife would bring a fucking five-million-dollar windfall with her? Why should my luck be any worse? Why shouldn't I end up with a woman who's inherited a fortune buried underground? Our chapter of the Wicked Warriors MC would be the luckiest bastards around.

Midnight speaks from behind us. "Makes sense. This area was littered with gold mines back in the day."

But what are the chances of finding one that's not already been worked out?

"I reckon Prez might be interested," I suggest, my eyes fixed on Raven's.

"I'm in," Scalpel says.

"Me too." Bonk backs him up.

Metalhead starts playing with fire when he points to Raven and asks, "What about her?"

Jack jerks her hair harder. "She'll do exactly what I say." Ignoring that he'd already lied and told us he owned the cabin, he adds, "And if she doesn't sign over the property, well, I'll inherit it when she's dead." His mouth quirks as if realising he can save paperwork by avoiding having to persuade her.

I jump in, scared he's going to kill her right in front of me now. "Hey, hold on, man. If you're going to do this, you're going to have to make it look like an accident. She turns up with a bullet in her brain, then who's the most likely suspect?"

His eyes widen as though he hadn't considered that, then he chuckles. "Plenty of places on this property for her to have a fatal accident."

The expression on Raven's face makes me want to simultaneously laugh and kiss the fuck out of her. She hasn't a doubt in her head that we're just playing him along and knows it wouldn't be her who would be having a mishap by falling into a ravine or such. She might not have trusted me to help her work through her issues, but she definitely has faith we're going to get her out of this.

She won't have to worry much longer. An almost imperceptible movement behind Jack catches my eye. Crumb has indeed found a way to enter the cabin silently and is approaching him from behind. I'd love for him to just shoot him, but with him holding Raven so close, there's a chance, one that my brother will be well aware of, that a bullet hitting Jack could travel through him and injure Raven as well.

I open my mouth to keep Jack talking when I realise the silence that had hit me earlier is being disturbed. Shadows have blocked out the sun, and the day has darkened so much it could be night. Leaves swirl up and buffet my legs as a strong wind blows. All precursors to a summer monsoon, except it's not summer now.

The air becomes electric as lightning flashes right overhead. A rumble of thunder sounds so loudly it makes even us Arizonians jump.

"*Boy!*"

What the fuck? I shake my head and stick my finger in my ear. I must be hearing things. The noise wasn't just clouds knocking together. That sounded like a voice roaring down from above.

"*Boy!*" it booms again, too loud to be human.

Along with the voice that seems to echo all around us, mingling with the thunder overhead, there's a loud stomping coming from inside the cabin, sounding like someone huge coming down the stairs. Crumb, a steady brother who did a few tours overseas, has lowered his gun and is looking in consternation in that direction, having completely taken his eye off Jack.

I can't blame him. Any threat Jack poses seems to be insignificant now.

"*Boy! Get your ass here.*"

Jack's face has paled as he lets go of Raven's hair. Released, she stumbles in my direction, and I swiftly swing her behind me, using her own momentum. But her brother doesn't even seem to notice he's lost his bargaining chip.

Slowly, very slowly, he turns and looks back into the cabin. Behind him, I see Crumb scrabbling out of the way as dust rises to take the form of an elderly, but impressively tall and strong man.

Jack screams and scrabbles backward toward me. When he's free of the door, he spins on his heels and starts to run.

The dust cloud elongates until it's just a head followed by a billowing cloud, and homes in on its target, now racing for the trees, and is gaining ground fast. If anything, it seems to be herding him in the direction it wants.

Raven, who'd been so terrified to hear her father's voice, doesn't seem overly concerned. She pulls at my hand and gets me moving after her brother and whatever the fuck it is following him.

The wind blows so hard it's difficult to stay on my feet, so I hold tightly to her. Lightning comes down, striking so close it makes the hairs on my neck stand up.

Metalhead, Scalpel, Bonkers, Midnight, and Crumb are running just behind us as if they are drawn by an invisible magnet, unable to stay back and let this play out.

Jack's screaming and I can see his steps starting to falter, demonstrating that even while running for his life, Jack isn't particularly fit. He pauses to get his breath and the dust cloud surrounds him.

"You always were a worthless little shit."

Did I actually hear that or was it my imagination? I must admit I'd expected if a ghost had spoken, it would have been something more profound.

But Jack squeals as though he's been hit and sinks to his knees, covering his head with his hands. "I'm sorry, Pops. I was only joking," he screams.

"Last time you ever touch Raven," the voice bellows again.

A loud crack, a strong smell of ozone, and lightning so close my hair stands on end. A tree flares into flame and drops heavily, landing right on Jack, knocking his body to the ground. He starts screaming as his clothes start to burn.

He may have threatened to kill her, may have tried to rape her if I'm reading the signs right, but this is Raven's brother, so I hold her head into my chest, trying to avoid her looking at the man who's literally been struck down.

There's a strong smell of burning flesh but before it can permeate into my lungs, the wind conveniently changes direction and blows it away. Jack's screams die down, and then shut off completely. I stare, transfixed as his body seems to fold in on itself, his hands which had been held up in supplication become charred claws.

My brain has difficulty processing what's happened in the past few moments, and I'm not the only one. Metalhead and Bonkers are looking at me and I can read their expressions as well as the words that they mouth. Both of them plainly asking, *What the fuck?*

Midnight is standing his eyes wide, and his nostrils flared. Crumb's looking horrified and Scalpel's staring at Jack's body as if he knows he's far beyond the need for a medic now.

I thought we'd disproved ghosts exists. I don't know what I believe now.

Chapter Twenty-Five

RAVEN

Hearing my daddy's disembodied voice had terrified me. Hearing my grandaddy from beyond the grave, well, while it didn't make me want to dance with glee, what it didn't do was make me afraid. Instead, I'd had a burst of nostalgia, wishing I could see him in flesh-and-blood form again.

None of it scared me. Even with the violent storm blowing up out of nowhere, for some reason, I'd felt cocooned and safe.

I must be a bad person that I feel no remorse knowing Jack is dead, nor have compassion with the manner of his death. He deserves to burn in hell along with my daddy, and I believe I just had a front-row seat to what he has in store for the rest of eternity.

I can't feel compassion—it was always going to be either him or me, and I'd rather I was alive. Maybe it has less impact as I already thought Jack had died, his appearance like a spectre rising from the grave, only for my grandaddy to put him back where he belongs.

As Dwarf tries to usher me away, he seems tense and uneasy. Strangely, not one word's been exchanged between him and his brothers, no exclamation or questions about what happened.

While I have zero doubts my grandaddy's spirit saved me today, and that we've had evidence things exist that we didn't want to believe, in no way do I feel threatened. Instead, I feel loved and safe. But how can I explain something I feel deep inside, but which has no rational cause?

Already I have the feeling that over time none of us will speak about what happened today. Our brains will translate the events, putting them together in an explainable way, that it was an unseasonal storm which caused Jack's untimely demise. We'll find it easier to scoff and laugh that anything supernatural came into play. Deep down, though, I don't think I'll ever forget that Grandaddy saved the day.

Already things are returning to normal. The wind is dying down and the clouds part, allowing the sun to shine through, making patterns on the ground as we walk our way through the forest back to the cabin. I notice all the men are staying close, as if ready to protect each other. By the time we get to the edge of the forest, the dust has settled, and the air becomes clear.

As I go to walk toward the cabin, Dwarf holds me back. "Let us check it out first."

I'm about to smile at him and tell him there's no need when a shimmering cloud approaches us. As it draws nearer, I can see it's hundreds of butterflies, the kind Grandaddy and I used to watch back in the day. The sight brings back memories of walking through the meadow, hand in hand with the man who was more like a father to me than the one who'd borne that name.

Dwarf inhales sharply and releases my hand as the butterflies start to settle on me. I laugh, a high-pitched childish giggle, a sound of pure pleasure I've not emitted for years. The butterflies land on my hair, on my arms, and one brazenly on the tip of my nose. The flock seems to be made up of many species, and none that should be around this late in the year.

For a moment I'm lost in my childhood, my mind filled with the pleasant times and none of the bad. I smile, and laugh, and twirl, raising my hands. It's as if with their wings the butterflies are taking the weight I've been carrying away.

So lost in this magical world, I'm only vaguely aware that another half dozen or so motorcycles have just drawn up. Whether it's the arrival of more men, or whether it's just that their time has come, one by one, the butterflies leave, lifting from my skin then seeming to dissipate as they rise into the air.

I hold my breath until the last one disappears then turn to Dwarf to see his mouth open and a look of wonder on his face.

"He was here," Dwarf breathes out. Then his eyes narrow as they regard the cabin. It doesn't take a genius to know what he's thinking.

"He's gone. Can't you feel it?" I ask him, looking around, smelling the pine in the air and hearing the birdsong echoing around. The atmosphere has completely changed, and instead of being ominous, it's been replaced with calm.

Without waiting for Dwarf, I enter the cabin. It feels as though it's been cleansed, which, in some ways it has. Most of the dust has now gone. The irreverent thought that in addition to getting me free of Jack, my grandaddy cleaned the cabin as well, makes me giggle again like a child.

"There's nothing here."

"You fuckin' said that before."

I turn in time to see Bonk swipe Midnight around the back of his head.

"Ouch!" Midnight rubs his scalp, then shakes his head. "There wasn't when it was Jack's toys, but just now? His pops? Sent fuckin' shivers down my spine, Brother. Never experienced anything like that before."

"Will someone bring me up to date? Where the fuck's this Jack bastard?" I hear Toad's voice before I see him.

Bonk swings around. "Well, see, that fucker Jack had Raven hostage. We threatened him, it was a standoff. He said he'd let us share in the gold mine. Then Raven's grandaddy rose from the dead, frightened the shit out of him, then set him on fire with a stroke of lightning—"

"Will someone tell me the fuckin' truth?" Toad thunders. "Oh, and don't let Bonk have any more of what he's been smoking."

Metalhead, still looking paler than normal, approaches his president, giving a sideways glance to Bonk. "That is what happened."

Toad's eyes open wide, and his brows rise to his hairline. He looks around as if trying to find someone sane. "Scalpel?" He says it in a tone that suggests he's disappointed with his sergeant-at-arms.

Scalpel steps forward, holding out the palms of his hands. "Sorry, Prez, but Bonk summed it up nicely."

"What he said," Crumb confirms, before Toad can ask.

Midnight also adds his two-pennies worth. "Seems Raven's grandaddy took his revenge from the grave."

Raider snorts and comes alongside his prez. "What the fuck are they all on?"

Toad just turns to stare at his VP. "Fuck knows. But whatever it is, made them clean the cabin as well." His boot scuffs the floor, the action which earlier would have left marks.

Dwarf pulls himself to his full height, still coming nowhere close to meeting his brothers in stature, but his voice has regained its former strength when he stares straight into the eye of his prez. "Ain't lying. Can't explain it. Maybe in time it will make sense. But Jack's dead." He jerks his head in the direction of the forest. "He's down there, incinerated."

Toad doesn't look convinced, but waves toward Stumpy and Cash. "Go check it out," he demands.

Metalhead departs with them, presumably to show them where to go. As he walks out, I can hear him mumbling, "Ain't a fuckin' liar."

Dwarf goes to speak again, presumably to back up his friend, but Toad holds up his hand to silence him. "However it happened, I take it Jack is dead, and you had no need of the cavalry."

"He is." Speaking for the first time since he arrived, I command his attention. "And unbelievable as it sounds, something strange did happen. But if you're worried about ghosts hanging around, something tells me this cabin's been cleansed."

"Not worried," Toad lazily responds. "Never believed in ghosts and I'm not going to start now."

Dwarf opens his mouth, but I put my hand on his arm in warning. Whatever Toad believes doesn't matter one iota. The cabin's been left to the living, and that's all he needs to know.

A few minutes later, Stumpy and Cash return through the door, with Metalhead wearing an *I told you so* look behind them.

"Fucking burned body out in a clearing. Lightning-struck tree must have fallen on him. He's barely recognisable but no reason to doubt it's Raven's brother." Stumpy pauses and gives his opinion. "Reckon they're all spooked, and a perfectly normal storm shocked them."

Toad grins as though he thought that all along. Dwarf grinds his teeth but takes my cue and keeps quiet.

"Okay, so Jack's gone. Now what the fuck was that about a gold mine? Something else you've all been hallucinating about?"

Dwarf sucks in air but pulls me close and ignores the insult. "Have to admit we didn't quite get to the bottom of it, but Jack seemed to believe there was gold underneath the cabin. That's why he so desperately wanted it."

In my head, I run back over exactly what Jack had said. "He mentioned a partner," I remind him. "Should we be worried about someone else turning up?"

Dwarf glances at me, shakes his head, then looks at his brothers.

"I'd put good money on who it is," Cloud says. "That Bland fucker wouldn't have helped him for nothing."

That statement goes right over my head. "Who's Bland?"

Dwarf whispers, "The guy who had the know-how to set up the explosives."

Toad raises his chin in acknowledgment to Cloud, then focuses on me. "What's the likelihood of there being a gold mine here? You ever heard anything about it?"

I answer him honestly. "I was as shocked to hear about it as you were yourself. I haven't even heard any rumours. Of course, when I left, I was only a kid, and Grandaddy might have discovered something after I went. But I doubt it. If he'd found anything of the sort, he'd have investigated it." That's the kind of man that he was.

"He had a stroke," Dwarf reminds me. "Maybe finding out he was a potential millionaire caused it."

If so, I feel devastated for the man who's proved he loved me so much. Grandaddy would have been so excited, how cruel it would have been to have that chance snatched from him.

Toad is quiet for a moment and then pinches the bridge of his nose. Eventually he turns to me, looking and sounding serious. "This change things, Raven? You having second thoughts about selling the cabin? Now you know there could be more to it?"

None at all. To my mind, it changes nothing. "I made an agreement," I respond. "If there's gold here, how would I know how to excavate it?"

Toad looks at me astutely. "How about this? We pay what we've already agreed, then if anything comes of there being a gold mine here, we'll give you a percentage."

That sounds more than fair, and far more than I expected. Grinning, I nod my head, showing his compromise is more than reasonable.

"Hey, Prez. We're buying the cabin along with a corpse. What are we going to do about Jack?" Raider seems to be thinking of practicalities.

Addressing myself to him, I say the first thing that comes into my head. "I'll report finding his body to the cops. It's obvious it was a freak accident."

Toad grimaces. "The cabin's surrounded by motorcycle tracks. Personally, I'd like to keep the authorities out of it."

I know they're buying the cabin through a shell company of sorts, so can understand why they'd not want to be associated with it. The cops knowing they're here doesn't gel with them having a place off the grid.

"We could bury him in the forest. Who the fuck's going to come looking for him here?" Dwarf suggests.

"Bland?" Cloud counters.

Raider shrugs. "We can deal with one man. But the question is what does Raven want to do? It's her kin we're talking about."

If involving the authorities is not what they want, it doesn't much matter to me. "Kin who wanted to rape and kill me and did nothing but make my life a misery." I can't summon up an ounce of pity for my brother, however awful that makes me. "There's no other family to mourn his death. He's not worth a gravestone."

Toad understands my thoughts and raises his chin. "Dwarf. Why don't you take Raven back to the clubhouse? Some of us will stay here and deal with the cleanup."

Dwarf starts to say yes, then looks my way. "Give me a moment, Prez?" At Toad's nod, he wraps a hand around my arm and leads me outside.

He leads me to the fence and leans back against it, his arms crossed over his muscular chest. Standing in front of him, I mimic his pose.

"You want to come to the clubhouse, or go back home?" His tone gives me no suggestion of what answer he'd prefer.

I walked out on him a little more than a week ago yet had done nothing to stay in touch. Is he asking because it's what Toad instructed, but not what he wants?

Before Jack had turned up, I'd been coming to accept I knew I'd made a mistake walking out on him and not giving us a chance. When Jack had stolen me away, it had solidified things in my head.

Dwarf had gotten under the barriers I'd set up to protect myself. If I hadn't been knocked back with spectres of my father and brother, I might have been more inclined to stay.

Am I being offered a second chance? Or this time, will it be Dwarf that walks away?

I risk a glance at him, noting he's staring out into the forest, and not watching me. Is it because he's dreading my answer? And what's the right one, anyway?

Remembering how he'd turned up at the cabin at such an opportune time, I ask, "Why did you come here today?" It seems a coincidence that they arrived to save me from being raped at just the right time. If they hadn't turned up, I have no doubt by now I'd be dead. The thought makes me shiver.

I don't know what I expect him to say. After the other inexplicable events of today, I wouldn't be surprised if he'd acted on a premonition. But maybe the club just wanted to check on the investment they were about to make, and serendipity came into play.

"Natalie," Dwarf answers, without turning to look at me. "She heard you say Jack was there, got worried when you didn't answer your phone, found you weren't in your apartment, and tracked down the club." He shrugs. "I take it you've been talking about me."

Natalie. Bless her for looking out for me. I realise there'll be nothing I can do that will show the immensity of my gratitude to her. I suck in air, realising how close I'd come to facing the worst thing a woman can face, and one, for me, that sadly was all too familiar.

"It was just a thought Jack might bring you here," Dwarf continues. His next intake of breath causes his body to shudder. "Raven, seeing you like that, hurt..." He trembles again.

"Natalie thinks I'm a fool," I tell him.

"For?"

Knowing my heart's going to be broken if he doesn't take this the right way, I take a leap. "For letting Jack scare me away."

"From your inheritance?" he asks in an emotionless tone.

"From you," I correct.

"From me?" His head turns slightly.

Is that hope in his voice? Hardly daring to breathe, I admit, "My experience with men isn't great, Dwarf. I found my feelings for you so intense after only a couple of days it unnerved me. Then finding Jack was behind everything that happened…"

Suddenly he moves. His hands are on my shoulders, bringing me around to face him. "You didn't contact me."

"I didn't know what to say." My own vulnerability must show in my face and my voice isn't as strong as I want it to be. "I'd left you without a decent explanation, thought you might have been glad to have me out of your way."

Dwarf looks up to the skies and then back down again. "I've never connected with a woman like I did you, Raven. It fuckin' killed me when you walked away." He sounds fierce as though wondering how I could ever doubt it.

"You didn't contact me." I throw his words back at him.

His eyes darken. "Raven, all my life women have used me to get close to my brothers. Each time I found a woman I liked, one of them managed to steal her away." His finger finds my lips to stop me from interrupting. "Not my brothers' fault, just mine for not understanding they were using me to find a better option."

"You are the better option." My statement is as fierce as his. Dwarf's brothers are great, but there's not one that would tempt me.

His eyes open, his nostrils flare, and for a moment he just stares, then he cries out, "Then why the fuck are we wasting time?" His arms come around me, crushing me to him, and his lips crash down on mine.

I grab at him like a drowning man catches on to a lifeline. My fingers curl into his t-shirt, holding so tightly, never wanting him to get away. When his tongue seeks entry, I open my mouth.

I've never been kissed this way, never been devoured as if he needs me more than he needs oxygen to breathe. Unfortunately, the pressure hurts the bruise on my jaw where Jack had hit me.

When I wince, he pulls away, pain in his own eyes as he places his hand against my cheek so gently.

"So fuckin' sorry. I got carried away."

Waving off his apology, I tell him, "When I'm healed, you can do that every minute of every day."

He grins at me, the expression transforming his face, again making me wonder why any woman could prefer someone else. Leaning into me, he places a gentler kiss on the undamaged side of my face, then tells me quietly, "I think I got the answer to the question. Clubhouse it is. But before we go, I want Scalpel to check you over."

I can feel his hard cock pressing against me, and how my own body is responding to his. So, releasing his shirt, I use my hands to cup his face. "I'll go anywhere with you, Dwarf. As long as it ends up with me in your bed. And if you need to, you can get Scalpel to give me the all clear."

Chapter Twenty-Six

DWARF

We only delayed long enough for Scalpel to reassure me that while bruised, she's got no serious injuries, and for me to give her the spare t-shirt out of my saddlebag to replace the one Jack had torn. Then we wait another moment for Raven to call her friend Natalie and reassure her she was alright. Raven was ebullient in her thanks for the alarm having been raised. With promises to tell Natalie everything all in good time, she ends the call and passes my phone back.

She's never been on a bike before, and while I was worried about the bruises that must be giving her pain, she dismisses them and shows me she's game. After a few instructions, she soon gets the hang of it. It feels a little unnatural having to compensate for someone riding pillion, but with her breasts fetched up tight against my back, and her pussy against my ass, I soon realise and appreciate the pros that come along with it.

Only her. It would always only ever be her. Now I understand how Toad so quickly fell in love with the woman he hadn't expected to develop feelings for. When you find the right one, time's of no consequence. I'm never going to let her go. I don't give a damn my life is here, and hers is in California, the practicalities will sort themselves out. It's being together that's important.

While desperate to get her back to the clubhouse, I take extra care, appreciating this is her first ride, and I don't want to scare her. If I have my way, she'll be riding up behind me for the rest of my life. I've waited so long for a woman to see me and no other, and now I've found her, I'm not going to let her go.

I know my brothers won't be far behind me, but today, I'm enjoying this time, just me and my woman on the road. My cock's already throbbing in anticipation of having her under me again. And this time, doing it properly. The only things going bump tonight will be my headboard against the wall.

For the first time since I made my home with the Wicked Warriors MC, I wish I didn't live in the clubhouse. All I can offer is little more than a frat house room. Raven deserves to be treated like a princess and not be subjected to the knowing leer of the prospect as we walk in.

Slightly ashamed, I walk her upstairs, but when we step through my door, her eyes are on me, and not on the furnishings.

"I'm a... I'm just going to use the bathroom." Her tone suggests reluctance for the necessary delay.

I turn her in that direction and risk a gentle pat to her ass. "Go freshen up," I tell her, knowing I'll be using the facilities after her.

While she's gone, I open the bedside table and make sure I've got a box of condoms stored there. Hoping she'll not think I'm presumptuous, I leave it on the top, opening it up and taking a foil-wrapped package out to speed up proceedings.

I hear the toilet flush, then water in the sink running. Feeling awkward, I hover at the end of the bed, then turn away and look out the window, trying not to look like I've been anxiously waiting. Nerves hit me. Only thinking of myself, I'd brought her straight up to my room for one reason, with no offer of hospitality nor having a discussion.

Is this what she wants?

I'm a confident man, but I don't want to blow this. While I'm still wondering how I can rectify the situation, I feel her arms come around me, her chin resting on my shoulder.

"We fit perfectly," she murmurs. As I turn around, my arms reciprocating her gesture, she grins and continues, "I don't get a neck ache when I kiss you."

"You're perfect for me," I tell her, realising expectation is making me breathless. I can't resist pushing my cock against her. "And we already know we fit."

Her hands move from my shoulders and go to the bottom of my shirt. "Last time I didn't get to see you."

"Hold that thought," I tell her quickly. "I need a piss."

She snorts and teases, "So romantic."

I'm back as fast as I can make it. This time, when she starts to lift my shirt, I raise my arms so she can do it more easily, then help her by reaching back with my hand, grabbing the neck, and ripping it off completely.

With widened eyes, she caresses my muscles and traces the tats. Her touch is both gentle and arousing, and I have to hold myself back to give her a chance to explore. I want to take charge, tear her shirt off, and worship her body in ways I didn't have time for before.

I notice enticing things about her—the way she's biting her lips, her tongue appearing then disappearing as she concentrates on her task, the gleam in her eyes as she focuses on tracing her fingers around my nipples. No woman has ever worshipped my body in this way before. I admit I'm enjoying being the recipient, but hell, I want to play too.

My hands twitch as I try to keep them at my sides.

But when she leans forward and takes one of my nipples into her mouth and sucks on it hard, keeping hands off is something I can no longer do.

Growling, I take hold of the t-shirt I'd given to her. It's not one of my favourites, and hell, I wouldn't care even if it was, but I wrench it in two.

My violent and unexpected action has her pulling away. Her eyes widen and her lips curve. "I take it you're impatient."

"Like fuck I am. I want to touch you."

She grins, and instead of leaving things up to me, reaches around her back and undoes her bra. As she slips the straps down her arms, her breasts drop free. "Help yourself."

My voice unintentionally gruff, I respond, "I don't mind if I do."

Christ, but her tits are perfect. Plump enough to fit nicely into my hands, the nipples surrounded by dusky pink areolae. Playfully I pinch them between my fingertips, rolling them, loving that she throws back her head and gives a loud sigh.

As though I'm starving, I can't keep my mouth away. Dipping my head, I take one of the hardened buds between my lips and circle it with my tongue. Her intake of breath and the press of her body against me shows that it's something she likes. I oblige by paying the same attention to the other side.

"I want more," she hisses against me.

"Patience," I murmur, determined to take my time, and that this time the agenda will be all mine.

Nevertheless, I push her back toward my bed, gently encouraging her to lie down, and then going back to toy with her nipples again. Like her, though, I'm becoming impatient. I can smell her arousal and my animal brain seems to take over as I move my lips down her stomach. She flinches and not with pleasure as my hand touches her right side.

Raising my head, I notice the reddened area and the start of a bruise there.

Discerning what I'm looking at, she shakes her head. Her fingers come to my chin and raise it so I can look into her eyes, flinching once again at her bruised face and the damage Jack had done.

"He's gone," she states with determination. "But his touch is still here. I need you to take it away for me. Make me forget he was ever there."

"I don't want to hurt you."

"You won't. I'm just tender in parts, Dwarf."

I want to treat her like a piece of precious porcelain, while at the same time fucking her so hard to leave my own mark, one of ownership and a promise I'll never let anything hurt her ever again.

While I hesitate trying to control my inner beast, her hand pushes between us. She flicks open the button on her shorts, and inches her fingers inside.

With a cheeky grin, she informs me, "If you're not going to get the job done, I'll do it myself."

Growling, I wrench her hand away and pin her with my eyes. "Mine." My voice leaves no doubt that she, and everything about her, belongs to me now.

As soon as I release my hand, she grabs my denim-covered cock, her fingers firming around it. "Mine," she retorts, claiming me in return.

I'm certainly not going to argue. As long as she doesn't want me to cut it off and give it to her as a memento, I'm more than happy it belongs to her and her only. For a moment, I'm blinded by a wave of emotion that my dream of having that special woman at my side has been granted. And not just any woman, *Raven.* A woman so perfect she should be running a mile, but instead she seems to want me as much as I do her. Overwhelmed, my mouth opens and words come out that I never thought I'd say.

"I love you."

Her eyes come to mine and study me as if to read my intention. What she sees must satisfy her, as with a sigh she responds, "I don't understand how this has happened between us, but I love you too." Then her eyes roll as she adds, "Now will you please fuck me?"

That's my girl.

Suppressing my chuckle, I rip her shorts and panties off her.

She might be impatient, but she'll have to wait for my cock. For now, I can't wait to taste her.

Pushing her legs apart, I dive in. Not much finesse is involved as I suck, tongue and torture her, but that doesn't seem to matter a damn. When I curl up two fingers inside her, her muscles first pulse then go into spasm. She screams my name so loudly, no one within hearing distance would be left in any doubt what we're doing. I'm half grateful and half disappointed that I've not heard the sound of motorcycles yet to show my brothers have returned.

None of those fuckers would think of stealing her off me when I can satisfy my woman like that.

I bring her down gently, then ramp her up to the edge once again. By the time I've drawn three orgasms from her, she lies back sated on my bed.

And I'll be fucked at how good she looks lying there. Her skin's flushed and aglow with orgasmic pleasure. Her pupils are large, and there's a smile on her face which would rival the Cheshire cat who's been given a big bowl of cream. Her hair, like a cascade of a waterfall at midnight, lies over my pillow.

The sweat on her brow gives a sheen that makes me proud, and her lungs still heave.

Fuck, I can't wait any longer to be inside her. Quickly I divest myself of my clothing, sheath myself with latex, then dropping to the bed once more, position myself at her entrance.

"Ready?" I ask, mainly to warn her.

"Fuck yes," she replies.

Her pussy is soft and wet with her copious moisture thanks to my ministrations before. My cock glides in easily, so I immediately immerse myself to the hilt. Her gasp is matched by my own groan at the feeling of coming home. Once would never have been enough to satisfy me.

For a second, I thank Jack that he brought her back to me and gave me a second chance.

It might be a mood killer, but it drives me to ask, "Were you ever going to return if Jack hadn't appeared?"

As if this is the moment to cement our relationship, she places a hand to my cheek, and replies to what could have been a mood killer with the words that I most want. "I wouldn't have been able to stay away. Jack just made it easier."

"Thank fuck he was useful for something."

Her laugh vibrates all the way down my cock, and I can't remain still anymore. I thrust at the same time she pushes back.

We fit well and seem to automatically synchronise our movements. I can't ever remember feeling like this fucking someone before. But then, previously, emotions have never come into it.

I've never stared into someone's eyes, seeing love shining back at me. I've never vowed that this is the only cunt I'll ever sink into until the day that I die. Somehow the intense feelings that flood through me elevate this from a physical experience to one that transcends the highest plane.

I try to make it last but know I won't go the distance. Thank fuck she seems to be there with me, as her head's thrown back and her mouth's open wide. Knowing I'm losing it, I strum my fingers against her clit and am rewarded by a tamping down of her inner muscles.

"Come with me." It's a cry, a plea, as I beg for her to take pity on me.

And thank fuck, she does. "Dwarf, oh my God, Dwarf!"

Yeah, I'll be her fucking deity, as she'll be mine. If she'll let me, I'm going to worship her for the rest of our lives.

Semen squirts out in the condom, so fucking much, my own orgasm seems extended, wave after wave of pure pleasure going on and on.

When I finally manage to gasp in air again, I look down into her beautiful eyes.

"I fuckin' love you, Raven."

She gives me a rapturous smile. "And I fucking love you right back."

Chapter Twenty-Seven

RAVEN

If choosing one's mate was based only on physical compatibility, then with Dwarf I've won the jackpot. Though I suspect the perfectness of our union is heavily fuelled by the feelings we have.

After my fourth orgasm, I feel too languid to move. I'm only just aware that Dwarf leaves me to deal with the condom before returning and pulling me into his arms.

"Get your head down for a couple of hours, babe."

I'm not going to argue. A bone-deep tiredness has come over me, and I give in to the impulse to close my eyes. But sleep doesn't come immediately. Instead, I relive the terrors of the previous night, of that awful journey in the trunk of Jack's car, being battered about, of the horror of those hours being in his company, and how close he'd come to raping me.

I press my lips together tight to stop a whimper coming out.

"Relax, babe. It's over. You're safe and with me. I'll never let anything hurt you again."

Dwarf must be some kind of mind reader, as he pulls me closer and tightens his hold. I feel cocooned in his embrace. Surprisingly, it reminds me of the only times a male has ever held me before with affection and no ulterior motive. It reminds me of my grandaddy, and the times I felt safe in my childhood.

I've not had time to analyse what happened earlier until now, but Dwarf's arms give me the safety to remember the events again.

"I suppose I'm going to have to believe in ghosts now."

"Ghosts?" Dwarf pulls me on top of him and looks up into my eyes. "I think there was some powerful energy in that cabin, Raven. Not sure I'm going to believe there are spirits all around, but maybe something of your grandaddy had lingered to make sure everything turned out right. He always tried his best to protect you."

He had, getting me away immediately when he realised what had been happening, and making sure my father could never do it again. Maybe some part of him had stayed because he knew Jack was bad to the bone.

"It wasn't coincidence, was it?"

"I could tell you a sudden thunderstorm blew up, that freak lightning took Jack out, but I heard his voice, Raven." He pauses, and I see him frowning.

Reaching out my hand, I stroke his cheek, feeling the softness of his short beard. "What is it?"

"Just realised I better treat you right. Else your grandaddy might come after me."

I snort a laugh. "Too fuckin' right."

He doesn't laugh back. Instead, he wraps one of his hands in my hair, and stares intensely at my face. "I'll make it my life's work to make you happy, Raven. I don't need any threats to keep me in line."

He's such a good man, and I was so wrong to ever run from him. But as I'd told him moments before, I'd have come back, once I'd pulled my head out of my ass. I'm only grateful he's giving me a second chance and wants me.

"I'd love you to move here, Raven, but if that's what it takes and your life's in California, I'll transfer to the NorCal chapter. I've met War, the prez, and I'm sure he'd have me."

I like Dwarf and his club too much to do that to him. "I'm moving here." Sure, I have Natalie in San Francisco, but she'd encourage me to follow my heart. It was her who pointed out I can do what I do anywhere, and if I'm good enough, my services will always be in demand. Though, as I tell him, "It might take time to establish myself."

"That doesn't matter," he replies. "I've lived at the clubhouse for next to nothing. I have a bit put aside. More than enough to put a deposit down on a house."

"I'm not going to leech off you, Dwarf. I'll pay my way. With what I'll have from the sale of the cabin, we might be able to buy outright."

His eyes suddenly twinkle. "Might be able to buy a fuckin' mansion if that gold mine works out. With my share and yours, babe, I reckon we'd do alright."

"Do you really think I've inherited a gold mine?" I can't believe my grandaddy would have sat on that. But maybe by the time he'd found what he had, he was too old and infirm to do anything about it.

"Is the presence of a gold mine more of a stretch than a ghost?"

Again, I snort. I suppose both are equally fantastical.

Dwarf suddenly sits up, taking me with him. "You're covered in bruises, babe. Let me run you a bath, then you can have a soak and take a nap."

"While you…?"

He chuckles. "While I go and see what a fuckin' mess they've made of my kitchen and try and get something edible cooked up. Something healthy with vitamins that will keep Ruby happy and disguise the greens for Midnight."

"Midnight?" My brow creases.

"Yeah, he's allergic to veggies." He rolls his eyes. "So, I have to be devious. You know the man actually believes Spaghetti Bolognese only has meat in it?"

"I can't really cook," I admit, biting my lip.

"Not a game changer, Raven. I'll happily do all that shit while you keep me happy in other ways."

How did I manage to find this man? He's perfect for me. I think on his suggestion. "A good soak in the bath sounds great. So does catching up on my sleep." I wink. "And then eating a gourmet meal cooked by my man."

He barks a laugh. "Doubt it will be anything gourmet tonight, but it will be edible."

Moments later, he's run a bath and placed a good heap of Epsom salts in it, stuff he had from when he gets sore after a long ride. He offers to wash my back, but I send him off with a smile. I'm too worn out to take anything further right now.

I relish the feeling of being looked after, from the just-right temperature of the bath to the towels he placed to warm over the rails. After finding myself almost dosing off in the water, I get out and dry myself.

Then, I collapse in Dwarf's comfortable bed, and immediately fall asleep. Surprisingly, no dreams haunt me.

"Babe?"

A gentle hand is shaking me awake. Lazily, I open my bleary eyes. God, his face. If this is what I'm going to see every morning for the rest of my life, I'll have no complaints.

"Boys are back, and I'm just about finishing dinner. You okay to get up and come down? I've laid a fresh shirt out for you, and Ruby's left you some jeans she says are too tight for her, but may be perfect for you."

That was kind of her. I'll have to sort the practicalities and go back to San Francisco to pack up my stuff. But thinking about that can wait for tomorrow.

Apologetically, Dwarf leaves me alone so he can go finish his preparations. I brush my teeth then slip into my bra and his t-shirt which swamps me so much it makes me laugh. The jeans though fit like they were made for me. And so they should. Ruby had forgotten to remove the tag. She'd clearly bought them for me. I'll thank her and make sure I pay her back.

Descending the stairs, I feel a little nervous, though I don't know why. Now I've committed to Dwarf, these men will be my family, and I want them to accept me. So far, I've been nothing but trouble.

I see eyes narrowing as I reach the main room, and my face reddens. I know Dwarf's shirt looks ridiculous, but I've tried to tie it to one side to make the most of it. Pulling back my shoulders, I try to brazen it out, and decide to follow the aroma that will lead me to my man's domain.

Toad scowls as he catches sight of me, but it's Bonk who stops my steps.

"Fuck, Dwarf must love you." As my eyes narrow, he continues, "Looking like you do now." It's then I notice his eyes aren't on my oversized apparel, but on my jaw.

"Wish we could dig that fucker up and kill him our way." Metalhead comes over to back him up. "That sore, darlin'?"

"Here." Ruby comes running up, glaring at the men. "Don't crowd her. Raven, I've got you some painkillers."

"That's my fuckin' job," Scalpel calls out.

"Yeah?" Ruby retorts. "Well, you weren't doing it."

"Simmer down, Princess." Toad holds out his hand to her and pulls her close. Once she's snuggled beside him, he looks at me again. "Once we've eaten, we're going to have a meeting. You're invited."

From the looks around me, I gather I should be treating this as an honour. But as I've no idea what it's about, I don't know how to react.

I'm saved when Dwarf calls out that the food is ready and have to step back to avoid being stampeded. Someone, I think Midnight, mentions "thank fuck, Dwarf's back."

As I go to fill my own plate, I pick up more of the conversation. Apparently, Dwarf hasn't cooked properly for about ten days, which coincides with the timing that I walked away. The thought I'd affected him should make me guilty, but instead, it reinforces my desire to stay. It's a concrete demonstration of how much he feels for me.

However, if I'd been wavering, Dwarf's fried chicken steak would probably have persuaded me to stay.

After we've been eating for a while, Dwarf, sitting beside me, leans in close. "If you don't quit moaning like that every time you put your fork in your mouth, I'm going to have to take you back upstairs."

"No need," I tell him, having swallowed, and yes, moaned around another mouthful. "This steak is orgasmic enough for me."

"But you'd prefer my cock," he says confidently.

I shrug. "The jury's out on that right now."

We obviously weren't speaking quietly enough.

Bonk snorts. "I missed Dwarf's cooking, but not quite to the point where I've creamed my jeans and have to go and change them."

Bonk's pronouncement gets the whole table looking at him. He's holding his finished plate up in one hand, while with the other he caresses his cock. Playing to the audience, he flexes his hips.

"Happens to me too, Brother," Crumb commiserates, though he fails to keep the grin off his face.

Toad stands, taking his plate and Ruby's, his face resembling that of a long-suffering parent. Before he leaves the kitchen, he turns. "Dwarf, Metalhead, Raider and Cloud. Assuming you don't need to change your pants, be in my office in five minutes." He walks off, shaking his head.

A couple of minutes later, Dwarf takes my licked-clean plate from me. Yeah, while I wasn't quite so uncouth to put my tongue on it, I had been surreptitiously wiping up the excess sauce and sucking it off my finger. When Dwarf had caught me, he'd made a show of adjusting himself.

"Come on, babe. Prez needs to talk to you."

Suddenly I'm nervous, knowing that Toad is the boss of this crew. "Is he going to be okay with me staying with you?"

Dwarf swings around, hearing the concern in my voice. "Of course, he is. I claimed you at the table. You're my ol' lady." He pushes my hair back from my face. "You've just gained a family as well as me."

His statement warms me, and I breathe easier as I follow Dwarf when he leads the way. He raps twice on Toad's closed door before entering.

Metalhead kicks out a seat for me, while Dwarf stays standing. Toad gives me his approximation of a smile—his real ones are reserved for Ruby I've noticed—and nods as I sit.

"Got bad news for you." As my face blanches, Dwarf's hand rests on my shoulder. "Jack was wrong about you sitting on a gold mine." He nods toward Cloud who reaches down and picks up a small bag. He empties the contents out on Toad's desk.

When Toad lifts his chin, I reach out my hand and pick up one of the rocks. It's got a metallic feel and has flashes of gold in it. Confused, I raise my eyes.

"Jack's gold?" I ask, reverently tracing my fingers over it.

"Fool's gold," Toad snorts. "No doubt about it. Jack must have thought it was the real thing."

I never thought my brother was the brightest bulb in the box and hadn't really suspected the cabin was sitting over a gold mine, but the dream was nice while we had it. I don't really know whether to be disappointed or amused. "So, we're not going to become rich?"

Toad chuckles softly. "Doesn't look like it. Oh, we'll keep an eye out when we're working up at the cabin, but I suspect that's all there is."

Sighing, I say, "Jack always was a fool." He'd been prepared to kill me and died himself because of a worthless pile of rocks.

"Yeah," Metalhead speaks, his hand brushing his hair back. "We found these in a safe. Whether your grandaddy thought they were real, or whether Jack found them and put them there himself, we'll never know."

My shoulders rise and lower. Easy come, easy go. It would have been too much to hope for that Grandaddy had left me more than he had. But, as the squeeze on my shoulder reminds me, he'd left me more riches than he'd ever know. If he hadn't left me the cabin, I'd never have found Dwarf, and he enriches my life more than any gold ever could.

Dwarf's staring at the worthless rocks. He looks like there's something on his mind. His brow furrows as he raises his chin to Toad. "We know there's no real gold there, but what about Jack's partner, Bland?"

Cloud waggles his fingers. "He might be waiting for Jack to contact him, tell him everything's gone to plan."

"And when he doesn't?" I ask, worried that he's a loose end hanging around.

Toad places his hands flat on the desk. "Cloud's been trying to locate him, but it looks like he's gone underground. I reckon it's a sure bet he'll emerge sometime and come sniffing around."

"And what then? He was part of Jack's plan." I don't have any kind thoughts toward him.

Toad grins but there's nothing cheerful about it. "I'm kind of looking forward to him showing his face."

"You're going to kill him?"

"Now, now, Raven." Toad's grin widens. "I don't think I said anything like that." His tone suggests he means the exact opposite to what his words imply, but then he's hardly going to admit to a pre-planned murder.

"Whatever happens, we'll keep you out of it, Raven." Dwarf takes hold of my hand. "It's our cabin now. If, when, he comes back, we'll deal with him."

"I'll keep my ear to the ground," Cloud states, looking at me sympathetically.

Toad raises his chin, then his eyes harden. "Don't know if you want to hear this or not, Raven, but when we buried your brother, we dug in the most likely spot. Found a skeleton there already."

A shiver runs over me, a chilling blast like when a shadow moves over the sun. "My father?"

Toad raises and lowers his head. "That's what we assume." He stares at me for a moment. "You want we should mark the spot?"

My answer is immediate. "Yes, so I know where to avoid."

Behind me, Dwarf snorts and says softly, "That's my girl."

Toad tosses me a look of respect, then leaning back, he links his hands behind his head. "We," he indicates his VP and sergeant-at-arms, "and our brothers, have been doing some planning. We're going to start on the cabin as soon as we can, get the structure stabilised and solar panels installed." I nod to show that's what I was expecting. "Dwarf, here, tells me you're shifting your business here. It makes sense to give the contract for the interior decorating to you unless you have an objection to it."

"Wouldn't blame you if you never wanted to step foot in the place again."

I glance at Metalhead and give him a nod while gathering my thoughts together. Part of me never wants to return to the cabin again, but a far larger part wants to grasp the opportunity offered. I'd love to be able to let my imagination loose and design an interior that would be sympathetic to the original structure but also suit the MC's purpose.

But there's something we haven't discussed. "You don't know what I charge."

Toad snorts. "We'll pay you a fair price and Dwarf can whore himself out for the rest. I'm sure you'll take payment in orgasms."

I flush red, but don't object, seems a good enough way of payment to me. Though I do have to wonder whether this is the way the MC normally conducts its business. The thought makes me grin as I reach up to squeeze Dwarf's hand that's still resting on my shoulder.

I tell them, "I'd love to. It would be a great way to kick-start my business in Arizona." Eager, now I've made the decision, I ask, "Have you any idea what you'd be using it for?"

The skin around Toad's eyes crinkles. "I can see it being used by us and other chapters—"

Raider snorts. "Yeah, if Mo is any example, they'll be jumping at it."

"Yeah?" Metalhead raises his eyebrow. "What did the old bastard from West Virginia have to say?"

Raider scratches his nose and thinks for a moment as if trying to remember, then says in a deep gravelly voice, "I miss cannin' all them veggies from Papaw's garden. Lucky fuckers."

Toad snorts. "He thinks we're going back to the land?"

Dwarf chuckles. "Well, we'll have the space. Could pick his brains on growing our fruit and veg. He might have a fuckin' point."

With a low growl, Toad gets back to the subject in hand. "A place for men to stay, where perhaps we can entertain. A retreat for us and other chapters." He answers my question at last, then poses one of his own. "So, you'll do it?"

I nod. "I'll do it."

Of course, 'doing it' isn't as simple as just saying the three words. There's the question of where we're going to live for a start. While I don't think I've accumulated much over the years, it's far too much to fit into Dwarf's one room.

Having made the decision, though, neither of us want to delay. When I return to San Francisco, Dwarf comes along. The plan being, while I finish up work on the contracts I've yet to complete, he'll pack up my apartment and arrange a truck to take everything back to Arizona to be put into storage.

We decide to fly. Dwarf doesn't fancy eleven hours cooped in a cage, and I'm too new to riding to want to go all that way on his bike. When the plane touches down, it's to find Natalie waiting for us at the airport.

Running into her arms, I hug her tight. "I thought you were going to come over tonight?"

"I couldn't wait to see you, and to check you were really okay." Her eyes zoom in on my face. While most of my bruising has disappeared over the last couple of days, my jaw where Jack had hit me hard enough to knock me out, is still swollen. "Is that where he hit you?"

"Girl, I'm fine," I tell her. "And yeah, Jack clocked me one."

"He's really dead?"

I'd told her that already, but it seems she wants my reassurance again. "Dead and buried," I confirm.

"You kill him?" It's the first words she's posed to the man who accompanied me.

"Dwarf." With a smirk, Dwarf stretches out his hand and introduces himself. "And to answer you, no. I didn't have that pleasure. But I witnessed it so can attest, he won't be bothering Raven again."

"Thank fuck for that."

Her gratitude reminds me how much I have to be grateful for, and it's all down to her. "Nat, I'll never be able to thank you enough for—"

"Yes, you will," she interrupts, and gives Dwarf an appraising glance. Then she leans in and in a theatrical whisper, asks, "If his brothers are as hot as Dwarf, all I want is an invite to Arizona."

Dwarf snorts and grins. "I'd say you got a permanent invite."

"But you'll be disappointed," I add, then pause, seeing Dwarf frown. "I've snagged the hottest of them already."

"Fuck but I thought I couldn't love you more." He pulls me into him, and right in front of Natalie, gives me one of those kisses where he all but devours me.

When he finally lets me go and Natalie has fanned herself sufficiently, we leave the airport and I introduce Dwarf to the delights of San Francisco. It doesn't take long for him to make his view clear—he prefers the desert of Arizona to the city.

Chapter Twenty-Eight

DWARF

Six months later

I kick back my legs and nurse my beer, wondering how life could get any better. Leaning back my head, I turn my face up to the warmth of the spring sun, letting my ears soak in the sound of nature and the female voices.

Now the cabin's completed, the club has started spending some of the weekends here. It's a place we can all unwind and relax. A million miles away from when I'd first seen it.

At a picnic table, Ruby and Raven are discussing something, their heads bowed together. Once Raven had moved her business here, Ruby had become interested. Having been brought up with all the style her daddy's money could buy, Toad's woman actually had a good eye for colour and arrangements, and Raven had started to appreciate her.

They'd pooled ideas and the interior of the cabin was the better for it. Gone was the mould and the remnants of outdated furniture, and in came modern and comfortable couches and table and chairs. The four bedrooms above all had king-sized beds in them, and the two bedrooms downstairs each had a couple of bunks, enough to house quite a few members.

Solar panels had been installed so there was no longer a need for the ancient generator, and Cloud had somehow worked his magic with a series of boosters and other paraphernalia which now means the cabin is provided with Wi-Fi.

I, myself, had installed the kitchen which was a chef's dream.

It had been a long undertaking but was more or less finished.

A noise beside me gets me opening my eyes. "Prez." I nod respectfully as he drops down into a chair beside me. I don't fail to note how incongruous it looks that he's cuddling Rolo to him. A less manly dog could never be found.

Nevertheless, I reach over and let the tiny pooch sniff my fingers, then ruffle its ears.

"Lots has happened in a year," Toad starts, conversationally.

I raise my beer bottle to show I agree with him.

"Whoever thought you and I would end up with ol' ladies," he continues.

"Thought you'd be the last to fall," I tell him.

He chuckles. "Yeah, strange what women fancy."

I don't take umbrage. He's scarred as hell with a face that would frighten a baby, and me? Well, I'm no prize. Except we've both found women who want to ride through life by our sides.

"Raven and Ruby have made this more than a club." I point my beer bottle to the two women who are obviously yanking poor Bonk's chain about something. "They've made it a real family."

"They have that." He raises his own bottle to his lips and takes a long sip. "Hey, Dwarf, you ever think about having your own family?"

"Kids?"

"Uh-huh."

I grin. "Can't happen too soon for me, but it's Raven who needs to be ready. You?"

Toad grins. "We've started trying. And I must say, I like getting the practice in."

I clink my beer bottle to his. "Yeah, well, we're still rehearsing."

It makes me wonder how the dynamics of the club would change once we start procreating.

"Who's next?"

"What?"

Toad shrugs. "Well, if we ugly bastards have found our soulmates, surely there must be someone out there for Metal and Raider. Even Scalpel."

"Definitely Midnight," I offer. I might be a straight guy but the Native American would tempt even me if I wasn't. "But Bonk?"

Toad barks a laugh. "Now that would be a damn miracle."

"What are you two plotting?" Ruby dislodges Rolo, taking her into her arms, then plonking herself on Toad's lap.

To my delight, Raven eases herself down onto me and wraps her arms around me, but her words are for Prez, not me.

"Do you mind Natalie coming here one weekend?"

He shrugs. "Fine by me." Idly, his hand caresses Ruby's ass.

"Oh, that's good. Bonk wanted me to ask you."

"Bonk?" Toad and I say at the same time, then look at each other and burst out laughing.

Raven rolls her eyes and shares a glance with Ruby. "Men, I'll never understand them."

"Oh, we're easy to understand, darlin'." Toad winks her way, then somehow manages to stand, lifting his woman with him. Rolo, displaced, lands on the ground. Toad's heated eyes turn my way. "You up for some dog sitting?"

Chuckling, I tell him, "Yeah, we'll watch Rolo."

As he walks off with his princess in his arms, Raven stares after them. "Where are they going?"

"To get some practice in." I chuckle at my own joke.

She widens her eyes and shakes her head. Over the months she's gotten used to my brothers and doesn't bother questioning what they're doing. She leans her head back onto my chest, snuggling in. "Have I ever told you how happy I am?"

I don't need telling. I see it every day. And I'm certain she knows she makes me just as happy.

"Best fuckin' day ever when you ran into my bike."

Suddenly the wind blows up from nowhere, making leftover autumn leaves dance and swirl. Rolo runs off and starts chasing them.

I look up to the skies. "Yeah, Grandaddy. I won't let her be hurt again."

The breeze dies down as quickly as it had come up.

Raven looks at me sharply. "That was coincidence you know."

She's told me before she's certain her grandaddy's not still around. But I'm not so sure. And if she's got a spiritual guardian, it really wouldn't bother me.

I'm convinced I must have someone looking out for both me and her. Else why would I have been riding that road at the precise time when Raven needed me?

Again, I raise my face to the warmth of the sun and thank fuck how everything had turned out. There's only one small cloud on the horizon. We've never heard from Jack's partner Bland, despite our searching for him.

Still, I doubt it will matter much if he turns up. He won't be a match for me or my club.

Other Wicked Warriors Books

In Tickety Tock I mentioned two other chapters of the Wicked Warriors MC. Why not check them out (in fact, why not look at the whole of the series?).

Read about War, the president of the Nor Cal chapter in Midnight Ride, a Cinderella retelling by P.T Macias.

Discover Mo, the president of the Wicked Warriors in West Virginia in s Goldilocks retelling, Her Three Bears by M.D. Stewart.

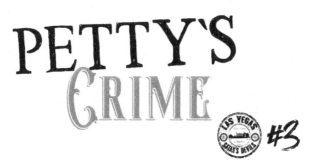

PETTY'S CRIME #3

Petty

I'm not the nicest person in the world, I know that. I've cultivated that world view. I'm a man's man, full of testosterone and with the balls to prove it.

I've spent years kidding everyone as to who I am, hiding the parts of me I'm ashamed of.

I didn't expect my nemesis to raise her head and step back into my life with the intention to destroy what I'd built.

I thought we were over, done and finished, but she had different ideas. No one could protect me from her, and I had no idea how to protect myself.

RoseLyn

I've a stalker after me and I am under the protection of the Satan's Devils' Security Services.

One of my bodyguards is Petty, and he's an absolute dick. He has no respect for anyone other than his brothers. If he wasn't good at his job, I'd have demanded he be replaced.

Though slowly I've come to discover there's something about

him, something I think only I can see. It lives beneath the persona he presents to the world.

Maybe as much as he's protecting me, I can save him?

It won't be easy. He's not going to let anyone in. But when his brothers all desert him, there's only one person he can turn to, and that's me.

Acknowledgements & Author's Note

Where do I get the ideas for my books from? Well, perhaps this is the craziest of them all.

I wrote *Warts an' All* as a one-off, part of the Bleeding Souls Saved by Love series. But as has happened before, readers quickly asked to read more of Wicked Warriors Arizona Chapter. I put that idea on the back burner.

My amazing husband had recently bought me a present—a bag (purse) with a real working clock on it. I only used it for special occasions, not wanting to damage it. But I didn't want to hide it away, so left it out on a table for all to see. The clock has quite a loud tick to it, and listening to it, the phrase *Tickety Tock* came into my head.

I immediately knew I wanted to write a book with that title, but at that time, had no idea what it would be about.

I used to love reading and writing horror novels (none of those works of mine have ever, or will ever, see the light of day). But I wondered whether I could weave some suspense and scary bits into a story, and gradually Dwarf and Raven's story began to take shape.

I had so much fun writing this book, and I hope you enjoyed reading it.

Grateful thanks as always to my beta readers, Sheri, Danena, Jo, Tami, Tera, Alex and Zoe.

Maggie Kern my friend, confidant and editor. I run out of accolades to give you, but so many thank yous for helping me with this book.

Darlene Tallman, thank you for proofreading this book. I really appreciate it. I'm sorry you weren't warned and read it too late at night.

I think Dar of Wicked Smart Designs has outdone herself with the cover for this book! She's taken a stock image and worked her incredible magic with it. I was blown away from the first time I saw it. Thank you so much, Dar.

Finally, last as always, but definitely not least, thanks to all of you, my wonderful readers who've taken a chance on this book. If it wasn't for your encouragement, I wouldn't keep writing. I have recently received messages and emails telling me how much you like my books, and I love reading everyone. A positive message inspires me to write more.

This book, like all of my works, has been to beta readers, through editing twice, to a proofreader and then to ARC readers, but there could still be the odd typo that's crept through. Please message me if you've found anything so I have a chance to correct the book. I love to hear from readers, even if you're pointing out something I've got wrong.

If you've enjoyed this book, please consider writing a review. Reviews are essential to us authors, and I appreciate and read them all.

The next book will feature another Satan's Devil, but there will be more Wicked Warriors on their way too.

Love and peace be with you all.

Manda

Other Works by Manda Mellett

Blood Brothers – A series about sexy dominant sheikhs and their bodyguards

Stolen Lives (#1) Nijad and Cara

Close Protection (#2) Jon and Mia

Second Chances (#3) Kadar and Zoe

Identity Crisis (#4) Sean and Vanessa

Dark Horses (#5) Jasim and Janna

Hard Choices (#6) Aiza

Satan's Devils MC - Arizona Chapter

Turning Wheels (Blood Brothers #3.5, Satan's Devils #1) Wraith and Sophie

Drummer's Beat (#2) Drummer and Sam

Slick Running (#3) Slick and Ella

Targeting Dart (#4) Dart and Alex

Heart Broken (#5) Heart and Marc

Peg's Stand (#6) Peg and Darcy

Rock Bottom (#7) Rock and Becca

Joker's Fool (#8) Joker and Lady

Mouse Trapped (#9) Mouse and Mariana

Blade's Edge (#10) Blade and Tash

Heart Mended: A Satan's Devils MC Novella

Truck Stopped (#11) Truck & Allie

Satan's Devils MC Boxset 1 Books 1-5

Satan's Devils MC Boxset 2 Books 6-8

Satan's Devils MC Boxset 3 Books 9-11

Satan's Devils MC - Colorado Chapter

Paladin's Hell (#1) Paladin and Jayden

Demon's Angel (#2) Demon and Violet

Devil's Due (#3) Beef and Steph

Devil's Dilemma (#4) Pyro and Mel

Ink's Devil (#5) Ink and Beth

Devil's Spawn (#6)

Satan's Devils MC - Next Generation

Amy's Santa (#1) Wizard and Amy

Hawk's Cry (#2) Hawk and Olivia

Twisted Throttle (#3) Throttle and Gwen

Saving Marvel (#4) Marvel and Virginia

Satan's Devils MC - San Diego Chapter

Being Lost (#1)

Grumbler's Ride (#2)

Avenging Devil Part 1 (#3)

Avenging Devil Part 2 (#4)

Satan's Devils MC - Utah Chapter

Road Tripped (#1)

Stormy's Thunder (#2)

Satan's Devils MC - Las Vegas Chapter

Red's Peril - Part 1

Red's Peril - Part 2

Wicked Warriors Arizona Chapter

Warts an' All

Stay in Touch

Email: manda@mandamellett.com

Website: www.mandamellett.com

Sign up for my newsletter to hear about new releases in the Satan's Devils and Blood Brothers series.

Facebook reader group: https://www.facebook.com/groups/mandasbadboys/

 facebook.com/mandamellett
twitter.com/manda_mellett

About the Author

Manda's life's always seemed a bit weird, starting with a childhood that even today she's still trying to make sense of, then losing her parents in the late teens. Going from the tragic to the bizarre, who else could be unlucky enough to have had two car accidents, neither her fault, one involving a nun, and another involving a police woman?

There isn't enough space to list everything that's happened to Manda, or what she's learned from it. But by using the rich fabric of her personal life, psychology degree, varied work experiences, and amazing characters she's met, Manda is able to populate her books with believable in-depth characters and enjoys pitting them against situations which challenge them. Her books are full of suspense, twists and turns and the unexpected.

Manda lives in the beautiful countryside of Essex in the UK, the area's claim to fame being the Wilkin's Jam Factory at nearby Tiptree. She can usually find jars of jam which remind her of home wherever she goes. As well as writing books and reading, Manda loves walking her dogs and keeping fit. She lives with her husband of over 30 years, who, along with her son, is her greatest fan and supporter.

Manda is thankful that one of the more unusual, and at the time unpleasant, turns her life took, now enables her to spend her time writing. Confirming, in her view, every cloud has a silver lining.

Photo by Carmel Jane Photography